Live And Let Bite

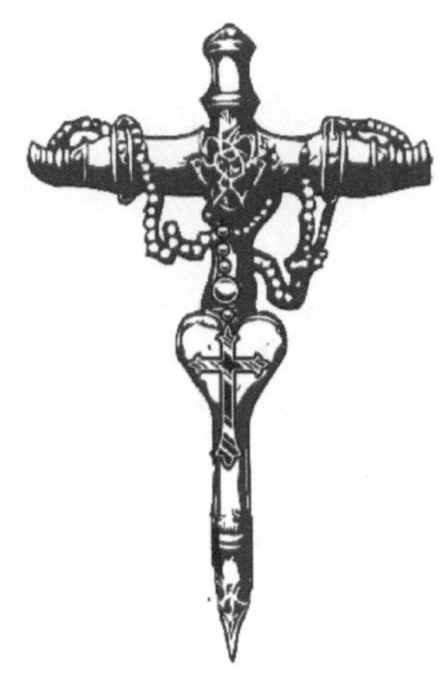

Love At First Bite

Book Three

By Declan Finn

Three Ravens Publishing
Chickamauga, GA USA

Live And Let Bite: Love At First Bite Book Three By Declan Finn

Published by Three Ravens Publishing

threeravenspublishing@gmail.com

P O Box 851, Chickamauga, Ga 30707

https://www.threeravenspublishing.com

Copyright © 2023 by Declan Finn

Credits:

Live and Let Bite: Love at First Bite Book Three was written by Declan Finn

Cover art by: Steve Beaulieu

Live and Let Bite: Love at First Bite Book Three by: Declan Finn /Three Ravens Publishing – 2nd edition, 2023

Live and Let Bite: Love at First Bite Book Three by: Declan Finn /Silver Empire – 1st edition, 2018

Ebook ISBN: 978-1-951768-75-1
Trade Paperback ISBN: 978-1-951768-76-8
Hardback ISBN: 978-1-951768-77-5

Dedicated to all those who made this book possible.

Table of Contents

Prologue

Dear Amanda

San Francisco, September

Marco Catalano sat down at his laptop and started to compose an email. For a man who had just gone toe-to-toe with a demon with as much worry as the average citizen might have against a mugger, the email terrified him out of all proportion.

Dearest Amanda,

I have a secret to tell you. Not too surprising, is it? My very smile must appear to be a mask at times.

In fact, I have two secrets to tell you. Neither may surprise you. Or both will. Though which would surprise you, or surprise you more, I couldn't begin to say or guess. After all, if there's anyone who knows me better than my father or my confessor, it would be you.

I've told you before about the night I lost Lily for the first time. Yes, it was before I met you, but I think I told that story vividly enough. It was a mugging. The man held me at knifepoint, and I killed him. I told you the truth in that I did have to kill him. I made a mess of it. What could have been a quick disable or kill turned into a bloody mess. I hurt him. And I kept on hurting him until he stopped moving.

What I didn't tell you is that I liked hurting him. I liked making him suffer. I enjoyed making him bleed and die.

In short, Amanda, I am a monster. You need blood to live, and you have only killed when you needed to, but I'm the one who enjoys it. I enjoy the stab, the slice, the twist of the knife.

However, I've been made aware that I might not be quite so insidious and monstrous a human being as I thought. My time in prayer and church and confession may not be 100% for naught.

My second secret is at the same time both much more innocent, yet much creepier at the same time, given secret #1.

I love you, Amanda. That is my big secret.

It sounds stupid to say it, but I love everything about you. I love your accent. Your hair. Your smile. I love how smart you are. I love how you think. I love your eyes and the way they sparkle. I like just being around you. I even like who I am when I'm around you.

Do you remember what I told you in the graveyard as we "pretended" to make out and profess our love to each other so that we could bait Mikhail's vampires? I wasn't pretending. Everything I said to you was true. Everything I did, I meant.

No matter what, Amanda, I will always love you.

Marco

Marco reached to click "send."
And then, just like that, it was away.

Chapter 1

Love Bites

New York City, September

Lady Jennifer Bosley, President of the New York City Vampires Association, was not only powerful but very, very rich. Not Bernie Madoff rich, or Bill Gates rich, but she was *rich*, as in "old world, old money, I can buy and sell China ten times" *rich*. She was not "the 1%" but the 0.0001%. She had founding stock in Bell Telephone. If anyone had known she existed, or if she had all of her money in the same place under one name, she would have been one of the top ten richest entities on the planet, including nations.

Like many other wealthy vampires, she bought entire apartment complexes, and left the outside alone, turning the inside into a luxurious palace. On the outside, it looked like a gang-ridden neighborhood had declared war on her building. Inside, it looked like a modern-day palace.

But Jennifer Bosley herself was surprisingly relaxed. She came in wearing dark green jogging pants and top, as though she had just come in from a run. Her basic attitude was such that she knew she was rich, and she didn't need to prove it to anyone. Her form was curvy, and she moved with effortless grace. Her blonde hair terminated at the base of her neck, with her hair at the sides tucked behind her ears. Her full lips were unadorned, and her brown eyes cut through whatever she saw.

Amanda Colt sat on the other side of the desk, and she *wasn't* particularly rich. To normal people, as she lived in her East 70th Street apartment, she was rich. To vampires, she was comfortable. It was an area where the cops had a good response time, and people walked the streets at night. Insanely wealthy vampires (the types that lived in castles and estates, if they could) merely called her type "well invested: the nouveaux riches of the vampire world." She only had founding stock in Apple, IBM, and Microsoft. If she broke two hundred (next century), she might be considered part of the club.

Amanda Colt wasn't particularly powerful, either. She was as strong as the average vampire, maybe stronger (she had odd bursts of ability that surprised her, but that didn't count). She didn't have a nest, and her sphere of influence had only recently started. Until recently, her only power was, really, the power to turn heads.

She was about as intimidating as a chipmunk, which was unusual enough for New York, but as sexy as the one that got away - you know, *that* one - only better looking. She was about 5'6," with long red-gold hair that went to the small of her back in a golden fall, eyes that were a warm, liquid Frangelico brown with her Siberia-pale skin. Her dress was casual and form-fitting. Tight jeans and a sweater that should have covered her thoroughly, but somehow managed to be quite snug. Granted, it was a very nice form with curves that a Volvo would hug. Marco and every other person who had ever talked about her appearance would be the first to say that it would be hard for anyone who met her to say that she didn't look good in everything she wore.

"So, love," Bosley began as informally as ever, her London accent slipping in. "You're gonna wait until at least Christmas? You love Marco; he may love you, for all you know."

Amanda sat back in the chair. Bosley's occasional casualness kept throwing her for a loop. *"Da."*

Bosley leaned forward, put down her wine glass, and picked up a picture from her blotter. "This him?"

Amanda blinked and focused a little. "How did you -"

"It's called Facebook, inn'it?" Bosley smiled. She kicked back in the chair, sweeping her glass in one hand, and holding onto the picture in the other. "Nice lookin' fella."

Amanda squeezed her eyes shut, as though to clear them. The conversation was a little surreal. She wasn't exactly up on "girl talk." Maybe it had to do with being Russian. Perhaps it had to do with being a vampire. Perhaps Bosley was just strange. "He is. Little on the young side, though."

Bosley gave her an amused glance. "Listen, mate, when you reach, well, our *general* age, human age doesn't exactly count for much. Know what I mean? Forty, twenty, makes little difference after you hit the first-century mark. See what I mean?"

"Perhaps." Amanda looked off to the side. "I wouldn't know. My life has been quiet for a vampire, I suppose."

Bosley nodded sagely. "I know how that can be. For the first few weeks, I was like that all the time."

"I… found a job."

Bosley looked at her. "Really? Well, then, I can only imagine how that went." She looked back to the pic of Marco. "You have a nice fella here." Bosley grinned. "Like I told him, if anything happens to you, I'll be happy to take him in."

Amanda tried not to laugh. "Be careful. He might just take *you* in."

"Indeed. So, while you're busy waiting for Christmas to come, what are you gonna do in the meantime?"

Amanda shrugged. "No idea. Honestly. I will probably just go out and continue vampire control duties."

Bosley's grin downgraded to a smile. "Don't think so."

Amanda's eyebrows shot up. "Really? Are you telling me not to?"

"Nope. I'm telling you that you can relax a bit. Your police officers and the mob guys have been playing nice, ever since the bombing incident took out your boyfriend's hospital." She looked off to one side and smiled slightly. "Also, I've started putting the arm on some of the lesser of the known quantities."

Amanda blinked. "Why would you do this?"

"A few reasons. One, I like you well enough to do you a solid. Second, I told you, I don't like terrorists. We lost plenty of people on September 11th, and I have no intention of playing nice with anyone who'd touch that sort of thing. Heck, from what you told me of the demon's plans, he was in on the attack in 2001. But since I can't openly move against whoever's involved in this, you're going to have to do all the work. If that means I suppress the local nuisance so you can take some names, I'll do it. Remember how I dug you out of the rubble so you could go play hero and slay a dragon? Well, that's about all I can do. Just don't think I'm a vampire *ex machina*."

Amanda's eyes narrowed, and she thought through the implications. When she and Marco had first met, there was an insurgency of vampires within New York, led by a vampire named Mikhail the Bear. He'd been busy raising a vampire army all over the planet and had settled in New York to make a new division. She and Marco had stopped him with the help of two local street gangs, as well as a government agent named Merle Kraft. However, before anyone could have an extended conversation with Mikhail, he had been assassinated by a redheaded vampire that had tossed Amanda off a roof.

Then "Mister Day" showed up after Marco had gone to San Francisco. Day had blown up the hospital that Marco's father worked in, to run him to ground. The effort worked, even though Day was destroyed, not easily but eventually. It was obvious that Day was part of Mikhail's band of killers. Day had even admitted it.

Which meant that there were others out there. Others who thought nothing about killing thousands in a single stroke.

"Thank you," Amanda said aloud, though she was still deep in thought. "I suppose I will have to kill a great many people by the time I'm done."

Bosley smiled. "Perhaps. But you never know how convincing you can be when you put your mind to it."

Chapter 2

Bite Me

Afghanistan, December 8th

Merlin Kraft looked at the mountains. Tora Bora was a labyrinth of interlinking caves that looked like someone had tried to make Swiss cheese out of Tatooine.

He lifted a thermal scope to his eye, then switched to night vision, then back again. The sentry appeared on the night vision goggles, but not on the thermal scope.

Crud, vampire. Damn it to hell. Welcome to Christmas in freaking Afghanistan. If anyone *ever* tries to drag me to a beach ever again after this, I will personally start breaking things.

"So, Merle, can we lase the target and let a *missile* take them out *this* time?" George asked.

Merle didn't reply. George knew as well as anyone that Merle needed to get into this cave before they blew it up. But then again, Merle wouldn't let George in until he scouted out the skill level of the vampires inside. Even then, Merle was wary. He was the only human being who could match the physical speed of the vampires. Though George could at least go toe-to-toe with them physically. The whole lycanthrope thing helped. *There are times I have the feeling that I only manage to survive because the vampires consistently underestimate me since I'm merely human.*

Merle switched back to night vision, then zoomed in. The vampire looked as though his face had almost been burned off. Remembering back to the vampires he had encountered in Brooklyn and San Francisco, Merle knew the higher-level ones were the most deformed, their faces projecting the state of their souls like the portrait of Dorian Gray. This was almost certainly a job for the snipers.

Merle looked over his shoulder at Carl Ramirez and nodded. Ramirez carried the .50-caliber Galil sniper rifle, which was technically an anti-vehicle weapon, perfect for dealing with vampires - one bullet could decapitate.

Merle straightened as much as he could with the vampire pack. At that moment, he had enough gear to arm any member of *Lord of the Rings* - two short swords on the back, a light broadsword on his hip, an arrow gun in a thigh holster, a squirt gun with holy water and a pouch filled to the brim with Throwing Stars of David, and that is not a misprint. There was also a

Kabar knife. There was no room for an assault rifle, and a handgun was useless for Merle.

He sighed to himself. *Yes, that's right. After weeks in the country, with enough terrorists to kill me dozens of times over, I, Merle Kraft, still haven't learned how to shoot someone with a simple handgun.*

Merle moved into position shortly before clicking his radio transmitter twice, sending the signal.

As much as he wanted the files inside the cave, Merle wasn't willing to let anyone gets eaten. During the four months in the country, his team had discovered that vampires were a consistently arrogant bunch, and in most cases, there was no sign of anyone trying to burn documents in their possession. There were large sections of the Al-Qaeda / ISIS hierarchy regretting those decisions.

The problem with fighting in Tora Bora was that, aside from Merle, the army would usually call an air strike down on ISIS ass, burying everyone under tons of rubble.

But Merle wasn't an army man or even army intelligence. A government agent, of sorts and he still had a tiny situation to do with a United Nations scandal.

Though plenty of people in my chain of command keep telling me it's a dead issue, with the appearance of "Mister Day" at the UN, I suspect it's an undead issue. And you can't spell undead without UN.

Merle nearly sighed at the thought but readjusted his attention to the vampire. Merle watched the sentry for a few minutes, getting his pattern down. Most vampires used their hyper-acute senses to monitor the area, but this one was visibly vigilant.

However, vigilance didn't work in this instance when, a half-hour later, out of relative nowhere, Merle dropped behind the vampire and slashed through his neck with a quick swipe of short swords.

The vampire fell over, and the others inside had felt the death. Within a matter of moments, the sound of bat wings fluttered down the cave. Merle blinked, then back-flipped down the mountain, eventually landing in the valley below. The bats exploded out of the cave in a puff of smoke, fluttering down towards him.

Merle smiled as the vampire bats came onwards.

A calling as a pyrotechnics man suddenly appealed to Merle. This had something to do with the fact that the entire mountainside, from the mouth of the cave to mere yards away from his feet, erupted in a burst of flame, piercing the darkness and the bats as well.

Inside the cave, where Merle didn't want to risk incinerating any documents, several flash-bangs went off, producing "bangs" more than 300 decibels, and a flash seven times brighter than the sun. Flash-bangs near humans caused bleeding from the eyes and ruptured eardrums.

Merle wanted to note what would happen to vampires who had hearing and sight easily twice that of humans.

The effect was better than he had hoped - Merle thought that possibly ten percent of the vampires who survived the firebombs would be incapacitated or even killed by the flash-bangs (which gave off their own ultraviolet rays). He got half of them.

However, that left thirty vampires with splitting headaches and an urge to kill something.

The first vampires that came after him played it cautious and swirled out of the mouth of the cave as fog but reformed halfway down the mountain as big and burly vampires who had grown Taliban-regulation beards, lest the religious police behead them.

The vampires looked at each other. Merle folded his arms waiting for them to decide how to attack. After a moment, he sighed, drew the automatic arrow launcher, and fired, recreating Saint Sebastian statues of each of them. Visions of Roman Catholic school classmates calling on Saint Pincushion flitted through his memory as they all disintegrated. Merle shook his head and tucked away the arrow launcher as another vampire leapt out of the cave. Merle whirled. The short swords blazed in the moonlight, rending arms and legs from the latest attacker. Another came out in a direct charge, trying to rush him.

Merle swung, and the vampire blocked a blade with a forearm. Merle blocked a swing from him with the other blade.

"Crap," he muttered. The vampire was so strong, he had made his skin hard enough to deflect blades. *This was bad.*

Merle back-flipped, kicking the vampire under the chin with his steel-toed boots.

The vampire tottered back, unprepared for the blow. His hard-as-stone skin had made him top-heavy. *At least I know that he's not a full-powered vampire, they don't need to concentrate on being invulnerable, they just are.*

The vampire glared, readying himself for his next attack when his head exploded.

Carl Ramirez chambered another round in his sniper rifle, ready for the next fang-banger to attack. The vampires must have noticed that their comrade had been shot because the next attack didn't come single-file, but widespread, like a shotgun move on a football team.

Merle reached to the small of his back, then swiped his hand in front of him, throwing out multiple, six-pointed throwing stars. The stars penetrated the chests of his attackers, and they fell, most of them dead, but a few merely fell to the ground crying out in pain.

Thank You, God, for not being picky, he prayed.

However, by this point, the whole hoard of vampires poured out of the cave mouth, including those previously disabled by the flash-bangs.

Merle grimaced, drew the arrow gun, and started firing.

"Now," he barked out.

Now George Berkeley attacked.

The entire ridgeline above the vampires exploded in fire, and all of it heading their way. There were blasts from incendiary grenades, two flamethrowers, and a host of tracer rounds that were all white-hot phosphorus and no lead. The remaining vampires were ash in a matter of moments.

Merle scrambled up the mountainside, heading straight for the cave mouth. He toggled on the radio, stating, "All clear. Move out, team, and get your package ready."

George frowned, as usual. Merle insisted on staying behind to collect evidence personally after clearing the area of hostiles and sent the rest of the men back to base before the cleanup crew arrived.

George sighed, secured his weapon, then radioed for the bombers to come in. "Merle, you've got the usual."

"Confirmed."

Below, Merle strolled into the cave, eyes darting into the night. There were still two vampires on the ground with bleeding eyes and ears, groaning in pain. He finished them off with two swipes, then moved on.

At the back end of the tunnel, there were several booklets of compact computer disks and flash drives. He quickly gathered each one, in turn, slipping them into his backpack, and recording with a digital camera what paper documents he didn't have room for.

Merle came to the last pile and noted something strange. One booklet was a three-ring binder filled with paper, but the cover had type in English. He opened it, then noted the pages written in French and Arabic as well... *Oh crap...*

There, on the booklet cover, was an emblem Merle recognized. An image of the planet wreathed on both sides.

It was the symbol of the United Nations.

Darn.

Merle grabbed the book as he turned and sprinted for the tunnel's mouth. He had been driven by the urgency the evidence dictated... and not the new sounds coming from the depths of the mountain.

His arrival had woken something up… and it was hungry.

George stood at the ridge, glancing at the mountain range with binoculars. What took Merle so long, he didn't know, but it was more worrisome than usual. No soldier in his right mind faced anything without at least some measure of fear. But Merle's team was special, due to its quarry. But Merle never cut his own extraction as close as now, not with the cleanup crew on its way.

Suddenly, Merle propelled himself out of the mouth of the cave, which made George worry more - Merle usually appeared behind him, not in front. (George never understood it, but knew enough not to ask)

"Oh shit."

A wave of creatures came out of the mountain after Merle. Some looked like they were vampires, but the rest looked like rejects from a Hollywood creature shop, thrown away, half finished. Somewhere human-ish, missing an arm or a leg, some running, some galloping on three limbs. Some looked like deformed dogs or bats or rats. Some were black masses of scar tissue and burns, baying like hounds at the moon.

There was, however, one entity which bore more than a superficial resemblance to a human being, but only if a human could survive with third-degree burns over the entire body.

Merle whirled, throwing full spreads of Throwing Stars of David, and they worked, cutting into the black wave, but only shallowly. He repeated the maneuver, now firing with the arrow gun. It ran out of arrows quickly, and he dropped it.

At which point, the cleanup crew arrived.

The "cleanup crew" took the form of a very large bomb called a daisy cutter, delivered by airplane, and resulted in a fireball with a 900-foot blast radius.

George closed his eyes as the fireball created a small dawn, not so much for the brightness, but for Merle. As much as he liked Kraft, there was no way in hell anyone could survive that, vampire or man.

"That one was close."

Berkeley looked over his shoulder at Merle, who looked tired, covered in sweat, and the cuffs of his windbreaker were slightly singed.

"Do I even want to know?" George asked.

"Probably not. I need to get back to New York."

George cocked his head. *Back to New York?* "Why?"

"We've got some problems."

Chapter 3

Suckers

New York City, December 9th

Amanda Colt entered the bar with caution. Calling it a dive would have been charitable; it was slightly wider than a large walk-in closet. It was a vampire bar, yes, but it doubled as a singles place in Greenwich Village, the place in New York for gays and lesbians to gather, as well as assorted freaks - vampires, the occasional pedophile, and people who had an unhealthy interest in leather.

It was called "Suckers," possibly because it sucked, but more likely because the owners, half the patrons, and plenty of the wait staff, happened to have sharp teeth - which was the reason most of the bar stools, chairs, and paneling were made of metal, and not wood.

The moment Amanda stepped in, the bar froze, and even the music in the jukebox seemed to mute. A vampire of her level never came to this sort of place. Mostly because of taste and class. There are some things respectable vampires don't touch.

Then there were these vampires - Pookas, mid-level demon-pretenders, the outlaw bikers of the vampire world. They weren't excessively evil, merely gypsies, tramps, thieves, brigands, brawlers, drunkards, letches, a menagerie of various and sundry sins that could easily be forgiven if they were in the slightest bit repentant. In this crowd, anyone who had the virtue of helping a little old lady across the street would light up like a neon sign in Utah.

A few years ago, when she had been trying to find someone to associate with that *wasn't* Marco, she had allowed herself to be chased away from a place like this.

Now, it wasn't a matter of being social.

Amanda glanced over the patrons and decided not to waste any time being subtle since it probably wouldn't have worked anyway.

"Hello," she said simply. "A friend of mine is in trouble. Marco Catalano." Her gaze swept over the entire bar. "You all know him. You all met him. All of you fear him. Explain to me what has been sent after him this time, and I will let you all walk away."

One of them, a big beefy vampire who had been a member of the Pagans Motorcycle gang in life, snarled and laughed. "Your pet human is lunch meat, and we all know it."

Amanda eyed him a moment, then smiled. This was someone she wanted to talk with. His name was Little Nero—dubbed that by a vampire old enough to have watched Edward G. Robinson's film *Little Cesar* in the theater and knew enough of the original Nero to realize that this guy fits the bill.

He was also the only person in the room that qualified as evil.

Most importantly, he would be someone in the know. This was more along Amanda's desired target. The demon known as "Day"—or Asmodeus, as most knew him—qualified as an upper-level demon. He had been a demon who certainly operated within the world constrained by certain limitations. Anyone under the rank of evil would probably not have heard whispers of him so Little Nero might have at least heard *something*.

The only problem would be getting him without interference from the rest of the bar's patrons.

Well, that's easy.

Amanda leapt to her left and casually ripped off a metal sheet from the bar counter and spun. The sheet metal cut off Little Nero's right arm, then embedded itself in the wall. She reached to the small of her back and drew two small vials of holy water, throwing both at his knees with pinpoint accuracy, effectively kneecapping him.

Nero screamed once more, blinked, then fell over.

Amanda Colt stepped on his neck within an eye blink, glaring at everyone else in the room. "Would anyone else like to have a conversation?"

She met their eyes, daring them to step forward. Not that she wanted them to. After all, it really was easier to win a fight that never started in the first place.

One person stepped forward. Nero's drinking buddy. Possibly because he felt an obligation to pay some lip service to support Nero.

Amanda understood. And even respected it.

This is why, by the second step, she only threw a stake through each kneecap.

Amanda stared down at the vampire beneath her and drew a wooden spike from her left ankle holster.

Placing it next to Nero's eye, she murmured, "What shall we talk about today?"

Amanda moved into the Blood Bank and sat down at the bar. Patrick Lynch smiled at her from the other end of the bar. He nodded in her direction and finished up with his current customer.

Patrick Lynch looked like a standard Irish cop-out of an 1880s period piece. This made sense, as he *was* an Irish cop from the 1880s.

Lynch walked up to her with a broad smile. "Taking a break from cracking some heads, lassie?"

Amanda smiled slightly. "I have been around."

"Aye. With a two-by-four, from what I've heard.

Amanda cocked her head and studied him a moment. "How many relatives do you have working bars in town?"

Lynch barked a laugh. "God, lass. I've lost count. I had ten. They're scattered about, here and there. Lost a few from natural causes, thank God. It feels like I'm still raising their grandkids."

She blinked. "Really? You still have contact with your family?"

"Of course." He grabbed a towel and started wiping down the bar. "I've got so many great-great-grandkids, nieces, and nephews, it's almost stupid." He placed both hands on the bar and leaned forward. "So, what are you up to? Worried about your man?"

Amanda nodded slowly. Lynch frowned thoughtfully, obviously chewing something over.

She didn't know what went through his mind, but then, she never really had a grasp on the bartender's line of thought. When she and Marco first tried to strong-arm his customers, he had run them out. When Marco had his own, private chat with Lynch, he had supplied them with places to turn in their hunt for Mikhail the Bear, denying him areas of influence within the city. Then, not long ago, Lynch had come to her aid against a vampire who ran a competing club.

Are these friends? Really? Welcome to vampire politics.

"I've heard of a lot of threats against Marco since that first day," he started. "I try to keep meself out of it because they're just noise. You know what I mean. But recently, the noises stopped."

Amanda frowned. "Is it the NYC-VA?"

Lynch scoffed. "That British hussy Bosley? Wouldn't be bothered. She can quell actions, not thoughts, not even if she wanted to. She knows that a vampire who's yapping is better than one who's quiet."

"You think one of them is going to move?"

He shook his head. "Wrong kind of quiet."

She nodded, and he continued. "Besides, the lad is still in parts unknown, isn't he? None of these twits would be bothered crossing the street to jump Marco.

I can't imagine them crossing city, state, longitude or latitude lines to hunt him down. Can ye?"

Amanda shook her head. "Not really." She frowned. What she had heard over the past few months, combined with Lynch's own observations, led her to only one conclusion.

"Thank you, Patrick. I must go see someone."

Amanda Colt walked up to the brownstone's door and rang the bell.

The one who answered the door was tall, thin, with a smattering of salt in his otherwise black hair.

Doctor Robert Catalano smiled. "Amanda, please, come in. What brings you here at this hour?"

Amanda slid past him and headed for the living room.

"We're in here," Robert said, pointing to the front parlor, which she already passed.

Amanda blinked. "Oh." She didn't have fond memories of that room.

Robert held the door for her. She walked in and blinked. Monsignor William Rodgers, Roman Catholic priest, sat on the couch. The other one was Ibrahim "Bram" Javaherian, a young Persian Catholic who worked as a Vatican Ninja.

Amanda made sure to sit across from Ibrahim. The chair he sat in was a replacement, the last one having been used as a stake to run through Marco's ex-girlfriend, a vampire at the time. "What brings all of you here?"

Rodgers grinned. "I'm here every few weeks."

Amanda looked at Ibrahim and raised an eyebrow. "I didn't know you were a regular."

Ibrahim smiled. "Only recently. Ever since the incident with Mister Day, we figured that it would be a good idea to have a bodyguard around here."

"So, we are all feeling wary?"

"That's one way to put it," Robert said as he sat next to Rodgers. "I've been given a few bits here and there about what happened back in September. Right now, I'm just glad that this creature didn't wear a suicide vest when he met Marco. Otherwise, we wouldn't have had enough parts to have buried him."

Amanda winced. Marco wouldn't have been the only one to have been killed in that engagement, had that happened. Asmodeus had been a difficult creature to dispatch, and at the end of the day, had been exorcised most unusually.

"I can only guess he didn't think he needed it." Amanda leaned forward, looking from one to the other. "However, I think whatever we went up against in the spring is behind all of this. The forces behind Mikhail the Bear sent Day after Marco, and I can't imagine that they'll stop now. Does anyone else?"

Ibrahim laughed. "That's sort of the reason I'm here. They blew up a hospital last time to get at Marco. Imagine what they'd do next. That makes Rodgers a target, also the good doctor here. You can take care of yourself, obviously."

Amanda shook her head. "Mikhail's assassin was a redheaded vampire of unnatural speed - even for one of my kind. She could probably kill me as easily as Mikhail. She speared him through his heart from atop a roof. But if I died, there would be no trace. Just ashes in the street."

"Point taken."

Robert raised his hand with a chagrined little smile. "Pardon me, but what exactly does all this add up to?"

Rodgers shook his head. "All we know is that Marco made himself a target."

"Yes, but *why Marco?*" Robert looked around. "This is my son we're talking about here, right? He hasn't become a vampire, has he?" he asked Amanda. "He hasn't become SpecOps," he said to Bram. "He's not even a commando priest," he told Rodgers. "So, what makes him so dangerous that they've sent a demon and a vampire hitman?"

Amanda nodded. Ever since her conversation with Jennifer Bosley, all those months ago, she had thought of little else. Even she spoke, she wasn't entirely certain of her answer. "Mikhail walked the earth for centuries, building up an army. He knew enough about military tactics to be considered… well, he did not suck?" She smiled a little. "But here is thing about it," she continued, her articles dropping as her Russian accent thickened, "he was good militarily, and he was good as strategist. Marco bested him. We had Ninjas, and street gangs, and cops, and Mafia, but no one had been able to best him before. No one. Then here comes Marco. Marco who…"

Amanda blinked and drifted off a moment, back to that battle with the evil Russian vampire. "Wait. During the battle. Marco invited Mikhail into his brain. Dared him. Mikhail screamed. He dropped Marco. He tried to run from Marco."

Robert frowned. "Really? Something in Marco's head scared off a centuries-old vampire?" He nodded slowly. "This is a cause of concern or pride?"

"Honestly?" Rodgers said. "I don't know."

"Well, what could have done it?" He glanced at Amanda. "You'd know, right? What would drive a vampire from someone's head?"

Amanda shrugged. "*Nyet* idea." She tucked a strand of hair over her ear. "I've been vampire for 100 years and have never been driven from anyone's brain. Ever. But Marco is unique."

The three men chuckled. Bram gave her his warm smile. "Tell us something we don't know."

Amanda considered it for a moment and nodded. "He has looked into my eyes, and then used it to talk to me, entering *my* mind."

Rodgers blinked. He moved the cigar away from his mouth as he shifted in his chair. "Was this a one-time event, or -?"

"He has done it twice," she elaborated. "Last time, he could edit his thoughts."

Ibrahim and Rodgers exchanged a look. Robert raised a finger, as though asking for a point of order. "Is that impressive?"

"That's unheard of," the priest explained.

Robert looked to Amanda, and she nodded.

Robert shrugged. "He's always been very controlled. I think even as a baby, he only screamed until we showed up to attend to the problem. But does that mean he has ESP or something like that?"

"I haven't noticed," Amanda answered. The others nodded, as though her answer was the *only* answer.

"He's got great mental control, and he's smart on a tactical level, and apparently can scare vampires." Robert looked at the three of them. "That's it? That's *all* Marco has going for him?"

"Actually, no," Ibrahim said. "He's good. I don't mean morally - I don't know him that well. But he's really good at whatever it is he does. Remember when Enrico had you hostage?" he asked Robert. "Marco walked in like he was a different person and stared them down like they were just annoying."

Amanda frowned, more to herself than anyone else. "His smell changed."

Robert arched a brow. "Really? Is that a shift in body chemistry that we're talking about?"

"Sort of. There are subtleties involved. But the question becomes whether or not Marco's ability to… change is something of interest to the enemy that makes him a threat."

"Are we sure he's not a selkie?" Ibrahim joked.

"A shapeshifter?" Rodgers asked. "No, I don't believe so."

"He tastes human," Amanda said.

Robert choked, and then coughed, and looked at Amanda, one eyebrow arched. "I'm sorry. What?"

"His blood tastes human. Between the medical tests he would have had growing up, and me, I can't believe that something so enormous would have avoided detection."

Rodgers took a long drag on his cigar, and slowly let the smoke drift out from between his lips. "You know," he began, unleashing a cloud of smoke, making him look like a dragon, "there are stories of people who could resist vampire mind control and people who could repel vampires. Usually, those two groups don't overlap, mainly because ones who repelled vampires never allowed any close enough to try mind control."

"Who are they?" Amanda asked.

"Saints," Rodgers answered. "Ignatius Loyola, the founder of the Jesuits, resisted mind control. I think Thomas Aquinas actively repelled them." He laughed. "We won't even go into the Inquisition."

"The Inquisition went after vamp-" Robert asked. He caught himself. "Of *course* the Inquisition went after vampires. What other reason would there be?"

"The usual ones," Rodger said. "A new state seeking to secure power by driving out anyone who could be a threat. After hundreds of years of Moorish rule in Spain, getting rid of heretics, Muslims, and any theoretical Jewish collaborators seemed like a good idea at the time." He puffed on his cigar a little. "Keep in mind, the Inquisition had better courts than the civilian, so much better that regular criminals blasphemed in court to get into them. And, at the time, the Inquisition was a highly-advanced concept. Usually, a government would just send in an army, slaughter whole towns and be done with it. The Inquisition also spent a good chunk of time hunting out vampires. Usually by touching a cross to their foreheads and moving on."

Robert shook his head. "Can we stay on point? No matter why these people want Marco, they're not going to be content with letting him wander free, are they? Doesn't that mean he's in trouble?"

"Yes," Amanda said. She rose from her chair. "Pardon me, but I need to book a flight to San Francisco."

Chapter 4

Live and Let Bite

San Francisco, December 10th

He sat at the bar of the club and wondered if he shouldn't burn the place down. It wasn't a vampire haven, though it was a stalking ground. That wasn't why he wanted to burn it down but considered it a good idea on general principles. Flashing lights and loudly deafening noises weren't his idea of a good time. He preferred some nice music in the background as he read a book.

Heck, had the music even been something good, like Nightwish or Dragonforce, he might not have minded the volume (okay, some Dragonforce songs at maximum volume would probably lead to bleeding eardrums, but that would still have been preferable to some of the garbage on the speakers).

He chuckled. Not that I'm a snob or anything.

He looked over the bar with his omnipresent Scaramouche smile – for he was born with the gift of laughter and the sense that the world was mad.

Someone touched him on the arm, and he turned. The blonde was utterly stunning. Marco's face didn't even shift a little, and he made certain to look at her lips. "Hi there."

She gave him a toothy grin. "You're cute," she called to him.

He leaned into her, almost so that he could put his lips to her ear. "Could you repeat that?" he asked at normal volume.

Unseen by anyone else, his left hand drew out a syringe. The needle was thin enough to be barely felt upon penetration but sharp enough to penetrate most cloth. As he spoke in the blonde woman's ear, he stuck her in the belly and injected the contents straight into her abdomen.

The woman stopped, blinked, jerked, and tore off for the bathroom.

She never came out.

He sighed and shook his head.

The bartender looked at him. "You scare off another one? What do you say to them, dude?"

Marco Catalano shrugged, his smile still amused. *Fifty CCs of Holy Water into the guts of a vampire.* "No idea."

Someone touched him on the arm. Marco felt a well of rage flare up from his stomach. His smile stayed; it didn't reach his eyes. He spun on the stool again, ready to just tear the next vampire's head off.

In this case, it was a petite redhead. Yana Rosenberg's hand recoiled like she'd been burned. "Marco."

"Yana," he muttered, turning back to the bar.

"Are you okay?"

Marco's eyes narrowed, and his smile tightened with suppressed rage before turning back to the smile. "I'm fine. Thank you. Now get lost. You're scaring off the vampires."

Yana grabbed his arm and pulled. "Come on, Marco, you've been here too long and -"

Marco swung around so fast as though moving to strike her. His hand came up, and she flinched before a blow landed. Instead, it was just his finger pointing right between her eyes.

"You listen to me, you petty little witch," he snarled. "I don't give a crap what you have to say. Take your fashionable, San Francisco lesbian Wiccan stereotype drivel and leave me be. The only woman - the only *person* - I give a *damn* about is three thousand miles away, and has ignored me for almost four months. So *pardon* me if I don't take your self-serving advice. Now get out. Get eaten by a vampire or something. Because we both know that without me and George, you, Tara and Tiffany would have been eaten *months* ago."

"But Marco -"

Marco pushed past her, nearly hip-checking her into the crowd. "If you're not going to leave me alone, then I'll just leave."

Marco made his way through the club, pushing and shoving anyone who didn't get out of his way fast enough. This led to one rugby player taking a swing at him. Marco ducked, came up with a knee to the groin, then stomped down on the man's instep. The rugby guy bent down low enough for Marco to clock him in the face with an elbow.

Marco went out the back way, kicking the door open. It was the back alley, just like he expected. The stench of foul matter emanating from the dumpster was its own special sort of hell.

"You've been killing my people here for the last week, *Marco*."

Marco looked off to the side. The gathering of vampires wore the standard black leather "We've seen too many movies" look. The only distinguishing mark was a red armband on each arm. Of course, it had a peace symbol in the middle.

Marco arched a brow, smiled back. "How very San Francisco."

The leader shrugged. He was about the size of a standard fullback - two meters tall, one wide. He had the brightest blue eyes that Marco had seen in a while.

"You've been killing my people. Mostly my women."

Marco gave his own shrug. "Actually, I've been sticking them with holy water. Heck, had they picked up anyone else in the bar, they would never have known I was there. Next time, you should shop in singles bars."

The leader took a step forward, and Marco nodded. The leader blinked, confused.

The confusion grew when the flaming arrows rained down on the group of vampires. The ground ignited under them.

The leader whirled as his cadre burned alive. While he was distracted by the death of all his dreams, Marco leaped on his back, ramming a stake into the side of his throat and punching out, cutting everything from the windpipe to blood vessels.

The next stab was to the kidneys. Had the vampire been alive, it would have been a death so painful that he couldn't even scream. The vampiric nature of the creature prevented him from dying but didn't spare him any of the pain.

Marco also didn't spare him any pain. He stabbed the vampire in the side, the ball joint of the shoulder, the shoulder plexus, and basically everywhere but the heart. The wooden stake made certain that none of the wounds would heal immediately, and that all of them hurt. The vampire fell to one knee.

Then Marco got nasty.

Marco tossed aside the stake and brought out a crucifix from the canvas sheath under his jacket. He stabbed away again, this time in all the wounds he'd already made, cauterizing them open. Each stab of the crucifix burned even worse than the stakes.

The vampire fell face first onto the concrete. Marco flipped him over, straddled his blood-soaked chest, and continued to pummel him, the crucifix still in one hand.

Had Marco's team not cut off the alleyway after the vampires entered it, or if Yana hadn't chained the exit behind him, there would have been some danger of a passerby coming through. Had an outside observer spied Marco beating a vampire to death, they would have called the cops.

Had they seen his eyes, they would have run for their lives.

The vampire saw glimpses of the hate and rage burning in Marco's eyes as he was slowly beaten to death. They were filled with such darkness, he had a passing thought that Marco may have been a demon.

The strangest part of all was Marco's face. With the eyes of a mass murderer, he had a small, sardonic smile on his lips.

Marco merely continued to beat him to death. He changed his tactics and started to stab the vampire in the front - again, everywhere but the heart.

After two minutes of nonstop striking, Marco staggered back, off the vampire. He pulled out a small atomizer with his left hand and sprayed the vampire down with holy water.

Marco, panting, looked down at the vampire, death still in his eyes like a bad case of jaundice. "Your throat is going to heal, little man. But you've killed too many people in this city. It's time for you and your people to leave. All of you. I am sick of you. I'm sick of vampires. I'm sick of demons. Most of all, I'm sick of San Francisco. My new policy on vampires is simple: genocide."

He took a deep breath, stood, and reached behind the foul dumpster. He had dropped a stink bomb in the dumpster every day for the past week so that it would cover the smell of napalm that he had laid down during the day.

Marco came back with an ax. And a smile.

"Don't move. This won't hurt… for long." As he raised the ax, he said, "No one expects the Marco Inquisition."

The body of the vampire leader had been dropped off at a known vampire hangout. To be accurate, what had been delivered were an upper torso, an arm, and a head. There was no belly button. Or anything below that.

Pinned to the vampire's chest was a flash drive. It had a video of the entire incident, from the initial fireball to the ax. The picture was unclear, so the human attacker's face was obscured. But as the ax came out, an electronic voice came up with a simple statement.

To the vampires of San Francisco that dwell on the dark side, we have a message.

The first leg to go punctuated the statement.

Stop feeding on the people of San Francisco. Find an alternate food source, or there will be consequences.

On the video, the ax came down again.

This is your final warning.

The video proceeded with the ax.

The vampire couldn't even scream.

"Marco?" Yana asked down the dorm hallway.

Marco stopped in mid-stride, only a few feet from his room. *Curses, foiled again.*

He turned around, his smile still in place. "Yes?"

She walked up to him, and said, as sincere and as concerned as any overly-empathetic person could be, asked, "Are you all right?"

Marco was briefly torn between being dismissive or being confused. He opted for the latter and arched an eyebrow. "Why *wouldn't* I be fine? We got them."

"That's not an answer."

Marco nodded. "You're learning." He paused, thought it over a moment, and he didn't sigh so much as deflate. "Come on in."

Marco let Yana in, a perfect gentleman. He stood dancer-straight and even bowed a little as she passed.

Yana was one of the most insecure cute women that he knew. Red-haired, green-eyed, petite, nerdy, smart as a whip, she was his type all over… except she was a gay Wiccan who was so touchy-feely San Franciscan, he was shocked she'd lived this long.

Marco was no-one's type, really. He topped out at 5'9", a dancer's build, acerbic, violent, and a temper that could lay waste to the city, but a genius all over.

"So, what's up?" he asked.

"You seem… angrier than usual?"

Marco gave a short, sharp laugh. "Is that a question or a statement?"

"Yes?"

Marco gave into the temptation and rolled his eyes. "I … was … *acting*. The vampires saw me blow you off, concluded that I was alone, then went out to ambush me. According to script."

"What about how we'd be dead for months without you?"

Marco paused. "Acting."

"How I'm the lesbian witch?"

Marco paused, wondering exactly what wasn't getting through. "Did I mention *acting*? And isn't that a descriptor you yourself have used? Also, isn't 'lesbian witch' a quarter of San Francisco's population? With 'gay semi-Catholic' being another?"

"And how the *only* person you care about is thousands of miles away and ignoring you for months?"

Marco blinked. He looked off to the side and said nothing for a moment. He ran his tongue over his teeth. "Acting."

"Uh huh." Yana frowned. "How stupid do you think we all are?"

Marco scoffed. "Tiffany *does* lower the average group IQ."

"Marco…"

"Don't worry about it."

"How can I *not* worry about it? You don't have any problems going on murderous rampages -"

"Hey!" Marco objected. "It doesn't count if they're all vampires."

"And I know that you don't kill *people* because…?"

He considered it for a long moment. "Okay, good point. But you can't prove that I've killed any people in San Francisco because no bodies have turned up."

"Look, Marco… talk to Amanda. Both of us know that she's the reason–"

Marco's eyes went flat and dead. The smile stayed but didn't touch his eyes. Yana took a reflexive step back. "What do you think I've been *doing* since September? I've sent Amanda several emails. *Months ago*. The only reason I even know she's even *alive* is that she occasionally drops by my father to visit, and *he* tells me what's going on. I thought something went wrong when she headed back for New York because she never even told me *she'd arrived.*"

He took two long steps towards her, and she took another step back, afraid she'd be run over. "You know the funny part, Yana? I sent her an email telling her that I love her right after she left. It's been weeks. Which means she must have read my emails by now. Hell, she couldn't even be bothered to give me a reply. Which means that she's rejected my feelings for her. Even worse? She's also jettisoned our friendship too. Now I'm stuck *here*, in this rotten garbage can of a village called San Fran-freaking-cisco. So, no, Yana, I'm *fine*. I am just. *Perfectly. Fine.*"

"No, you're not," she said quietly. "You're not fine. You just hacked someone to pieces."

"Evil vampire. Had it coming. Kill people for fun and food, you get hacked into itty bitty pieces and left to fate and the good graces of your fellow vampires." Marco paused, then waved her away as he turned back towards his bookcases. He took a moment, a long breath, and turned back. "Merle brought me here."

It was Yana's turn to scoff. "Duh. We lost Sarah, *then* you show up? It wasn't hard to figure out something was up."

Marco gave a little nod, acknowledging the deduction. "My mission was to leave a San Francisco that can defend itself from vampires. I'm going to do that, no matter what I have to do. If I have to create a desert out of the vampire community and call it peace, I will. It's bad enough that we had a demon that came here specifically for me. The vampires need to be taught that they can't screw around with us. They can't just come here and play with the population without punishment. If they don't want to meet horrible, terrifying ends, then they play by the rules."

"But the bit with the ax -"

Marco spread his hands, palms up, and gave a little shrug. "As opposed to what? A stake to the heart? A head cut off? No. Too quick. Too neat. The *threat* of Hell is nice, but it's hard to imagine. Being hacked to pieces by an insane human and left to rot? That's a bit more real to them. And the idea that I'm real *should* scare the hell out of them."

"But Marco -"

He held up his hands. "Yana, stop. Just stop. I don't care. I don't care what you have to say. I really don't. Don't you see? That's the problem. I like you well enough, even Tara and Rory, and Lord help me, I even like Tiffany to some extent. I will lead. I will help. I will come to the rescue. I will stop a bullet for any of you. Because I came and accepted responsibility for you all. But you know what? I don't give a single *damn* for your opinion of my personal life."

Yana stomped her foot. "I care about you and your life. You're going to self-destruct if you keep going like this."

Marco's eyes narrowed. He closed to within inches of her. His voice was low and calm, and barely above a whisper. "Yana, do you really want me, a straight Catholic male, commenting on your relationship with your girlfriend?"

"Of course not!"

"Then why should you expect *me* to listen to *your* comments on *my* relationships?" He pointed. "There's the door. Goodnight."

Chapter 5

Blue Blood

New York City (December 10th... still)

Merle Kraft walked into New York City's One Police Plaza and merely looked around the office building, hoping that he wasn't about to get mugged by reality - or a bunch of cops with nightsticks.

Despite being a secret agent with connections to the government and the FBI, Merle had no idea what he was doing in the headquarters of the NYPD. All he knew was, after an 11-hour flight from Israel to New York, he had arrived at Kennedy airport, only to find the police waiting for him. They wanted to bring him to the Police Commissioner.

Merle smiled genially, then went along quietly.

On the top floor of 1PP, Police Commissioner Ray Wilson sat behind his desk, and welcomed Merle with a nod, barely looking up from the paperwork on his desk. Wilson was a large fellow, tall, with a full head of dark hair. It was a surprise for someone who was his age - Merle knew it was in the sixties, but he looked more mid-fifties. If the vague hints in the PC's bio were to be believed, his conditioning probably had something to do with being Naval Intelligence in Vietnam… which, to Merle's mind meant "I used to be a SEAL."

Personally, Merle thought he looked more like Teddy Roosevelt.

"Hello, sir. You wanted to see me?"

"Yes please, have a seat." Wilson turned through some more pages. "If you ever wonder why there is a minimal police presence in high-crime areas sometimes, it's because that every time a police officer even needs to look at a suspect cross-eyed, he has to fill out a stack of papers about, oh, yea high." He held his hand about a foot over the desktop. "I should know because I'm the one who gets all of the forms in triplicate."

Merle chuckled as he sat. "Shouldn't there be a hundred guys between a street incident and your desk?"

"Maybe. But that's what it feels like." Wilson looked up from his desk, his black wire-framed glasses making him look like an owl. He set the papers aside, leaned back, and folded his hands across his stomach.

"One of the last times you were in town, you made inquiries with one of my detectives about a Marco Catalano and an Amanda Colt."

Merle nodded. "Yes, sir?"

"This brought you to my attention."

Merle arched a brow. He was a federal agent who had asked for a street-level perspective on two citizens. Wasn't that was real Feds did? "Why?"

"Because you are a government employee that no one likes to talk about, asking one of my officers about citizens in my fair city. You had no obvious reason for it. You had just wrapped up a case here that ended in the decapitation of someone whose body had completely disappeared. I hope you don't mind me saying so, but that looked fishy as hell."

Merle chuckled. "Yes, I can believe that. Trust me, I think a great many projects I'm sucked into have the smell of salmon about them."

"Right. Since then, you had been staying out of my city. So what you were doing has been none of my concern, and none of my business. However, now that your ex-wife and your son are in San Francisco, there is no reason for you to be in my town *except* on matters that are my business. Therefore, I think it's time that you and I have a talk."

Merle wasn't about to argue. "Okay. How do you figure?"

"I made a few inquiries. There are a great many things I don't think *you* understand about your position."

Merle frowned, skeptical. His position wasn't nearly as covert as he was promised, but that the NYPD's PC knew things about his job that Merle himself didn't? Unlikely. "*My* position? What would you know about my position?"

"To begin with, Mister Kraft, you were a cost-saving measure."

"*A what?*" I could understand if I was a minority hire, but cost-saving?

Wilson nodded. "You see, back in the 90s, we already had a team in the government. More than a few teams. The Initiative, as you know it, came later."

Merle sat, blinked, and tried to do some math. "You had teams, *plural?* Vampires and ghoulies aren't new to the government? And somehow, *you* have known the whole time?"

The Commissioner paused a moment. "You're aware of my record?"

Merle nodded. "You've been a cop since you left Vietnam. You've been Commissioner in several cities, mostly setting up methods of patrolling to prevent crime."

"That's not all I've been setting up." The PC leaned back in his chair, his hands behind his head. "When I was in Nam, I also ran missions into Laos and Cambodia. I won't say they were all *missions*. There were a few times where we simply got lost; that isn't a euphemism, that's the fact of navigating in a jungle that crosses barely existent borders. However, I can tell you that my men and I ran into some strange crap. And by strange, I mean your kind of strange, things with fangs and fur, and occasionally scales. We had special training because we tended to run into a lot of this stuff. About half the folks who worked the tunnels in Nam had similar run-ins, and we all kept in touch. Because when there's a network of tunnels running under an entire country, trust me, things that like the dark will migrate there.

"About the early 90s, most of the guys running 'special' missions had been laid off, or cut back, part of the 'Peace Dividend.'" Wilson scoffed. "Peace Dividend. Right." He coughed and cleared his throat.

"Anyway, beastie attacks had been down. The Cold War was over. The idiot in the Oval Office decided that we weren't going to be involved in the world as much anymore. If our boys weren't running into these creatures, we weren't going to be using special teams, or have special training. And if we stopped hiring and training, well, it's just less likely for 'this sort of thing' to get out into the media, right?"

The Commissioner growled to himself. "We won't even go into that part. Anyway, someone decided that when weird stuff started showing up in America, then it was time to start bringing someone in who could handle it locally. Someone with, well, initiative."

Merle narrowed his eyes. "Me? Great. Why didn't they clue me? I didn't even know *vampires* were real until the past year. Heck, why didn't they get some of the old band back together and give me someone to work with?"

The PC shook his head. "From what I heard, some of the higher-ups in some fringe eco-groups were put in charge of the EPA in that administration, and so they declared that the dangerous things we knew about were put on a classified endangered species list. Not only were they to be protected, but they were also to be protected by completely denying their existence on every level of government."

"That means I'm left to myself." Merle sighed. "Such *mishegas*. Is it at all possible to bring in some of these guys from the old days?"

The Commissioner rolled his eyes. "Son, most of these men have been cashiered for more than 20 years. I include the ones who weren't outright thrown out of the Army or served in other branches. Now they've been hired by private military contractors."

Merle thought it over a moment. Just because the US had stopped running into vampires and lycanthropes and whatnot, didn't mean that they had just gone away. Like the "Peace Dividend" BS, just because the White House ignored threats didn't mean that they had just gone away. In fact, if the US had stopped caring, and assuming that the nations of the world had already done as much as they could, that meant someone had to pick up the slack.

"Don't tell me that PMCs have their own monster hunting squads?"

The PC waggled his eyebrows. "Okay, then. I won't."

Merle processed this a bit more. "We ran into them in the sandbox after 9/11, didn't we? Iraq, Afghanistan, Pakistan. That's one of the reasons that the PMCs were brought in, isn't it? They had the special hunters, and the regular military hadn't."

The PC nodded. "Got it in one. As the Secretary of Defense said, they had to go to war with the military they had, not the one they wanted. It was easier to hire

PMCs than to recruit and train soldiers to fight a single type of enemy. The military tried to start building back up, but -"

Merle held up a hand in the "stop" gesture of a cop halting traffic. "But let me guess, the *next* administration decided that we didn't need a special monster squad, we just needed Predator drones for predators?"

PC Wilson didn't even smile. "Precisely. Meaning that if you want a monster squad, you're going to have to assemble it yourself."

"There's a difference between 'Some Assembly Required' and just getting an empty box and a diagram without any parts."

"You're doing a good job already. In fact, I think you're already doing better than you think you are."

"How?"

Wilson smiled tightly. "Back in Nam, most soldiers hadn't said anything after their first encounter, because no one wanted to be dragged into a rubber room. But we were almost prepared for our second, and by then, someone had found out what we were doing and why. We had been read into the situation, and we had the facts of life explained to us by one of the higher-ups."

"Okay. That's to be expected, I suppose."

"Remember how I mentioned you came to my attention?"

"Yes. I had Kristen run a background check on Amanda and Marco. Why?"

PC Wilson reached into his desk, pulled out a sheet of paper, and slid it in front of Merle. It was a copy of a New York City ID for Amanda. "*She's* why you came to my attention. *She* was the government agent who briefed my men. The woman known as Amanda Colt used to have your job. She was one of the people fired as a cost-saving measure. You're *her* replacement."

Merle gaped at the photo. "Son of a bitch."

Chapter 6

In Cold Blood

San Francisco (still December 10th… yes, it's a long night)

Yana stormed outside, an image which, from the outside, might look something like a five-year-old trying to be serious and angry and hurt. She was genuinely all of the above, but the movements matched too closely to avoid the comparison.

How could Marco not realize what he was doing? To himself? To people around him? He was terrifying in his rage, and not just to vampires.

Okay, fine, he was *always* scary, but before, Marco was the right *kind* of scary. It had gotten worse ever since Amanda left in September, but after he had come back from Thanksgiving, he was inconsolable.

Maybe inconsolable isn't the right word. Always angry. Always burning hot.

Yana took a deep breath and tried to focus herself. She tried to draw upon nature, the crisp night air, the quiet, the moisture in the air, the element of calm.

Maybe I should burn something else.

She then reached into her pocket and slipped out a marijuana cigarette. She quietly lit up and inhaled deeply. It would help her relax enough to commune with nature.

This was one that had one of the "extra bonuses" along with it. In small doses, amphetamines worked *just* enough as performance enhancers. Thankfully, Yana had enough access to the chemistry lab to brew her own. She never made that much, so the quantities went unnoticed. But right now, she needed to focus on nature to balance out Marco's negativity cloud.

"Want to party, little girl?"

Yana opened her eyes. She couldn't tell if the abomination in front of her was human, but he had the decidedly predatory look in his eye. It reminded Yana of Marco, only in a much less pleasant context.

A hand came up, grabbed his elbow, and flipped him like a rag doll, slamming him face-first into the pavement.

"Puny rapist."

Yana blinked and wondered if the vision before her was a result of the drugs. There stood Amanda Colt, as large as life and twice as lovely.

Yana could understand what Marco saw in Amanda. She was stunning. Literally, if one went by the poor dumb sap face-planted in the concrete.

Yana absently took another drag on her cigarette. Amanda's nose crinkled, as though she smelled something dead and decayed. "Really?"

Yana blinked. "What?"

"Meth?"

Yana looked down at her joint as though it had magically appeared there. "You can tell?"

"Coyotes won't eat bodies of meth addicts because they can smell the chemicals," Amanda said. "Do you think vampires cannot?"

Yana sighed. She had smoked most of it, so she dropped it on the ground. She ran up to Amanda and hugged her. "I'm so happy you're back in town! This is going to be so great!"

Amanda reflexively put an arm around Yana's waist. For a long moment, the San Franciscan enjoyed the warm, yielding sense of Amanda's body against her. Just because Yana had Tara didn't mean she was dead.

Then Yana broke the hug, reared back, and punched Amanda in the arm. "What took you so long! How could you just disappear on Marco! He loves you, and you do this to him!" She kept punching with each exclamation point. She tried slapping at Amanda at few times.

Amanda gave her a look like she was insane. "Are you done?"

Yana threw her hands up, then straight down, hands balled into fists. "No, I'm not done. How could you do that to Marco? How could you hurt him like that?"

Amanda blinked, squeezed her eyes shut, obviously confused. "Do what to Marco? I've been busy, that's all. And what are you talking about, he loves me? You really are high."

Yana tried to push Amanda away but instead ended up with something more groping the vampire and pushing herself away. "Oh shut up. Everyone sees that he loves you. Everyone. Don't you love him, too?"

Amanda sighed, looked down at the attacker, his arm still in her grip. She took his hand and crushed it in hers. When he finished screaming, she said, "You are getting off easy tonight," making it sounds like *You arrr gettink ov e-z.* "Run now."

Once he fled, Amanda turned back to Yana. "Let us talk, you and I."

Amanda felt disoriented. She had gotten off the plane not *that* long ago. Why did it feel like the entire world had been warped when she wasn't looking? Had her time away really had an effect on anyone? Including Marco?

Hurt *Marco*? Please. No one could *hurt* Marco emotionally. The man had a psyche like an Abrams tank, and mental control to rival Svengali. Marco had survived without Amanda for years. And they had only known each other for a little over a year. The idea that her absence for a little over three measly months could affect him? Ridiculous.

Amanda took Yana by the shoulder and started moving her back to the dorm hall.

As Amanda half-led, half-dragged Yana, she pondered what the San Franciscan had told her. It was a puzzle, really. There was no way in which Marco could have been in love with her without having made a move by now. Impossible. He would have said *something*, at *some* time. It wasn't as if like Marco was *shy*. He was incredibly open about his thoughts. Anytime someone pissed him off, someone would be hurt. He was the first to make his displeasure with someone known, the first to express whatever was on his mind.

Then again, did he express *positive* emotions easily?

No. Not really. When Marco'd had to kill his own ex-girlfriend, he rationalized it to Amanda. He dismissed it. He *had* to kill her. He had to have felt more than that unless he was a sociopath.

So… Was it possible that Marco had hidden feelings from her?

Maybe? After a fashion?

No. Again. Not possible. It would have been completely out of character for him. Just because he hid his feelings didn't mean that he would have hidden that, does it? Feelings about Lily could have been considered a weakness, and he didn't like showing weakness… or at least didn't go out of the way to show softer sides of himself. But to not express that he loved Amanda?

Why would he do such a thing?

It was possibly just wishful thinking. Amanda *wanted* to believe it. It would have been so… Terrifying, actually. She couldn't conceive of it if he *did* love her.

But if he did, theoretically, love me…

Why hide it? Why go across the country? Why wouldn't he just *tell* her?

Amanda pondered it for another moment. Because there was one particular conversation, she'd had with Marco about this once before, exactly. It was one of the stranger conversations with Marco because he was falling asleep at the time. She had "joked" that she was the sort of woman men friend-zoned.

Maybe it's time to ask follow-up questions on that conversation.

Amanda finally guided Yana to her dorm room and had her open the door.

As they entered, Amanda was caught flat-footed. Yana's girlfriend Tara was curled up on top of her sheets, curled up into the fetal position. This wouldn't be a problem if she weren't wearing only her undergarments.

"Of course." Amanda rolled her eyes and closed the door behind her. "Now, tell me all about Marco's *decline* in my absence."

Yana gaped, and blinked, and frowned, not having expected to *think* this late at night. "I have a video."

The video was on YouTube. The only title on it was "Bad@$$ Student Drops Bully like a Ton of Bricks." The date was from mid-November. The opening of the video started with someone who was easily 6'9" and a basketball player striking his girlfriend in the middle of a hallway.

The only reason that Amanda noticed Marco in the background was the walk. He stood out as he approaching in a controlled, oh-so-casual manner. It was so casual it was clearly faked. He kept his hands in his white windbreaker the whole way. When he finally came close to the attacker, the height disparity was painful to look at. There was being a head shorter, and then there was Marco coming up to the man's armpit.

Marco raised his knee, as though he was going to simply take another step. Except the knee came up past his hips before the foot shot straight out. The kick hit the basketball player's knee on the side, hyperextending the knee joint.

The attacker almost went down, but quickly adjusted to the injured leg. He whirled on Marco, backhanding him. Marco had met the strike with both forearms, then grabbed the offending hand. He dug his thumbs into the back of the hand, with his fingers digging into the palm. Grip established, he twisted the arm, and the sound it made was like very loud Rice Krispies.

Then Marco folded the wrist forward, almost, so it was flat against the forearm.

Marco moved closer. The dark blue eyes she so liked were even darker, and colder, like an overcast day in the Arctic.

Marco said something to him. Even though Amanda couldn't hear it, she could read his lips. "Touch her again, loser, and you'll wish I was this gentle."

The attacker reached back for the small of his back. Marco's gaze followed the movement. The camera's angle revealed the knife Marco was reaching for.

And Marco *waited*. He knew something was coming but couldn't have known what. But Marco *waited* for it to happen. Marco *wanted* there to be a weapon.

This was no longer a fight. This was an excuse.

The knife hand came up, landing in Marco's waiting grasp. He took the hand and guided it, turning over the hand, and slammed it into the attacker's opposite shoulder. Amanda winced. The knife point had gone into the ball joint.

Marco's knee came up again, and he stomped once more, into the other kneecap, dislocating it as well.

Worst of all? It wasn't that Marco's smile didn't even flicker. That was normal for him. The worst of all was that Marco could have stopped the attacker with the first—maybe the second—blow, without crippling him. The basketball player would never fully recover and would require months of physical therapy to regain even basic functionality of all of his limbs. If ever.

"How did this man with the knife stay standing after?" Amanda now asked.

"PCP, it seems."

"What happened after?"

Yana frowned. "Nothing. There was talk of lawyers, and someone said that, practically, Marco was well within his rights to kill him once the knife came out. But that none of the hits before the knife were really that bad. 'Reasonable force,' as though any of that was reasonable."

"I need to talk to the others."

The first one Amanda talked with was Tara. She had to be awakened.

Tara was a dirty blonde, with wide, sad eyes, broad forehead, and something very drab about her. With makeup, there was always just something about her that was off. She was pleasant enough, amiable, but so relatively low-key that Tara was almost a void in space and time. Most people emanated some sort of life force. Tara almost nullified it. If Amanda could see auras, she would lay money that Tara would be made invisible by hers.

Tara gave her insecure little smile. "Marco's been giving off bad juju for a while now."

Hi. Have you met Marco? I knew he was different from the first moment I entered the same room. And you're insisting that you're a perceptive, aura-reading Wiccan? You wouldn't make a good high-school guidance counselor.

"How so?" Amanda asked.

"He's been getting angrier and angrier. If I thought he was sexually active, I'd say he wasn't getting any. But it's more like he's frustrated with the world. He wants to do harm to something. The best thing I can say about him is that he's only hurting people who won't be stopped any other way. He's not even picking fights, you know? He sees something, he doesn't say something, he just *stops* it." Tara looked at Yana. "But he was like that a little when he got here. Remember that rapist? He stopped that one cold, then stomped on his junk a bit? I think it was our first night out with him?"

Amanda nodded. That sounded like something Marco would do. "But now?"

"Now?" Tara answered. "I think the rapist would have needed an ambulance to leave the cemetery. It's like that thing with the ax."

"What ax?"

Once the raw video footage of Marco in the alley with the ax was over, Amanda cleared her throat. "Well. That was… horrible."

Tara nodded. "I don't think anyone, but Rory thought it was a good idea. But Merle and George aren't here. Rory's really the only person that Marco will take advice from."

Amanda nodded slowly. That didn't help unless she knew exactly what they were saying. To some extent, Rory was right - violence was the only language that enemy vampires would understand. They wouldn't get the message otherwise. But still, that Marco was able to do it was part of the problem. Most people she knew couldn't have done that, to heck with someone like Marco, who's only experienced with combat was mostly this year.

Like when his father was kidnapped, he is what he needs to be, she thought. *To hack the vampire to pieces is one thing. To break the abuser piece by piece? What need did that fill?*

As for ignoring advice… "Why? What have you been suggesting?"

"A little less blood," Tara said.

Amanda didn't face-palm, but it was a near run thing. "How so?"

"That we just kill them and be done with it. Maybe injure a few and find out if any vampires reform."

Yana looked up from her bed. The redhead had laid her head down a while back, seemingly tired of the conversation. "Maybe a vampire jail."

Really? Well, that is spectacularly idiotic, even for a pair of touchy-feely Wicca San Franciscans. "Indeed," she said aloud. "Perhaps I should talk to Rory."

"Aye, and the lad has been coming along just wonderful, hasn't he?" Rory said.

Even though Rory was about five-feet tall with Day-Glo red hair, Amanda knew that he had looked different when he'd been alive as the Irish rebel Sean Treacy. The man had been quick on the trigger during the First War of Irish Independence. Amanda hadn't been in the area at the time, mostly because she had been having enough trouble with the Russian Civil War and its ramifications, but what she knew of Treacy was that he would be the first to shed blood in almost any given situation.

So, maybe Amanda shouldn't have been *that* surprised that Rory thought Marco was actually getting *better* the more he inflicted pain.

"Doesn't he have the right idea?" Rory continued. "Send the bastards a message. Straighten up, or be sent home in pieces? Isn't that the only way to beat the idea into their heads? Now, if you ask me - which you did - I think that we should have been doing that months ago. If we did, wouldn't Sarah Ann still be alive? I'm surprised it took Marco to come up with the idea. Wouldn't know it to look at him, would you?"

Maybe not. Though it should concern us all that Marco came up with the concept, and not a killer 80 years his senior.

But Amanda understood. "Sarah Ann" was Marco's predecessor, who had been torn apart in a battle against vampires. It made sense that Rory would think that these tactics may have saved her.

"I want to see what happens next with him, I really do," Rory continued. "If this keeps up, we may not need him around here soon."

Amanda cocked her head. "How do you figure?"

Rory lit a cigarette and inhaled. "You remember that little rampage he went on that drew Asmodeus here? Well, after that, didn't the local vampire population know there was a new sheriff in town? And that the sheriff was cranky? Marco sends crystal-clear messages. In fact, after the bit with the ax ..." Rory cut himself off and thought for a moment. "You know that before this year, there weren't enough vampires in San Francisco to warrant an SFVA, right?"

Amanda nodded. "I never understood that."

Rory shrugged. "Too cool to be comfortable for the likes of us – unless you're used to it. Too many drugs in the bloodstream of the general population. Too many homeless who are too dirty to eat. Too much literally *shite* in the streets is a turn-off. A number of things. But at the current rate of speed, Marco may be able to go home by Christmas, and stay there if he wanted."

The very idea made Amanda's heart skip a beat without her thinking about it.

Rory blinked. He slowly inhaled and looked at Amanda closely. "You? And Marco? Really?" He gave a thoughtful little frown and nodded. "Good for the lad. I could think of much worse, for both of you."

"It is slightly more complicated than that."

Rory waved it off. "When isn't it? But I'm sure you'll both do fine. In fact, I like the idea a lot. Come to think of it, does he even know you're in town yet?"

Amanda shook her head. "I wanted to know where the land mines were."

Rory smiled. "Could have used you back during the Troubles."

Chapter 7

Spytalk

New York City, December 11th

Merle Kraft walked up to the Church of Saints Anthony-Alphonsus, a Catholic church in the midst of Greenpoint. It was built in the 1850s, and it looked like it must have been the pinnacle of construction back then. It had a 240-foot spire the color of iron which shot straight up to the sky, with a red brick face trimmed in white limestone. The inside was cavernous and Gothic like someone had tried to construct a small Saint Patrick's Cathedral in a space, not half as large.

The priest of this particular church was a slightly pudgy, older black man, mildly wrinkled. He had thick plastic frames for his glasses, though the lenses weren't that thick. He looked about as harmless as Father Brown.

However, Merle knew that this was possibly the most dangerous priest in all of New York since Father Rodgers was in command of a team of Vatican Ninjas.

Rodgers smiled and shook hands with Merle. "Welcome, Mister Kraft. Good to see you again. Been a while. How has Afghanistan been treating you?"

"Strangely. I was clearing out a vampire cave and found documents that led back to the whole, strange connection with the United Nations. I don't get it. Because some of them were trade agreements, some were about force deployments."

The priest frowned. "Come back with me."

Once the two were seated around a small table in the rectory, and coffee had been poured, Rodgers continued. "Describe exactly what's going on in Afghanistan right now?"

"I'm going back and forth," Merle explained. "The President doesn't want to really commit to either end of the sandbox, and barely wants to acknowledge that there might be vampires there. It's been a bit of a problem, to tell you the truth. Seriously, the man is a bit of a moron. Instead of just going all-in, he wants to basically send squads on small missions against the resurgent Taliban or the Islamic State. You'd think he was putting in the bare minimum if it weren't for the fact that we've seen his bare minimum with all the hashtag nonsense."

Rodgers frowned, thoughtful. "Tell me, do you think that the missions you're sent on are rogue? Unsanctioned?"

Merle frowned, and not thoughtfully. "That would just be odd. Granted, I've been given my own team, we are considered SpecOps, and they've taken a lot of instructions from the CIA in the past, but I haven't heard a whisper of being unsanctioned. Incursions into a foreign country?"

The priest shrugged. "All it takes is for someone to say 'Fix it, but don't tell me about it,' then you're off to Belmont."

"You mean the horse races, right? Oy vey. Politics."

Rodgers nodded. "So, what can I help you with? If you're asking about the United Nations, we haven't heard anything. The local vampires have been quiet lately. The Vatican is considering taking my men out of the area, to tell the truth. My men are in high demand. We won't even talk about Hendershot resenting the resources put on Robert Catalano."

"Really?" Merle asked. "I would have thought given the amount of help that Marco has given, protecting his father would have been a small investment."

"Ignore that Hendershot and Marco never got along _"

"Marco didn't get along with someone? I'm shocked," Merle snarked.

"- but we've got our sniper keeping an eye on the house almost every night. We just don't have many Swiss Guards around the world who specialize in anti-vampire operations. Hendershot and his people have been here for nearly a year."

Merle nodded. "Okay. Your guys are spread a little thin. I got that. However, I know that the UN has something to do with the vampire problem. Who should I talk to?"

"I could ask Enrico."

"Who?"

The man known simply as Enrico was tall but more elegant than most Mafia knee breakers. He was as relaxed as he might be for a standard business meeting. Enrico was less DeNiro and Pacino of Mafia movies, and more Michael Rennie of the original Day the Earth Stood Still. He was of medium build, with thick cheekbones and slicked-back hair.

He would have looked as out of place in a rectory as a tarantula on a wedding cake. Which is why they were meeting in his home in the middle of Bensonhurst.

"The United Nations?" Enrico asked smoothly. "The big ugly glass building around Turtle Bay? What does that have to do with vampires?"

"If I knew that, I wouldn't be here," Merle answered.

The mobster nodded. "As you have asked for my expertise, I also invited someone else over, hope you don't mind."

Merle cocked his head to one side and arched his brows. "Really? Why? Who is it?"

"Me."

Merle looked over his shoulder. The woman was so pretty she practically glowed … he would have even thought *sparkled* if he wasn't worried she could read his mind. She had a wide, beaming smile, blonde hair that stopped just before her shoulders, and warm brown eyes. She wore a warm-looking chocolate business suit.

Merle reached out and took her hand. "Merle Kraft."

"Jennifer Bosley."

Merle blinked. "Odd question, are you a vampire, by any chance?"

Bosley nodded. "Quite. Shall we sit?"

Merle sighed as Bosley walked past him. *Why is it that all the hot ones are dead? And why am I so hip-deep in vampires lately?*

After they settled into Enrico's marvelously well-furnished sitting room (with blackout curtains), Bosley sat forward, legs primly crossed, hands folded in her lap, and began, "Why do you believe that the United Nations has anything to do with vampires?"

"UN documents found in vampire caves in the sandbox. The most recent batch was very, very recent. As in 'this week' recent. The first time I stumbled across vampires, they were murdering FBI and MI-6 agents sniffing around the UN. They damn near killed me for doing the same. You can see why I might think there's a pattern. The one thing I don't know is what the hell they're *doing.*"

Bosley frowned. Her big brown eyes focused just past Merle, visibly turning it over in her mind. "To tell you the truth, I'm certain that you're right. You are onto something. You'd have to be, really, wouldn't you? I'm somewhat familiar with what's been going on. I am, after all, friends with Amanda Colt. And if you're not connected with her and Marco Catalano, I'd be surprised."

Merle nodded slowly. "Of *course* you're friends. How did you and Enrico meet up?"

"After Marco's father had his hospital blown up," Enrico answered. "Miss Bosley and I worked together to get Miss Colt out from under the pile of rubble that was that wing of the hospital."

"Neither of us," Bosley noted, "are particularly fond of terrorists. As I told Mistress Colt, that is a line few vampires tolerate."

"Right." Merle looked off to one side, trying to think of his next play and his next question. "Is there anyone you two could tap? If you're already against these people, a little extra support won't hurt."

Bosley and Enrico shared a look. "Possibly," she said. "It might take time, though. Have you talked to Amanda?"

Merle shrugged. "Not since September. I've been busy. Why?"

"She's been hunting down any leads behind Asmodeus," Bosley explained. "If he's connected, then she'd be the one to ask. I've put out some feelers, but nothing specifically connected to the United Nations. Will there be anything else? We have an appointment."

Merle didn't really hear her. "Hmm?"

"We have another appointment after this," Enrico echoed. "We're working on a philanthropic endeavor together."

"Oh? Should I ask what the mob and vampires are working on?"

"Rebuilding the hospital," Bosley told him.

Merle looked from one to the other, with a little smirk and a raised eyebrow. "Are you trying to buy goodwill from Marco, or hope it leads into a *quid pro quo* down the road?"

She beamed at him with the full wattage of her brilliant smile. "Yes."

Merle chuckled. "Yeah, good luck with that. I don't think Marco has goodwill to spare."

Bosley shrugged. "I haven't even met the lad yet in person. He sounds positively charming, though."

"That's one word for it. I'm not even sure *I* can get goodwill out of Marco now, and he's kinda working for me."

"Marco doesn't really work for anybody," came a new voice.

Merle stood, taking the hand of Doctor Robert Catalano. "Sir. Good to meet you again."

Robert nodded. "Been a while. My son hasn't broken anything new lately, has he?"

"Not that I've been informed of. Though I heard something about a YouTube video? I haven't had much time to catch up while I've been… away."

Robert looked at Merle closely, studying him. "Which end of the sandbox?"

Merle made certain not to flinch. "I can't confirm or deny."

"Oh please," Bosley said, still in the chair. "A tan like that, you've either been at a beach ten hours a day, or you've been to the Middle East."

Enrico nodded. "Sorry. It's not that hard to guess."

Merle rolled his eyes and paused. He listened for a moment, then looked at the vampire, meeting her eyes. "Listen. Do you notice something?"

Jennifer Bosley and Merle actually held the look for a moment. The spy and the vampire, in that span of time, had an entire conversation in their heads - coordination, strategy, tactics, and most importantly, the first move. Because the thing that Merle *felt*, and Bosley *knew* was something very simple.

There were no more guards around the house.

Five seconds later, gunfire filled the room.

San Francisco

Marco always felt like he was a great argument for religion.

Whenever someone tried to argue that "Oh, without religion, it's not like anyone is going to become a mass murderer," Marco just laughed in their faces. He didn't know if he would be a mass murderer, a spree killer, or a serial killer, but he knew that there would be a string of bodies behind him wherever he went.

But his faith didn't like that, his God was against it, and every document of the church that Marco got his hands on didn't approve.

But even Marco knew that he was starting to spiral.

When he was growing up, Marco had idly considered various and sundry ways of fighting off everyone in the room if he needed to. When he had to kill his first human being, he upgraded the plan to *killing* everyone in the room.

Now it was just getting ridiculous.

Marco walked down the street, hallways, walkways, and everywhere he went, he sized up a human being, broke them down into quick observations and component parts, and reassembled them regarding weak points and angles of attack.

It was only through the grace of God and a thorough prayer life that he hadn't acted on it.

Then again, it helped that he spent many an evening taking out his aggression on the forces of darkness.

This was normally the part of any Physician Assistant program where the entire class would have broken up into their little cliques, study groups, book projects, that sort of thing.

Marco wouldn't want to be tempted to do something at the first sign of stupid. He really did know all of this already. Mostly because he was easily bored and read medical textbooks for fun.

Maybe that's why I'm cranky all the time. I feel like I'm hip-deep in stupid, trying to explain thermodynamics to cavemen. Oh, who am I kidding? Even cavemen understood fire. These people are working so hard at things that I understood when I was twelve, I might as well be explaining things to them with Lego.

The truly sad part is that these people have to be brilliant just to make it in the front door. They have to be at least as smart as anyone else I know. Maybe it's San Francisco…

I didn't exactly like the people back at NY Screw, either…

Maybe I'm just cranky. Maybe he could learn new ways to kill people with scalpels.

"Hey, Marco!"

He didn't look towards the sound of the new voice. He wasn't particularly happy with Yana, but he knew that she couldn't exactly be punished for it. After all, she was only trying to help.

But then again, as one of the interview preppers told us: Even lawyers *think they help people. If only her version of help wasn't telling me how to run my life…*

"What can I do for you, Yana?"

"Some of the people in my Pharm class want to form a study group. Want to help?"

"How many of them are fellow Wiccans who are taking pharmacology in part for recreation?"

"Um, all of them. How did you guess?"

Maybe there's another reason I'm homicidal. "Have you ever considered that I'm not a fan of people who hope to be legal drug dealers when they grow up?"

"Why?"

Oh for frig's sake! "What's the sudden rush to get me socialized? Or are these friends of yours failing because they think it's fun to lace marijuana with uppers?"

"I just thought that you might want to be around other people!"

God save me from perky people. In fact, just shoot me right now.

New York City

A bullet storm wouldn't have been a problem for Jennifer Bosley, except the holes blasting through the blackout curtains also filled Enrico's living room with sunlight.

In short, it was a torrent of death that no-one would have survived.

The men who swarmed in were dressed in full tactical gear, dressed in black from head to toe. They had enough automatic weapons to go to war with a few squad cars, and enough personnel to top the famous LA Shootout of the late 90s.

They came in through the front door, then they swept in from the back and side doors as well. Eight of them had wiped out everyone on the perimeter, and all of the guards between them and their targets.

But as the soldiers swarmed the living room, they found themselves facing an empty room with a massive hole in the floor. It was the sort of thing that a vampire could have created in a few seconds of punching through wood.

That led to a little problem for the attackers. As the gunmen formed a circle around the hole in the floor, they pondered their next move.

The first two soldiers to drop dead were taken from below. Silverware flew up from the basement with the speed of bullets, hurled with unerring accuracy by a pissed-off vampire who had grown up in a particularly bad London neighborhood.

The gunmen on either side immediately lifted their guns to fill the hole with gunfire. The gunmen who were probably *directly* above the knife thrower reached for their hand grenades.

Merle Kraft appeared behind the men with the grenades and threw *them* into the hole. With an angry vampire.

The remaining four gunmen refocused their attention to where their last two comrades had been a second ago. But Merle was already gone.

The door from the basement burst open, and Enrico wheeled around it, firing six shots in short order. None of these bullets pierced their body armor, but the impacts drove two more men down into the hole.

Jennifer Bosley would not go hungry today.

Merle Kraft appeared behind the last two men standing, pressing the tips of steak knives into the back of their necks. "Would you two like to be taken alive or undead?"

The gunman on Merle's left didn't hesitate. He slammed his rifle into his comrade's face, driving his head into Merle's weapon.

He quickly ended himself with his own gun.

Merle frowned. "Well, that was odd." He looked down into the hole. "Hey, Bosley, you have anything on those guys down there?"

"I have two stripped," she called back, "and they're covered in tattoos. Russian."

Merle quickly stripped down the thug with his head still attached, and found something different - tattoos in French, from the DGSE, their special forces.

Oh, now what? So, mercenaries. Have to be mercenaries. It's not like they'll work together willingly unless they were being paid to.

But wait, I started with freaking vampires, and now I'm fighting human gunmen? What the hell goes on here? Unless … they're humans serving *a vampire?*

"Miss Bosley," Merle called down into the basement, "I think it's time that we cover the topic of minions."

San Francisco

Amanda Colt had kept a close eye on the clock. One of the things with San Francisco was that sensing the sun wasn't just sensing the position. She could easily wander out into the heavy fog and not worry about being burnt to ash. She couldn't transform into a bat or mist, but she could walk around.

Right now, sleeping in Rory's crypt is getting claustrophobic.

Amanda had carried her dirt with her and had slept with it still in its zip-locked bags taped against her back. She usually slept with it under a mattress, but Rory was far more… traditional in his vampire sleeping arrangements. She would have considered a hotel, but she didn't want to have to deal with friendly, helpful maid service, especially if one opened the curtains for any reason.

She peered out of the crypt door once more. It was finally dark enough for her taste and headed out. She had talked to everyone she could, and she had finally run out of excuses.

She arrived at the dorms once more, and she needed Yana to meet her at the front to let her in.

It was time to visit Marco.

New York City

Enrico had a very nice basement.

After the assault upstairs, the cleanup, the conversations with the cops, and everything else was over, the easiest place for Jennifer Bosley to have a conversation with any of the others was in the basement.

Doctor Robert Catalano and Merle Kraft took seats in some beat-up but very comfortable recliners. Jennifer and Enrico shared a sofa that could have opened up into a bed.

"Minions are very much like your standard Renfield," Bosley began. She paused. "We all know who Renfield was in *Dracula*, right?"

Enrico shrugged. "Who?"

Bosley sighed patiently. "In Stoker's book, Renfield was under Dracula's control and influence. Also in the book, he becomes repentant, and killed by Dracula. But real minions are more like drug addicts, and the vampire they're linked to *is* their drug. They drink some of the vampire's blood - not a lot, but enough to give them far more strength than the average man. Addiction is almost instantaneous. Consumption of too much blood can turn them into vampires. Occasionally, minions have been mistaken for revenants - ghosts or zombies or some such. The blood provides a link between minion and vampire.

"These men and women are the vampire's eyes and ears during the day. The vampire can use their senses at will – all at once, if the vampire is strong enough."

Enrico frowned. "What happens if there are too many of them?"

"Imagine trying to keep track of a dozen televisions at the same time, all of them playing at full volume and point blank."

Enrico winced. "Oh. Can't be fun."

"It has some advantages. But keep in mind, if someone is old enough and powerful enough, controlling or guiding eight people may not be that difficult."

Merle gave a little smile. "Though it would be great in tactical situations. The vampire is basically networking a hive mind. No-one has to radio in positions, situations, or recon. The vampire sees all, knows all, and can relay it back to the operatives. I'd want to have something like that sometime."

"What I'd like to know," Robert said, "is how it works." The doctor looked around at the mobster, the vampire, and the spy, and thought over how to explain himself. "I know that the mechanism for vampirism is viral in nature. When a vampire bites someone, it supports the victim's recovery with enhanced strength. It's probably the only reason that many of the victims who were attacked last year were able to survive. But Amanda never mentioned being able to influence Marco in any way. Let's call that Stage 1 vampirism? The body is resisting, like fighting off a bad cold. This minion-status would be Stage 2, I presume. The vampire and the virus have a more permanent hook in the victim."

She grinned. "Very nicely put, Doctor. Yes, your analysis is very much how it breaks down."

"But does this level of influence extend to when the victim turns into a vampire?" Robert asked.

Bosley nodded, then hesitated, and shrugged. "It depends on a lot of things, does it not? If I created a new vampire, it's different than a minion. It's almost more of a partnership. One vampire can try to enforce their will on another, but she'd need to be a very powerful vampire to start with before they could try such a thing. There are plenty of variables, of course, but that's the gist of it."

Merle winced. "Ever heard of one that brought commandos on board? Because those weren't your run-of-the-mill dirtbags upstairs. Those were some grade-A gunmen. I'd say it's like Mikhail from a few months ago, but this is more dangerous. This is more SpecOps. This is more... oh crap."

Robert gave Merle a sidelong glance. "What?"

"This is more like the vampire bitch that *assassinated* Mikhail."

Chapter 8
Getting Back Together

San Francisco

He stayed still, terrifyingly still, holding the knife blade in one hand, waiting to strike. He summoned all his control and concentration into that one point. Without warning, he threw his brand-new throwing knife into the target.

A knock sounded against his door. He turned, the frown of concentration replaced by a tiny, almost omniscient smile. "If that's Yana, you can come in."

After living there for months, he'd gotten accustomed to never accepting visitors after dark without being very specific about who he invited in. He knew Yana's knock by now, but he liked being cautious anyway.

The cute redheaded witch walked into the room, as shy as ever, her smile as unsure as 20% of the words from her mouth. Her hair was cut short, almost curling around the neck and the shoulders, staying above the nape. He didn't like to think of advertising dinner to vampires, but he wasn't up on the latest in fashion, so he let it go.

"Hi. You busy?" Yana shyly asked.

"Not really. Is it time to go hunting now?"

The redhead simply smiled. Someone else stood behind Yana. The light inside his dorm suite wasn't as high as possible (he liked to work in minimal light for his knife throwing), so her face was in general darkness. Only those marvelous eyes stood out.

And then his heart stopped. *Oh no.*

Sure, he would never admit it, but he was scared of those eyes - terrified of what would happen if he looked in one day and never came out. Or if she saw what was in his heart.

But at that moment, he was more terrified of what he was going to do in that instant.

Marco forced his heart rate to slow down. He didn't want to give away what was in his heart. Now if *he* only knew what was in his heart. Did he want to grab her and hug her to him, or did he want to stab her? And even then, fatally, or non-fatally? The burning, hollow sensation in his chest filled his guts, his ears, his soul.

Wow. I knew I was angry at her. I just didn't know how angry.

"Um…"

Calm down. Calm down. Calm down.

Marco settled for his most used gambit - emotionally shutting down. It often happened when the rage grew uncontrollably, and his only options were to attack someone or become, terribly, terribly civilized. It was what he used whenever he got into a political conversation with classmates - or whenever he saw someone wearing a Che Guevara shirt … in San Francisco, this meant he was on guard like that half of his waking hours.

With that effort, Marco felt his entire body relax. He forced himself into his most charming smile and stepped forward, one hand forward in friendship. "It's a pleasure to see you again."

Amanda Colt smiled, stepped into the room, and hugged Marco off of his feet. "Brat," she commented.

He smiled and hugged her back. "But you love me anyway."

Amanda smiled as she let him down.

Yana looked from one to the other, blinking, thinking that these two must be dating… and then noted that Marco was totally oblivious to Amanda's obviously loving glance.

Marco straightened his polo shirt over his frame. It was black, to match his dark pants. "So, Amanda, when did you get into town? Please sit."

Amanda sat on the foot of Marco's bed, demurely crossing her legs. He remembered the last time she was in the same room, on the same bed, wearing a cheongsam. Now that she wore jeans and a long-sleeved t-shirt, he suddenly missed the cheongsam. It would have been something to rip off her and -

Marco forced himself into numbness. Relaxing.

"How many people have you been pissing off lately?" Amanda asked.

He smiled. "Oh, everyone who died once already… you just got back into town?"

Amanda smiled and didn't answer. "Have you been keeping up with the combat exercises?"

"Of course, wanna see?"

"Sure."

"Great." He smiled broadly and arched his eyebrows suggestively. "Let's roll around a little."

New York City

Merle Kraft walked around the United Nations building, considering how the setup would operate.

What possible use would a demon be to the UN? Or a vampire?

Or, better question, what use would the UN be to the forces of Darkness? Or for anyone else for that...

Wait a second... I felt something.

Merle turned, only to catch something blinking out of sight. Then he looked up - something moved from the roof of the UN. He crouched, hoping to be a smaller target. But what was hunting him closed nearer. The pressure against his skin was like pressing two magnets together by identical poles. The bottom of his gut had fallen out, as though an elevator had started to drop. This sinking feeling was he wouldn't be fast enough this time.

"I've got a crucifix, and I'm not afraid to use it," Merle whispered.

"Goody," came a soft brogue. "At least you'll be a challenge."

He spun to his feet and leapt to one side, moments before a fire hydrant was knocked out of the ground, taking the hit for him. He turned and saw something pluck the hydrant out of the air and hurl it at him. He jumped aside again, coming to his feet in a doorway arch.

In front of him stood a six-foot redhead of the blood-drinking variety. Her face looked as though someone had taken a blowtorch to it, leaving the face nigh unrecognizable as human - and the fangs didn't help the impression. If Merle could tell anything about her face, he knew she was glaring, mainly because of two, bright green pinpoints he guessed were eyes.

"You think you can fight me, little man?" she purred.

Merle blinked. "Certainly not."

"Good, then stay still, this won't hurt a bit."

She wheeled around, scooping a manhole cover from the street and hurled it at his neck.

Before she released it, however, he had already vanished.

A wooden stake stuck out of her arm, and she flinched, grimaced, then flicked her arm so hard the stake came back at Merle with the force of a bullet. He was already gone, and she leapt away, ripping a stop sign out of the ground, hurling it like a throwing ax at his new position. Merle moved once again, breathing heavily.

Why couldn't this witch even let me get close?

Merle was then lifted off the ground by the collar.

How did she manage to get in front of me?

"Had enough?" he gasped.

She smiled with sharp teeth.

With his left hand, Merle chopped on the inside of her arm, hitting the nerve point behind her wrist, so she dropped him. With his right, Merle fired a palm into her nose, driving the cartilage into her brain. With a quick spin kick, he snapped her head back, and Merle dropped to a crouch to sweep the legs out from under her. He pressed the advantage by throwing himself forward, crucifix first, and wound up with a kick to his face for the trouble.

He found himself on his back and in a lot of pain…

With a vampire standing over him.

San Francisco

Marco ducked and sidestepped under the right cross and hammered his thumb into her shoulder, numbing the muscle. He slid back before she could deliver a kick that could collapse his chest. By the time he made it back to his starting point, the effects of his blow had worn off, and she came at him again.

Amanda delivered a snap kick aimed high, and her foot landed in his waiting double block. He pushed. She fell backward, landed on her hands, and flipped back onto her feet. She pivoted to deliver a reverse back kick, but he dropped to one knee while she was still in mid-pivot and let the leg fly over his head as he sprang into her like a lineman breaking the other team's line. His shoulder landed in her stomach, and he wrapped his arms around her in the same motion.

His impact sent her off balance and added to his next move. He held onto her as he threw himself backward, dragging her with him.

It would have made an impressive throw if he had the impetus to do it, but the awkwardness of the move made him turn it into a wrestling slam against the mat, which would have worked had Amanda not slapped her hands against the mat and jerked her legs from his grasp. He fell to the mat as she pulled her legs over her head in a handstand. Before he could move, she backflipped and landed over Marco's chest, straddling him, his neck between her knees.

Marco blinked, a little stunned. "Wow. You've gotten even better."

She smiled. "I try."

Marco looked deep into Amanda's eyes, and felt, as he so often did, that he could be happy just to fall into them for the rest of his life and have no need to come out for oxygen, food or drink.

He could be happy … if the idea didn't scare the heck out of him.

Marco smiled. He needed to say something before his pulse quickened so she could hear it. The fact that he was near a very interesting part of her anatomy didn't help him and his situation at all.

Wait, we're sparring, my pulse is already up, he thought, his breath speeding up slightly. Amanda's weight on top of him, her heat against him, the way she looked with her skin lightly covered in sweat…

Think of something else, or this is going to end badly. "Hmm… you're all sweaty."

She grinned. "The first dirty thought that comes out of your head *will* be your last."

"Who? Me? I think?"

Marco blinked, then looked on Amanda with his clear blues. "We can stop wrestling now."

Amanda nodded and slid off of him… rather slowly. As slowly as possible without tipping him off that she wanted to prolong contact. Her own urges were a little bit too literally animal in nature.

"Um…" She cocked her head. "Marco, why have you never tried to… is it because I'm a vampire?"

He cocked his head, like a curious dog. His heart rate sped up, and he tried to make it decelerate before Amanda heard it. Did she mean…? Was she implying…?

Was she *disappointed* that he hadn't made a move on her?

Marco blinked once more and asked, "Is *what* because you're a vampire?"

Amanda heard his heart beating faster at the question. *He's getting nervous.*

She sighed. "Never mind."

And then the phone rang.

New York City

Merle blinked as the vampire towered over him.

"It's time fer a midnight snack, ye little bastard," she said. "A little payback for that daisy cutter in Afghanistan." She reached down and grabbed Merle by the shoulders, hauling him off the ground. "First you, then Catalano, then his little girlfriend, too."

He smiled. So *this* had been one of the creatures chasing him out of the cave the other day – that at least told him how she knew he'd be coming.

It also reminded Merle of what had worked even then. "How's your night vision?"

She never liked to play with her food before. "Perfect."

In a move that not even Nuala saw, Merle set off a charge of flash powder right in her face, the white-hot flame blinding her. Merle hit her with a quick triple-kick and a backspin kick that broke her neck and smacked her with the flat side of the crucifix.

The pain of the cross made her push off with both feet, sending her in a leap so fast that she was about a block away when she landed.

Merle had made a decision to be somewhere else when she got back.

San Francisco

"I'll get it," Tiffany called from the front register of the Artful Krafts shop.

Marco shrugged at Amanda. "At least she's good at taking notes."

"Is George hanging around?" Amanda inquired.

"He's in Afghanistan at the moment, with Merle."

She raised a brow. "Our Merle? Kraft Merle?"

No, the Queen of the Damned… Of course *Merle Kraft!* Marco thought. He simply nodded. He yawned, then looked at his watch. "Amazing, I'm actually kinda tired. You'd think I'd be better at staying up late given this town."

Amanda smiled. "Good night. Don't let the vampires bite."

He offered her his arm. She took it.

They left just as Tiffany hung up with Merle Kraft, telling her to keep Marco in sight.

"Harder! Harder! Faster, damnit!"

Tiffany jerked out of a boredom-induced stupor at the noises. Loud annoying people were irritating her - and oh dear, they might be scaring away the customers.

The blonde looked around the store, seeing no-one inside, but it was close… So it must have been outside.

She frowned. No-one was inside. Damn. There were no customers at all even to make loud, obnoxious sex sounds. That would be corrected soon.

Tiffany marched outside, her over-endowed chest leading the charge like a battering ram. She rounded the corner of the building, looking down into an alley. Rory was there, pressing a woman up against the wall, her back to his chest, and her legs occasionally thrashed as she cried out.

"Damnit!" Tiffany shrieked. "No sex by the store. That will scare away people with money!"

Rory looked up, and Tiffany saw a ring of blood around his mouth. The woman he held groaned and looked at the blonde with irritation.

"I'm a phlebotomist," she groaned. "I wanted to see how fast he could go."

"I don't care how phlegmatic you are, you can't have sex by the store, and that includes quickies!" Tiffany snapped.

Rory sighed. "She means that she works at a blood bank, and she wanted to know how many milliliters I could drain per second, okay?"

Tiffany rolled her eyes. "Just not by the store. Find a vampire bar or something."

Chapter 9

Passion Play

Amanda sat outside Marco's dorm room. She would make damned certain that nothing happened to him while she was around. She had come to San Francisco with the deliberate purpose of protecting him, and she was damned if he died on her watch. She would die first. Period. End sentence.

And the last thing she wanted was to be there, only a few feet away from Marco. Lying in bed. Maybe wearing nothing.

This is not a good line of thought.

Then she heard something.

It was from inside Marco's room.

Marco settled into his bed, in t-shirt and boxers, tossing the sheets over his form, and he gently closed his eyes, ready for sleep…

But it wouldn't come.

He frowned in frustration, and ground his teeth, then tossed himself one way, and then another. He growled and was suddenly uncomfortable in his own bed.

Marco sat up, running his fingers through his hair. He knew he was tired. Heck, he was exhausted. He hadn't slept well. And he knew why. Amanda. She had completely disappeared from his life without so much as a goodbye.

Let's face it, Marco, you're certainly glad she showed up again. Hell, you're ecstatic. You could think of nothing else when she got here other than "She's here, she's here, she's here…" Now, what's your problem? That she didn't… say… one, damn, thing before vanishing into the mists? That she hadn't even deigned to take a break to see you for -

The knock came so suddenly a wooden knife was in his hand before the sound waves had finished vibrating. "Who is it?"

"Me," Amanda said.

Marco cocked an eyebrow and absentmindedly tossed the blanket aside, standing. "Twist the knob gently right, left, right again, and tap on the door twice."

On the other side of the door, Amanda wrinkled her brow and did as he instructed. The door popped open, and she walked in on him. He stood in the center of the room in a t-shirt and boxers the way any other guy might stand in a full tuxedo, like a dancer with his hands at his side. A knife lay on the bed, completely ignored.

Amanda smiled and raised a brow at the knife. "I hope I'm not interrupting anything."

"Not in the least. I require so very little sleep nowadays… the resident annoyances have made sure of that. Will you sit? Desk, chair, or bed, makes no difference."

Amanda eyed the bed, then looked at him in his shirt and underwear - yeah, she'd jump him if it was the bed. "Chair."

Marco reached over and pulled a chair from the desk and turned it toward the bed. He held it for her as she sat down, and walked around to the bed, still standing. "So, how do you like the place? And what really brings you here?"

"Well, I… Are you going to sit?"

He nodded casually. He sat on the foot of the bed and deftly crossed one leg over another. She wondered how he managed not to flash her. "And?"

"I have been worried." She leaned forward, looking into his thoughtful eyes. She was tempted to rip his clothes off, and he was oblivious.

Instead, his mood changed. Something darker, and angrier, had come over him. "Really? Well, if you were, you could have at least said goodbye last time."

Amanda winced. "I know, but as I mentioned to you, I had been occupied -"

He arched his brows. "Better things to do, were there?"

She winced inside. Marco's tone was neutral, but she smelled his anger, his bitterness. How royally pissed he was. She couldn't even recall the last time she had sensed this level of rage pouring off him. And he had been so happy when Amanda had arrived that…

"Asmodeus," was her only answer.

Marco's eyes narrowed. "Was *that* the only reason? The demon we personally sent back to Hell?"

Amanda nodded. "I asked around the underground -"

He raised a hand. "Wait, you don't mean the vampire underground, do you?" He leaned forward. "You went talking to the Incontinents?"

She almost balked at the odd name he had labeled the lower-level vampires of the evil persuasion. She knew he took the classification from Aristotle's four levels of human behavior - virtuous, continent, incontinent, and vicious - but every time she heard that all she could think of was constipated vampires.

"They know enough to not challenge me, Marco."

One of his eyes twitched. They had both needed to chat with Incontinents, true. They weren't outright evil creatures, just not very friendly, and a few steps below a mere rogue.

But they both went in together. *Always. Together.* She had never considered talking to the riffraff before she met him, and he… well, he had never even heard of real vampires before he met her.

Amanda smiled despite herself. "You were there in spirit. They all remember what you did to the Recovery Room… and the Bloody Mary… and the Platelet. If they weren't afraid of me already, they'd be afraid because of you." She leaned forward and touched his knee. "Marco, Asmodeus is *serious*."

He nodded. "Yes, seriously dead…" He felt himself getting even more irritated than a moment ago.

And she was touching him.

Passion and annoyance fought for dominance within him, and he decided to sidestep them both.

"Did I show you some of my recent woodworking?" Marco asked. Without waiting for a reply, he strode over to his headboard and withdrew a foot-long wooden blade. He flipped it onto his middle finger to show that it was perfectly balanced in the center.

"Throwing knife," he said. "I don't like up close and personal with something ten times stronger than I am if I don't have to."

Amanda smiled tolerantly. "Can you throw well?"

Marco scooped up three knives from the nightstand (they had looked like letter openers) and tossed them at the bulletin board in a triangle and ended by smoothly taking the foot-long knife in hand and throwing it into the middle.

He stood dancer-straight and shrugged. "You could kinda say that." His eyes brightened. "Did I show you this one?"

Marco went to the night table drawer, yanked out a crucifix and stood, feet apart, his forward foot perpendicular to his back foot. He held it before him a moment before lunging forward, as with a foil, and ramming the sharpened bottom point towards Amanda, stopping inches from her heart. He felt fortunate that she didn't beat him to death with his soon-to-be-ripped-off arms.

Amanda looked at his feet. "Do that again."

He did. "You look like you're fencing again," she told him.

They had met over swords. They had stayed in the realm of friendship, somehow. Amanda smiled at the memories.

At what point did she realize she was in love with him? She couldn't answer. She couldn't even answer why except she knew Marco made her heart beat without her needing to concentrate on it. Sometimes, he could stop her heart with a look.

They had been such a large part of each other's lives, not being near him during the last few months had nearly killed her… again.

Marco went to his closet and opened the door. From the bottom, he withdrew a polished wooden box. He turned to her on the ball of his foot and presented it to her. Inside was a finely polished cavalry saber.

Her eyes widened. "Wow. Nice toy."

Marco smiled. "Turn around a minute."

Before she could, he had his shirt off, and Amanda wondered if Marco had even 1% fat on his body, and then how he looked so ordinary. He seemed to have an armor of muscle beneath the skin, but she hadn't even guessed at it.

He was in mid-reach for an item in the closet when he stopped and said, "Turn around."

Amanda had to stop her eyes from glowing with her desire. There wasn't that much cotton standing between her and his more interesting body parts. "Why? Afraid I'll see something I haven't before?"

She heard his heart accelerate. "A surprise."

A few moments later: "You can turn around."

Amanda sighed, turned, and opened her eyes. Marco had been replaced by a soldier in a navy blue military uniform with a white cap atop his head and the cavalry saber at his side.

Marco spread his arms. "What do you think?"

She bit her lip for a moment, wondering what to think. "Not bad. You never showed me that one before."

He nodded. "Xavier High School," he said. "You couldn't have shown up at the graduation ceremony even if you had known me… it was a rather bright and sunny day, as I recall. ROTC. Comes with the uniform and saber. They taught me how to fight, shoot, and use this." He patted the hilt of the sword.

Marco's hand gripped the sword handle, and the tension in his jaw suddenly jumped to the fore.

Amanda stepped forward, and he took a half-step, avoiding her. "Marco, what is it?"

"You left," he whispered. His hand reached for his belt buckle with slow, deliberate movements. He didn't trust himself with the sword on hand, and he put it off to one side. "You left me alone here for months. You didn't even write. You didn't even open a single email I sent you."

"Yes, I know. I told you I was -"

"*Busy*," he spat. "You were *busy*. I didn't even know if you were alive, but that's okay because you were *busy*. You were doing things for my protection. Seriously. Hi. *Have we met?* The first time you did this, it was funny. But you didn't know me then. You didn't understand me that well. It didn't really occur to me that you'd pull that again. Not really. After all, you knew me by now, didn't you? You understood a little bit about me. But no, you didn't even think about what your absence would do, did you? Did you even think of disappearing into thin air would even affect me a little?"

Amanda's eyes narrowed. The more he spoke, the more it hurt her. But it also pissed her off. "Why would it?" she asked with scorn. "You left for San Francisco, didn't you? You left *me* in the city without anyone else to deal with. You left *first*."

He stepped forward now, moving in on her. "You had everyone back in the city. *Everyone*. And we talked every *damned day* from the day I left until the day you disappeared. If I had bought it, you'd know about it in a matter of *hours*. If you died, there wouldn't even be a *body*. I would have never known something had happened to you. When you disappeared, I had nothing and *no-one*."

Amanda heard his heart beating faster. That was anger, wasn't it? But it didn't sound like Marco angry. She stepped right into him, staring him straight in the eye. He didn't blink, and neither did she. "If I completely disappeared, you would have known exactly what happened. I would have died. And then you could have gotten on with your life."

Marco scoffed. "*What* life? Tell me, what do I have? Minions in the gangs of New York, some paltry assistants in San Francisco, and my parents would like me to have a life eventually. I have *you*, and that's *it*."

Oh, really? He is going to play it like that, is he? "Because I am your *friend*?"

"No!" he barked. "Because I love you, damnit! Don't you get it? Why do you think Lily is deader than dead? She *threatened* you. She wanted me, she saw you as a threat, and I wouldn't have it. She would have killed you, if not that day, then soon enough. I wouldn't let her." He took a deep breath, and whispered, "I couldn't let her do that." He blinked. His eyes were wet, and he took several deep breaths, as though he was running a marathon. "I wasn't going to let her do that. It was her or you. I chose you."

Amanda let the silence settle in for a moment. She didn't have Marco's photographic memory, but she had something better - a spy's memory. There was a memory palace of her entire life. There was a place for Marco, of course.

Suddenly, many of their conversations had a different ring to them.

"Do you remember the cemetery?" she asked.

Marco's little smile returned. "You have no idea how much I remember the cemetery."

"You meant it, didn't you," she said, as a statement, not a question.

Marco nodded.

"You remembered what I said?" she asked.

"You started by asking me -"

"- Do you have any idea what you do to me? You make my body react involuntarily to you. I have perfect control, yet when you are near, your proximity controls me. I want to bite you every time we meet and hope I don't drain you completely. I want to run my hands over your body and give you a sample of everything you do to me."

Marco blinked, and his heart started racing once again. He whispered, "You didn't -"

"I meant it."

Marco's arms were around her before either of them knew what was happening. His lips were on hers in a crash, kissing her with a fury and a passion that like he was compelled. Amanda only backed up a step before she attacked him with equal fervor. Her arms wrapped around his neck, holding him to her, lest he escape.

As they kissed, Marco's hands slid down her back, and then into her pants. Amanda was worried that he was going to take her shirt off - *Would I stop him if he insisted?* - but that worry died quickly. He simply untucked her shirt, sliding his hands up along her spine, skin to skin. He needed to touch her. Amanda combed her fingers through his hair as her tongue penetrated his mouth and deepened the kiss.

Marco's upper body pressed against hers. And while his mouth and hands were extremely active, the rest of him was perfectly, perfectly still. She wondered why for a moment as she moved a little closer to him and found herself poked in the stomach.

Amanda gasped at the sensation and pulled away a bit to say something, but as her lips left his, his mouth kissed her chin, then proceeded to leave a trail of little kisses along her jaw.

"Isn't that awkward for you?" she gasped.

Marco's kisses reached her ear. When he spoke, it was less of a whisper and more of a quiet growl. "Don't move, or it'll be more awkward for both of us in the morning."

His mouth went to her neck as though he was going to devour her. His hand slipped along her spine, around her waist, to her stomach, slipped off for a second, and went reversed course. She was no longer being poked.

Amanda sighed as his teeth grazed the nerve that went down her neck into her shoulder. This couldn't last. He didn't know even a fraction of her life. They had only known each other a year and a half. She had been alive a hundred years, just as a vampire. She had secrets he couldn't even guess at. She had to stop this. She had to tell him everything. She had to -

The thought got cut off as his lips found her collarbone. She groaned, mostly in frustration. "Marco, you have to stop."

"Why?" he said into her throat. He had made a U-turn up the jugular. She could hear his smile. He was freaking teasing her now.

"There's so much you don't know. You can't love me -"

Marco stopped kissing her but didn't release her. His head came up just enough, so they were nose-to-nose.

His words came clipped and sharp and fast, as though he wanted to crack them out and get back to what they were doing. "How can I not love you? I know everything about you. You were in Afghanistan in the 80s, you said so yourself. There were three people in Afghanistan then, the Russians, the Afghanis, and the CIA. You weren't with the Soviets. That means you were CIA.

"The wall of your apartment has an Enfield rifle on your wall, a World War One weapon used by the British in the incursion into Russia with the Allied Expeditionary Force of the 1920s, filled with gunfire and blood on the snow. You have a World War II Thompson and a Vietnam-era M-16. Thus, you were in almost every major war of the twentieth century. But I can't see you taking a break from being a soldier in the off-years, so you were a spy. You served for about sixty years in four wars that I know of. How many smaller wars?"

Why am I even surprised he can do that? She thought. *Though why he's trying to sound like Basil Rathbone, I don't know.* "But the things I've done -"

"Like assassination?" he said. "Cloak and dagger, fang and claw, back-alley feeding in enemy territory? I've read history. I can guess. How many times do I have to tell people that I am a genius?"

Amanda was silent for a long moment. Marco now knew things about her that most people have never suspected. Ibrahim had guessed, but he was a Vatican Ninja and had heard some of her history as history before he had ever met her.

Which meant that it was her turn.

"Why is Yana scared of you? I could smell it."

Marco sighed, deflated. He almost sagged against her. "Remember the mugger?"

Amanda blinked. There was only one mugger that had ever made an impact on Marco's life. The mugger had jumped Marco and his sort-of-girlfriend Lily. Marco killed him. A lot. She nodded.

Marco continued. "As I told Yana, I kind of enjoyed it."

Marco met her eyes and let his own go dead of life and emotion. It was dark, and cold, and angry in there. Full of energy, raw bitterness, burning with a cold fire. "*This* is what I've not wanted you to see, Amanda. I stabbed the little bastard, and I enjoyed it. I even liked the fresh, warm blood covering my hands. I hurt him, and I wanted to keep on hurting him. I wanted him to suffer."

Amanda pushed him away, holding him at arm's length. She was shocked. She was appalled. She was hurt. She was ready to use his head as a basketball while it was still attached. "And *this* is what you were worried about me seeing? *This* is what kept you from telling me you loved me? *This* kept you at arm's length from me since we met?"

Marco's eyes softened, melting into a form of gentle kindness Amanda knew better. "Yes."

Without any warning, at a speed that Marco didn't see coming, he felt a smack knock his head back. He staggered a little.

"You *knew* I was a veteran of at least four wars," Amanda yelled at him. "You think you're the first man I've ever come across who thinks like that? Who acts that way? Would you have ever told me if we hadn't had this conversation?"

Marco shook his head, as though he expected it to rattle. "Why do you think I wanted you to check your email? I told you all about it. Then you disappeared for months. I thought you hated me."

Amanda blinked, her anger settling. "Oh."

Well, that's embarrassing, she thought. Her heart rate had spiked again. She hadn't even noticed it this time. *I guess Marco really can get my heart started… in more ways than one.* "What changed your mind?"

"I had someone give me a clearer viewpoint to my examination of conscience." He thought, *Wow. Do I even try saying my guardian angel told me? Nah. Too complicated.*

Amanda smiled, and her mind didn't have to travel far to change the subject. "How do you stand the uniform? You wear it like your underwear, completely comfortable."

Marco shrugged. "I've always felt more comfortable in decent clothes than in blue jeans. You can look fine in casual wear, mainly because you'd look fine in… just about anything."

She rolled her eyes. "*Da*, I hear that from most guys."

Marco made a little frown. "Hmm… pity, I always considered myself more attuned to reality than most men. But I suppose that beauty such as yours must serve to smack them in the face with the force of a hammer blow."

He stepped forward again and took her by the shoulders. "Now, where were we?" He drew her back to him, wrapping his arms around her shoulders. "I think you were telling me how I can't love you." His mouth moved to hers, and he muttered, "Let me show you."

This kiss started slowly, gentler, more tender. They barely touched each other's lips at first. Marco gave a deep, contented, rumbling sound that started deep in his chest and vibrated in hers.

Amanda grabbed Marco around the head and used that to control his center of balance as she leveraged him to another part of the room.

Or in plain terms, Amanda grabbed him and tossed him on the bed.

Amanda didn't jump after Marco, but bent down, putting her hands on the mattress, on either side of Marco's legs. She moved forward on her hands, then her hands and knees. As she crawled up the bed, Marco swore that she looked like a jungle cat coming to devour him.

As she came level with his belt, Marco's heart didn't quite stop, though it skipped a few beats as her hand reached for his pants.

When she pulled out his uniform jacket from the pants, he was one part relieved, one part disappointed. She undid the bottom button of his jacket, and he was a little confused. Then she lowered her lips to his stomach and started to kiss her way up his body.

Marco tried slowing his breathing as she worked up to his chest, but then her hair curtained her face, and dragged along his torso. Each strand of hair was a pinpoint of fire dragging slowly up his body.

By the time she made her to his collarbone, Marco had groaned and reached for Amanda. Only her hands shot up and grabbed his wrists, pinning them to either side of his head.

This time, she gave a contented little rumble, only hers came out more like a deep purr.

Her face lifted from his chest, so her hair was just grazing his skin… which made it even worse.

The fire burned in him so intensely he almost missed that her eyes were glowing. They always looked like deep amber, and now they were literally glowing.

"Poor human," she said, her lips going back to his collarbone. Her accent had gotten thicker, her voice huskier. "You invited the vampire in." She kissed the hollow of his throat. "Now she eats you." She kissed his carotid artery. "Slowly."

Marco didn't know whether to be turned on or scared. He was just happy that she was still on her hands and knees and didn't settle her body on his. Otherwise, he really, really hoped that her control was better than his.

And then Amanda kissed him lightly on the lips, and he wanted her to have very, very bad control. The first kiss lasted only a few seconds, a light touch of the lips, a quick swipe of the tongue just inside his lips. Then she pulled back as Marco tried to follow her lips when she pulled away.

She grinned. "I choose how I eat you."

Amanda met his eyes.

Anyone who pays attention to vampire lore knows that looking a vampire in the eyes all but invites them into your brain. Into this mix, add one 19-year-old human, a vampire who is 22 and holding, both in a heightened state of passion, love, and a pinch of lust. This results in the excitement and sheer joy in both people turning into an echo that reverberates in the minds of both of them, generating massive feedback.

Or, in other terms, their brains shorted out.

A few minutes later, they both woke up on the floor. They were in such a tangled mess of limbs, they weren't on top of each other as much as they were sprawled on the floor. They both took several deep gulps of air, grabbing and climbing up the mattress.

Marco looked at her, and said, in a strangled voice, "If this is us kissing, doing something more might just kill me."

Amanda just nodded.

Marco rested his chin on the bed for a moment, letting his breath slow. Amanda did the same. In her case, she was trying to block the hormones she could smell coming off him.

"Though I guess what we should do," he said, still out of breath. "Is keep kissing until we can get through it."

Amanda gave him a small smile this time. "Endurance training."

"Building stamina," he concurred.

"Something to get the heart rate up," she suggested.

"Exactly… once I catch my breath."

"Heh."

Marco let his eyes droop closed for a moment. Then he blinked. "Wait," he panted. "You went… whew… looking for news about Asmodeus. You wanted to back-trace him after he's dead."

Amanda looked at him like he was insane. "You want to discuss this *now*?"

"Because I kinda get that, now that I'm…" He blinked again, foggy. "Sorry, I'm slow right now. I'm calmer - that's the word."

Amanda groaned in frustration. "Yes, Marco?"

"Our dear, dead Mister Day was into politics. When we met Merle Kraft, he was dealing with vampires and the United Nations… They're interlinked, aren't they? Day and the UN."

Amanda had to blink to clear her mind. "I… I am not sure. I know something *bad* comes. I mean *evil*."

Marco raised a brow. "Amanda… you're here. Now. With me, instead of hunting down a lead that made you disappear for three months."

"You are complaining?" she said, her accent getting a little heavier.

His annoying little smile was firmly in place. "You're not holding out on me by any chance, are you?"

"Not at the moment." Amanda hesitated, unsure of how she should tell him. "I am not sure of anything specific. There's word of a vampire coming, one specifically bred for destruction."

"And you think," he took a deep breath. Still a little knocked around, "it's after me?"

She shrugged. "I don't know. The Incontinents I talked with were… unreliable. This creature is so high-level, the definitely evil ones have only heard *whispers* about it. Not even Mikhail is as high as the rumors say this one is, and Mikhail was practically a legend."

"Legends are flashy and showy," Marco muttered, peering intently at the sheets in thought. "If this is someone great and powerful on the Calamity Jane scale *and* unknown, then it's out of our usual league… this is a *smart* evil."

Amanda nodded. "The dumb evil isn't bright enough to reach real viciousness."

He smiled absently. "True… not creative enough to be so monstrous. But this… ever heard of anything like it?

Amanda sighed, trying to be patient. "Only if you count the Council?"

Marco nodded slowly. "Yes, you had mentioned that once before. Something that even master vampires could answer to. You never really went into detail."

She shrugged. "It is 'Stupid things that vampires believe in.' The boogeyman. Evil that wants to control the world."

"A vampire urban legend."

She gave a "so-so" wave with her hand. "A myth."

"So, the Council is the vampire version of black helicopters, or Protocols of the Elders of Zion, which were plagiarized from conspiracy theories about the Jesuits, going back to the 1500s?"

Amanda chuckled. "Exactly. It is like any of the others. It is supposed to be made of vampires and higher-ranking minions that sometimes coordinate mass movements of evil over the world."

Marco shook his head, then caught himself, still woozy from their make-out overload. He cleared his throat. "The theory is nice and novelesque, but the execution? I'm trying to imagine controlling someone on the level of Mikhail. Most dark side vampires aren't that easy to ride herd on as it is. The type of power a Council would need? Power over other master vampires? It's ridiculous. Even the Vampires Associations are local, and more of a coordinating body. Hell, it's a bureaucracy meant to keep everyone from killing each other, but that's less control and more referee."

Amanda climbed onto the bed, had a seat, leaning up against the headboard. This mood was not going to come back anytime soon. "You have it. It's not possible. The Vampires Associations have trouble keeping regular, upper-middle-class vampires in line. This would require master vampires answering to a single Council."

Marco nodded, granting her point. "For the moment, let's presume that this is real though. We're talking about an evil that had something like Day on board. He wasn't just a demon, but a Prince of Hell. Remember when I asked you what happened to vampires who were perfectly vicious? Demonic, even? You joked that you believed that they were dragged straight to Hell - because you had never heard of them. What if you never heard of them because all of them are recruited into something *like* a Council?"

She sighed. "There's no proof. And I *heard* of Mikhail the Bear before we met him. I could not identify him because we'd never met, but still…"

He grinned. "Again, because he's flashy." Marco finally crawled onto the mattress, staying at the foot of the bed. "Look at it this way, how many nests did he plant? You said it yourself, he had a tendency to migrate only after thoroughly entrenching a nest in any given area. If someone were controlling him, they'd necessarily control all of those nests as well. Now that he's dead, what happens next? Who takes over?"

She thought about it a moment. "An even better question would be how did Mikhail manage to control all of those nests at all? He could not be everywhere, so delegate control. He made an army."

"So who owns it now?"

"Good question."

Marco closed his eyes, and just let his head fall onto the bed. "I guess we won't answer it tonight."

Amanda studied his still form for a long moment. It was always odd when he fell into these states. He was almost peaceful, without his intense focus turned up to twelve.

She shifted around and lay down next to him. He wrapped an arm around her, drew her close, and put his face in her hair, breathing deeply. She buried her face in his chest and did the same. A bit of musk. A lot of anger. And now, a lot of pheromones.

After only a minute, Amanda could tell that Marco was still awake just by leaning against him.

"Marco…" she said softly, her voice tense with need.

"Sigh. I know." He shifted himself again. "Want to go kill something?"

Amanda groaned. "You want to do this *now*?"

Marco reached down, took her chin in his hand, and lifted her mouth to his. He kissed her gently. "You want a few good reasons?"

"Please."

"One." He kissed her again. "If we stay here like this, I don't think it will just be cuddling." Kiss. "Two. This took you away from me for *months*. And it won't take you away from me for even five more minutes if I can help it."

Amanda gave a toothy grin. "What did you have in mind?"

"Step one… bite me."

Amanda's eyes started to glow again. "You want to tempt fate like that?"

"I'm not tempting fate." He kissed her again. "I'm tempting you."

Amanda pulled him closer, then rolled on top of him. She ran her hands over his chest, spreading his uniform jacket. With a blur of motion, she took off her shirt and pressed herself against him. His stomach pressured against hers. She wrapped her arms around his bare back, under the jacket.

Marco slipped his arm out of the jacket sleeves and wrapped around her lower back, going for the bare skin contact. She lowered her lips to his neck and licked the skin, tasting him. She sucked on the skin a little, making him groan.

"Amanda, I thought we were -"

"Shh. I'm playing with my food."

Her fangs sank into his neck, and her lips closed around the skin. She didn't drink, but constantly ran her tongue over the punctures, constantly wetting it with her saliva, and with it, the vampire "virus." As the ultimate blood-borne virus, it served several purposes in the saliva. The most important part when she fed on a person was that the slight transfer of the virus in the saliva lent extra strength to the person being fed from. Yes, it would help them if they drank more fluids for the next few days, but the virus would prevent any overfeeding from being necessarily lethal.

Originally, Amanda told herself, and occasionally Marco, that the tongue-swiping refreshed the saliva-ridden virus. Now she had no qualms about tasting his skin just because. With only a few drops of his blood, his warmth filled her. He was good and solid against her; he was hers. His scent was all around her. The smell of home.

Chapter 10

Shot in the Dark

New York City

The Mafia guy known simply as "Enrico" poured himself a drink. He needed it after the little run-in with the gunmen in his own freaking home. Damn it, it used to be that people wouldn't pull this *Godfather II* crap in real life. Most people would simply settle for whacking him in a back alley.

"But *no*, they need to shoot up *everybody*."

"Talk to yourself often?" Robert asked.

"Only on my bad days."

He turned to the rest of the room, facing both Jennifer Bosley and Doctor Robert Catalano. For very good reasons (namely, a totally destroyed parlor), they had to adjourn the meeting about funding the recreation of the hospital. Much to Enrico's surprise, the good doctor recommended they reconvene at his own house. He was a real *paisan* for doing that. Enrico took months to trust Jennifer Bosley enough to invite her into his own home. That was before he knew that

Bosley was "virtuous" enough to walk in on her own if she so chose.

Robert smiled as he leaned back in his chair. "I can understand that."

Enrico raised his glass to him in salute. "You know, doc, you weren't all that thrown when the guns opened up."

Bosley chuckled. "Indeed. I was somewhat taken aback that you seemed not the slightest bit perturbed at being shot at."

Robert pointed outside. "I had a pitched battle on my front stoop last spring, remember? And I've worked in some of the lesser parts of the Bronx. Guns don't affect me. The only New Yorkers they do affect are the politicians who'd rather that their bodyguards and criminals be the only ones who have them."

"I can relate," came a voice behind Enrico.

Enrico turned, reaching for his gun. A hand clamped down on the wrist.

Enrico relaxed. "Mister Kraft. Can I help you with… something?"

Enrico looked him up and down. Merle's hair was frazzled, his windbreaker was rumbled to hell and gone, his eyes bloodshot, even though it wasn't late.

Merle's voice came fast and stressed. "I need you, or Bosley, or someone, to get me to an airport.

LaGuardia, JFK, I don't care which. I need out of here in short order, and on a plane back to San Francisco."

"That's okay, I can…" He sniffed the air a few times. "What did you do, swim in the East River?"

Merle's eyes narrowed. "Yes, actually. I had to get across Turtle Bay."

Robert frowned as he stood. "What's the matter?"

"Something is after your son."

Bosley's eyes narrowed. "Is it a vampire?"

"Yes. I think so. Probably. But I've already encountered her once in the desert, and, well… vampires *are* flammable, right? Bosley blinked, taken aback. "Yes. Dangerously so. We could probably be considered a fire hazard in crowded public places. Why do you ask?"

"Because I hit this thing with an FAE in the sandbox not too long ago, and she's still running around loose, and pissed, and really, really, wants to kill me." Merle looked right at Robert. "And she's after your son."

"I'll get the keys."

Bosley waved him off. "Nonsense, doctor." She opened her phone, tapped on a few keys, then sent off a text. "You'll be there in a few minutes, Mister Kraft. Now come, please, tell us about this creature that attacked you."

Enrico: "What did you just do?"

"I sent a text message to my helicopter to swing by and pick us up. Is LaGuardia all right?"

Merle slumped into a chair that was wrapped in vinyl, so he didn't damage the upholstery. "Um, sure. But… wait, you have a helicopter?"

Bosley laughed. It would have been sexier if it hadn't been for the flash of fang. "Of course I do. I'm a vampire with enough money to buy city blocks of Manhattan. Or even quality real estate. Of course I have a helicopter. You never know when you need to intercept some problem or other in the midst of the city."

"Of course. Why not?" Merle rolled his eyes. "I don't suppose you have a really fast jet I can borrow, too."

"Funny you should mention that…"

"Really? That too?"

"If that's a problem -"

Merle held up his hands. "Oh, no. No no no. That's fine. What'd you want to know?"

"Describe her."

"Size two redhead, six-one, long hair. If she were human, I would have her sent to the burn ward, or maybe wrap her up, so the scabs didn't peel away and turn her into a bag of blood. She has green eyes, I think. Long fingers, long arms, and really sharp facial features. Almost ax-like. The mouth and teeth jut out, almost like she'd more paleo than the meat-and-vegetable diet."

Bosley bunched up one corner of her mouth. "That sounds like Amanda's redhead from your little adventure with Mikhail the Bear."

"Do you know her?"

"After a fashion. I've put considerable research behind examining this since my discussion with Amanda in September. I'd come to think that this one is actually a vampire myth. Something like the Council, or something equally ridiculous. The short version? She's an assassin. The whispers I've heard have given only one name. Though, for obvious reasons, she's been referred to for the past twenty years as simply 'The Slayer.'"

"Why obvious?" Enrico asked.

"Because, my dear Enrico, she's the vampire one sends when you want to assassinate a vampire."

San Francisco

Rory the vampire walked into Artful Krafts and looked around. Tiffany was busy with shoppers, while Yana and Tara were off to the side at a corner table.

He walked over to the couple. "You look like you two need a drink."

The women shrugged. "I'm just tired," Yana insisted. She reached inside her jacket and pulled out a joint. "I need a smoke."

Tara frowned, reached out, and grabbed Yana's hand. "Maybe *not.*"

Rory sniffed. He could smell some of the chemicals coming off of it. He pulled out his own cigarettes and offered her one. "Have one of mine, lassie."

Yana's brow wrinkled. "Is that tobacco? Yuck."

Rory didn't roll his eyes. If he did, he might just do an implied face-palm so hard that it would blow them both away. "Indeed. So why not come out and share a drink with me. In fact, it's a Friday, ya? You can come out and share more than a few drinks with me."

"That depends," came a new voice from the door. "Are they legal to drink?"

At the door was a 5'3" athletic, golden-haired blonde (leaning heavily on the gold), with strands falling smoothly to the nape of her neck. Rich blue eyes set over smooth Celtic cheekbones locked onto the three of them. She wore a lightweight black sweatshirt with a zipper in front, opened partly at the neck, with a pair of black jeans.

"I'm Detective Kristen Kelly, San Francisco PD," she said in a voice to be heard in the back of the room.

At this point, most of the clientele started for the door.

Kelly stepped out of their way, letting them all go.

As she waited for the rush to pass, Rory palmed Yana's joint and stuck it in his cigarette pack. "And how can we help you, officer?"

"Detective," she corrected. She took a step or two down from the front door. "Now, all of you have been hanging around my ex-husband, Merle, for quite some time. He tends to deal with plenty of strange things. It's in his job description."

"He's not here," Tiffany said from behind the register. She had run out of money to count and was visibly pissed at the woman who had driven away her customers. "We don't know where he is. We don't know what he's doing. So leave. And send those people back in."

Rory gave the cop a great big grin. "We'd be happy to help you with anything we can, Detective. Anything at all. What exactly is this about?"

"A few months ago, we had reports of multiple desecrated graveyards. It looked like squatters had been attacked by Molotov cocktails. A lot of them. Yet, there were no bodies. No blood. Nothing. Which means anyone attacked had been taken away, and somehow didn't bleed any."

"And you think that Merle might be behind this?"

Kristen glared. "I didn't say that, did I? But there is a person of interest that I know that frequents this place."

Her cop's eyes looked around. "Where's Marco Catalano?"

Chapter 11

Danse Macabre

San Francisco

Back in the 1960s, there arose an institution called the "Church of Satan," and it managed to stand out like a sore thumb. Among the pleasant, pastel houses of San Francisco, it was an all-black home that looked like something out of an Alfred Hitchcock film.

The 8th Church of Satan, Reformed, was in the yet-to-be-Yuppified part of San Francisco in Haight Ashbury, commonly known as Hashbury, well known for the production of a certain plant of a similar name. It was located in an all-black warehouse, with no sign out front, back, or the side.

Inside the warehouse was a scene out of Dante's Inferno, if the second level of Dante's Hell was retrofitted with high-velocity, seizure-inducing, flashing strobe lights, triple-digit-decibel loudspeakers, and enough vibrations to shatter fine crystal and liquefy unstable internal organs.

Also known as a club.

The occupants of the warehouse only stayed within the basement - the ground floor was rendered unworthy to support life for street rats. The next level down had been turned into the new and improved domain fit for the damned, complete with a full bar, refrigeration units in the back, and a stage in front. The band played what was charitably called as "death metal" music, but only if the qualifications for it meant that the hearers sincerely wanted to die, preferably quickly and painlessly, rather than being blasted to death by the noise.

However, in this instance, most of the hearers were already dead…

Most of the vampires were young, at least three-quarters of them had died within the previous fifty years, and all of those between the ages of 16 and 26. They had "died" young and left good-looking corpses. Now they continued to enjoy their eternal youth, trying to keep up with the new music of each successive generation of teenagers. The vampires who were older and more experienced worked at the club - they were unimpressed and longed for the days of Elvis or the Andrews Sisters.

The vampires were all Incontinents, and they all would have hated the term. Most of them considered themselves "rebels from society," not evil in any way.

Most of them were the ancient "lesser evil," who could be deflected by a good quality cross, but who could rectify that problem by a visit to a confessional. One way or another, they were simply inconsequential in the grand scheme of life, and in the vampire kingdom, and thus no-one of greater status ever worried if they knew anything - what would they do about it?

However, this made them a useful font of information. Their indifference was usually the guarantee of other people's confidentiality.

The remaining customers within the club were human servants and vampire wannabes. Some of these humans hung around to enjoy the sense of power. Some wanted to hang out with the "really cool" dark side. Some wanted to be vampires. Some came to enjoy the music and liked the tall, dark and bloodless look. Some came hoping that they would be eaten by the "barely legal" who had been undead before they were born.

All in all, most of the customers, both vampire and human, had read far too many novels. They had watched the vampire media, and they took their cues from there. They indulged in black leather, took to kinky sex, and did their best to imitate an Ann Rice novel. Half of the audience routinely tried ceremonies, Black Masses, dark rituals, but they typically ended up as sex orgies - less Satan, more basic hedonism. Everyone else had pastimes that generally included drinking blood from drug addicts, petty theft, and generally making a nuisance of themselves.

They were generally never caught by the police for the simple reason that they were just fast enough to get away, or just strong enough to leap over a wall. And if they were shot at long-ranges, policemen were far more likely to believe that they had missed than to believe that the target was undead. Any of the Incontinents who attracted too much attention were either brought in by the others or killed by a higher-level vampire.

Little did they realize the party was about to end, and the days of blood and roses were over.

The lead "singer" - if one could call any of that singing - on stage had his mouth wide open, screaming into the cordless microphone at the top of his lungs, and using all the power his vampire-enhanced diaphragm could produce.

However, that did not help him all that much when the microphone was rammed down his throat so hard it poked out the back of his head.

It didn't hurt so much as it stung. And it didn't sting for long, because a stake to the back of the head replaced it. This procedure might have caused permanent brain damage to any vampire, but in the singer's case, he wasn't using too much of his brain to start with. The end result would only be to keep him unconscious.

However, no-one had noticed this, because, being essentially 60-year-old teenagers, most of the vampires had drunk of a meth user shortly before. The band played on, and the volume was so loud that, between the music and the meth, even vampires were starting to go deaf.

Everyone noticed when the music stopped and was replaced by a new voice. "Sorry to break up the party, but I need some information. There's some crap going on in New York with the United Nations, a vampire named Mikhail the Bear, a demon that goes by Mister Day, and something wicked this way comes. I will be happy to take information on any or all subjects. The last one is near and dear to my heart since someone's coming to kill me."

Amanda smiled at Marco as he stood up on the stage, as though he was a comedian doing stand-up instead of someone on the menu.

Ironically, as she had listened to his plans, she realized just how much she had taken away from her time with him. Her training in intelligence gathering had taught her to be calm, quiet, casual, thoughtful, and most of all, subtle and discreet. Marco had yet to learn anything beyond thoughtful. His direct approach, with overwhelming force, had all the subtly of a Main Battle Tank, but it worked.

Most of the time.

The vampires around her grew restless. They were already disoriented and slow by the amount of drugs they'd sucked in. But their mood wasn't improving.

Still, the crowd didn't faze Marco. He raised a cell phone as vampires snarled in his direction. "I should probably mention that there are minor explosive charges set all over this place that will burn the entire institution down around your ears... thankfully, your circuit breakers are crappy to begin with."

Amanda smiled to herself. That much, at least, was true. She had installed the devices herself. Thankfully, with Amanda's experience and Marco's knowledge of chemistry, they had more than enough ways to improvise explosives.

Despite the threat, several vampires still drifted his way. "By the way, I'm Marco Catalano, pleased to meet you all."

Everyone stopped in their tracks.

Amanda looked around and blinked. Wondering what part of his reputation had gotten around to this end of the coast…

Well, he *had* killed an unkillable demon; maybe that had something to do with it. The audience paused, silent for a moment as they considered their options.

He smiled. "Ah, I see that my little video has gotten around. I guess I should have brought my ax.

"I want to speak to the Council," Marco continued. "If any of them would like to talk, I'll be happy to -"

As one, the vampires rushed the stage. Amanda's eyes widened at the violent response as the wave of people carried her closer to the stage.

I think Marco hit a button.

Marco merely sighed and slid a throwing knife from his left sleeve into his hand, and, with his aim and strength enhanced by the microorganisms transferred by Amanda's bite, hurled the stake across the room into a bottle of scotch… it was one of his flammable throwing stakes, which immediately ignited the bar, setting the back of the room on fire.

"That was a warning," he announced. He raised the phone again. "The next move burns the place down."

Everyone in the audience shifted. They were no longer generally confused, listless, petty evils. They were a mob. They were a herd. Suddenly, Amanda was reminded of all the things that human beings were capable of when the situation was right - said "situations" covered everything from riots to a soccer game that didn't go the right way.

For the first time in their association, Marco had finally, and disastrously, miscalculated, what the reaction would be. This was no longer the laid-back crowd they had anticipated or came in with.

They were now a mob about to riot.

Amanda leapt out from the crowd, grabbed Marco, and literally jumped over the bloodthirsty horde with him under one arm, reaching the stairs with ease.

As one, they ran up the stairs, and Amanda, with one of the portable mikes in hand, said, "Last chance, talk to us or -" A crossbow bolt flew past her head. She cleared her throat and muttered, "Well, if you want it *that* way…"

Amanda was about to turn and leave them all to their fates, when she noted that Marco stood there a moment, his eyes dark and deep and dangerous, and - "What are you doing?"

Marco concentrated a moment, and then, with full force, hurled a stake into the heart of the vampire armed with the crossbow. He looked at her briefly and said, "He tried to hurt you. Therefore, he dies."

He shrugged, and they left, locking the door behind them, leaving several crosses against the door. The fire from the bar had already spread across the floor.

Outside, Marco said, "Well, *that* got us nowhere. You'd think after Day they'd have some respect for me in this town."

Amanda smiled wearily, suddenly overwhelmed by both being so near to Marco in addition to the activity. *Just when I thought that being away from him would be* good *for me.* "I doubt that."

He sighed. "Bastards… then again, do you think I'm wrong about the Council now? We had their attention until I mentioned it." He paused and looked her over. "How're you doing?"

She turned, looking off into the alley, and sighed. "I'm okay. I'm just a little tired."

Amanda was half-afraid to look at him, lest she – jump him. She was too old to be attracted to Alpha-male doggerel, but damn, some of that was kinda sexy.

Granted, Marco was never Conan the Barbarian, nor was he remotely like a wrestler. But the over-the-top, yes-I-do-think-I'm-Tyrone-Power attitude was… strikingly attractive to her. And killing someone just because he took a shot at her - a shot that clearly missed - was either the act of a gentleman or… she didn't know, she just felt… unusually warm towards him. Alive a hundred years, and she was falling for something out of swashbuckler films… which was odd, she was never interested in men like those…

Or maybe it's just because he's *doing it.*

Amanda stood in the dark, rubbing her arms, staring into the shadows. A coat draped itself gently around her.

"We probably shouldn't stay out here," Marco said from behind her, holding her gently by the shoulders.

"I know." She hugged the coat tighter around herself and breathed deeply, bracing herself. She could smell him all over the jacket, and it was nice, a combination of clean soap, garlic, and a touch of musk.

"Unless you want to stay and warm yourself by the fire," he joked.

She turned to face him. Marco looked deeply into her eyes and saw a sadness there he'd never noticed before. One of terrible loneliness and desire, and a fear of never having… it, whatever the "it" was.

Is she going to attack me? He wondered.

Marco's thoughts paused as he wondered what definition of the verb "attack" he meant. Amanda slid into his arms and held him close. His ribs slowly bent against her grip.

"Just hold on," he whispered gently, hugging her back. "Don't worry, I won't break," he lied, calculating the pressure it actually took to snap human bone.

Chapter 12

Terror By Night

San Francisco

Amanda and Marco were still embracing outside the club when they heard a voice in the dark say, "It's about to get worse."

The two of them turned. Amanda blinked. "Merle?"

Merle Kraft came out of the shadows, his hair a mess and his jacket in tatters. "Listen, it's not safe here. For either of you. I think there's been a hit put out on you in the vampire underworld."

Marco blinked a moment, and then laughed, long and loud and hard.

Merle raised a brow. "I was attacked outside of the UN building by a very tall redhead."

Amanda started. Her eyes narrowed. "Redhead?"

Marco and Amanda exchanged a look, both of them remembering Mikhail's assassin.

Suddenly, Amanda tensed and then jumped onto him. "Down!"

Amanda dragged Marco to the ground as a light metal spear sped through the air where they had stood.

It impacted against a dumpster and went through, knocking it over.

Amanda and Marco rolled apart, the vampire taking a stake from Marco's jacket, the PA student slipping two from his sleeves. They came to their feet facing the same direction, feet apart, left arm outstretched as a shield, stakes ready to kill. Marco held his with the points toward the thumbs, and Amanda held hers upside down in her hand like a commando.

The next missile came right at Amanda through the shadows. Amanda grabbed it, spun, and used its momentum to toss it back at the attacker.

A shape darted out, leaping out at Amanda over the spear. A mop of long red hair framed the face of the most hideous vampire she'd ever seen, and two glowing green viper's eyes. Between the hair and the eyes were a mask of scar tissue, fresh burns, and lizard-like scales. The vampire had half of a nose – the left half. The jaw, mouth, and teeth were elongated, akin to neanderthal skulls.

Her first move was a swipe at Amanda's hand. The strike made Amanda's arm go numb. The stake flew into the wall, where it shattered on impact.

Amanda ducked in time for the backhand to soar over her head and punched for her opponent's stomach…

And into the assassin's waiting hand.

The vampire grabbed her hand, threw Amanda against the far wall of the alley, and was ready to leap atop her to finish the job.

Marco casually took aim and threw his blade as he dropped forward into a roll. With a blur, the vampire caught the knife and hurled it back at him with deadly accuracy, without looking. Marco would have been dead had he remained standing for even a split second longer. The splinters embedded themselves into the wall.

Marco's roll brought him to the vampire's feet, and he jammed both stakes into her flesh, one in her thigh and one in her side. He had two impact-firecrackers taped to the sides, and they went off when they pressed against her flesh, igniting the stakes and setting the vamp aflame. By that time, Marco had already bounced away, running for Amanda, leaving the vampire for dead… even as she rolled to put the fire out.

Marco slid to his knees, stopping at Amanda's side. He grabbed her shoulders and shook her firmly. Amanda's eyes snapped open, and she grabbed and rolled over him and threw one of his stakes into the vampire's back.

The vampire stopped moving and dropped to her staked knee. Both of her hands went for the stake protruding from her heart.

Merle made his move and led with a flying spin kick that knocked her head back and dropped her onto the ground. She blinked, as though she hadn't even felt it. All of her concentration was focused on the stake as she slowly drew it out of her heart and rolled to her side.

Marco and Amanda looked at each other. "That doesn't happen, does it?"

"No," she answered.

"This is bad, then, right?"

"You betcha."

The vampire turned, ripping both stakes from her lower body. Marco dropped, dragging Amanda with him as the stakes flew overhead, shattering brick and mortar. Merle jumped in again, and the vampire tossed him aside, slamming him against a brick wall.

Marco reached for the small of his back and drew out a water pistol. The attacking vampire became a cloud of mist, and swooped in under the stream of water, and came up, ripping the pistol from Marco's hand.

Without blinking, Amanda grabbed Marco, ripping two stakes from the inside of Marco's jacket and threw one straight for the assassin. The vampire smacked it aside, and it shattered. The two women were only yards apart when Marco put himself between them, rosary wrapped around one hand, and cross held up in the other.

The vampire smiled and stopped two feet away, leveling her glowing green eyes on Marco. "You think just holding those will hurt me?" she hissed in a brogue.

"No." Marco slammed the fist with the rosary wrapped around it into her nose, a hiss accompanying it, then slapping her with the flat side of the crucifix. "I expect *that* to hurt."

The vampire staggered a little, shaken. The center of her face smoked, and audibly sizzling, and so was the side of her face. It looked like she had been branded by both hits.

"I'll be seeing you," she snapped before she ran so fast, she might as well have evaporated.

Marco turned, saw Amanda was all right, then looked at Merle, slowly rising to his feet. "Thanks a lot."

Kraft shrugged. "I tried to warn you. Besides, I would've brought a squirt gun, but those post-9/11 security dweebs at the airport confiscated it. They didn't find my stakes, but they took my squirt gun."

Marco nodded absently. "We need to find the others in case they're in trouble."

Merle smirked. "That part's easy. You want the nearest nightclub."

Marco jerked his head over his shoulder at the door they had just come out of. "That *was* the nearest nightclub, and it should be halfway to charcoal by now."

On that part, Marco was wrong - the inside was almost all charcoal, the inhabitants of the club consumed by flames which had eaten through flesh and wood.

In the center of the room, admiring the damage with a chuckle among the charred remains, stood a dark man, in dark clothes, with dark purpose. The outfit was basic early 4-T magician - tux, tie, tails and top hat, complete with a cane that had a silver wolf's head and ruby eyes. He was black Irish - olive skin with sharp cheekbones, black hair, and eyes of deepest midnight blue. They were the eyes of a Kraft brother.

Dalf Kraft looked on the wreckage and smiled. He gazed over the flames, counting the numbers of the dead from this night. *This is what I call a good haul.*

"Are ye responsible for this mess?" hissed a voice from the corner.

Dalf looked over his shoulder at the redheaded creature of the night that had just tried to eat Marco Catalano. "I'm in collections, not destruction. You kill people. I just collect them."

The redhead narrowed her eyes. "Then you better help me collect Marco and Amanda. Lest someone kill *you.*"

Dalf's eyes became hooded as his eyebrows arched and his smile widened. "Oh really, Nuala, darling, whatever shall we do with you?"

Rory, the redheaded vampire with the thick brogue, looked into his shot glass. Well, that sucked.

Going twenty rounds with the Detective that Merle called his ex had been a pain. He'd been a vampire for nearly a hundred years, and he had never had to be quite that evasive.

Maybe I should see the sunrise.

There were days that he examined his life, and counted all of the people he missed, like his friend Dan Breen. While the kids in San Francisco had adopted him, they were still… kids. They treated this like it was some kind of game.

Well, Sean, didn't you? He thought to himself. *Gunning down Brits was fun, wasn't it? Now, you can't even use your own bloody name. Sean Treacy would be a name to turn heads back home, and a turned head is the last thing that you need.*

The former IRA gunman ordered another shot.

"Shouldn't you hold off?" Yana asked next to him.

Rory looked at her, sighed, and grabbed the glass. "Can't break my liver, now can I?"

"Cheers, bloodsucker."

Rory looked over his shoulder at Marco and blinked. "What's wrong?"

"Amanda and I were just attacked by a vampire who doesn't want to die. Since this is a public place, she can walk in. I don't want to get eaten. Anyone who agrees will pretty much leave right about now." He looked at Yana. "You coming?"

She looked blankly and nodded. "Oh, you -"

"- want you to come and play," Marco interrupted.

* * *

Amanda waited in the alley, waiting for something to happen. The redheaded creature had nearly put down both her *and* Marco, not to mention Merle… which meant that this was *bad*.

Maybe that she survived a stake to the heart should also warn you, yes?

Amanda shook her head, her thoughts drifting between what she wanted, and what was happening around her. The two merged and blurred as she replayed the fight. This newcomer had thrashed the three of them without a problem…

Although Marco had managed to perform amazingly well for a human. He had anticipated her moves, dodged them, and had stood between her and Amanda. He basically put one over on a vampire that was at least two centuries old.

Yes, that was one thing she was certain of. The creature had even *smelled* old and stank of age and evil. There was also no way for someone to have gotten to that level of power without being either prolific or had plenty of time to practice her craft.

In this case, it was almost certainly lots of practice.

And the power… being stabbed in the heart and surviving… the next step, undoubtedly, had to be soul fire. Assuming that she didn't already have access to it.

Amanda paused, then shook her head at that thought. If the vampire had soul fire, she would have used it, and everyone would have been cooked. It was basically the ultimate in vampire weaponry, and it would have been used on them as soon as she ran into problems. But still, the power displayed in that one confrontation was immense, impressive and borderline impossible. The fact that Marco had even managed to slow her down was…

Actually, it was a turn-on. Her heart gave a little lurch, as did several other body parts…It was replaced by a sudden emptiness. She couldn't have him, no matter what her body told her, what she wanted of him, or from him. Despite everything they had gone through, she should know better. She should know it wouldn't work in the long run. Hell, the long-term implications would have been worse. Really, what could they expect? A brief interlude? A good friendship that becomes something more… until he remembered that he was dating someone who occasionally saw him as food?

Nyet… won't happen. It can't…

The cold began to slip into her bones, into her very marrow.

Marco stepped out of the club as Merle and Rory gathered Yana, Tara, and Tiffany.

Amanda was standing in the dark, her back to him. He admired the way she held herself, confident, casual, calm, with a languid posture he found… quite alluring. His own heart began to beat faster as he recalled the look in her eyes, that look of hunger - he had come to the conclusion that it wasn't for blood. "Amanda?"

She didn't move, didn't flinch, and barely breathed when she said, "*Da?*"

"We're ready to go."

She nodded, again, barely. "*Da.*"

He tapped her on the shoulder. "Hello, anyone there? Signs of life?"

She blinked and stared at him. "I heard you."

Voice flat, plus dead, plus distant, equals not good. "How about I walk you to a safe, vampire-proof, private home, and then we can meet in the morning over at Artful Krafts. Okay?"

"Sure. Why not?"

The constant numbness finally started to worry him. He put an arm around Amanda's shoulders and walked next to her down the alley.

Marco walked his "living corpse" into George Berkeley's home - Tiffany had the keys - and sat her on the couch. Yana and Tara soon followed. Tara looked in on them, and Marco nodded, a general signal telling her he'd handle it.

"I can't get warm," Amanda whispered softly.

He nodded, then glanced toward the stairs, making sure everyone had gone up. "This ever happen before?"

She nodded. "It is rare."

Marco took her hand between both of his, and she was relatively warm for a corpse. He rubbed both hands against hers, trying to generate some heat. "Psychological effects. Your body's registering the deficiency as a coldness."

"Huh?" she responded blankly. She wasn't even looking at him.

"It's my best guess. Your mind, your soul - the Greek nouns are interchangeable - feels a deficiency of... something. Your body is registering this lack as a cold sensation."

He kept one hand in his and reached the other one to her cheek to make her focus on him. "Unfortunately, I'm neither a theologian nor a psychologist; I'm just a well-read PA student. I do know we should get some sleep - both of us. You have your Ziploc bags of dirt?"

Amanda nodded. "In my pockets."

Marco slid his hands up her body, then fluidly slipped one under her legs. He scooped her up in both arms, and slowly carried her up the stairs.

After taking directions about where to put Amanda, Marco arrived at the guest room and gently deposited her in the bed. He slipped his jacket off of her, draped it over the nearest chair, and then slipped her shoes off. He swept her body with his eyes, checking for stakes, and once he was sure she wouldn't roll over onto one of them in the middle of the night, he pulled the covers over her and tucked her in as though she was a child. He kissed her gently on the forehead and started walking slowly out of the room.

"Where are you going?" she asked.

He turned to face her. "Back to my dorm."

Amanda rolled her eyes. "A vampire just tried to kill the both of us, if you have not noticed. She could have followed us here, and I do not want you going out alone."

He nodded. "Okay, I'll sleep on the couch."

She raised a brow. "Merle is sleeping there, remember?"

Marco thought for a moment. "Fine." He grabbed the chair and dragged it toward himself.

Amanda sighed. "Don't be ridiculous." She swept the corner of the covers over. "Get in."

Marco waggled his eyebrows. "Are you sure you trust me?"

"I trust you," she said. "Nothing can happen."

"Oh boy, do you underestimate your sex appeal." Marco slipped his pants and shirt off quickly. Marco took his shoes off and slid into bed. He turned to face her, and she turned away.

He leaned over her shoulder a little, and whispered, "The only reason this isn't undue temptation is that I'm too tired to do anything."

Marco rolled back, lying flat on his back, arms crossed over his chest like a mummy, as he felt her restlessly tossing next to him - she didn't sleep well in the dark. After ten minutes, he rolled onto his side and put a hand on her shoulder, turning her to face him.

"Mind if I try something that might help you sleep better?" he asked.

"Okay."

Marco carefully slid his arms around Amanda, one hand to her neck and the other to the base of her spine. He moved his fingertips over her skin at those spots with a fine caress. She moaned a little as he felt the small spasms along her spine as she relaxed. He continued to stroke these nerve centers. She wrapped her arms around him and fell asleep in his arms.

Once she finally stopped moving, Marco smiled. Certainly, he respected anyone that could rip his arms out. But he also respected and appreciated Amanda personally. She had a mind like his and was strong enough to take on almost any five vampires.

And at the same time, she was… pleasant to hold onto.

Marco held onto her and didn't let go.

Chapter 13

Fallout

San Francisco, December 12th

Amanda opened her eyes right at Marco. His eyes were already wide open and awake, staring right into hers just as she awoke. It was amazing just how deep and blue they were.

And he was still touching her, his fingers traveling lightly over her upper arms, and down her back. It was gentle and comforting and unleashed a whole collection of emotions that she was grateful he couldn't pick up on.

Her eyes flicked to the clock over his shoulder on the wall - nine in the morning. Amanda rolled out of bed, suddenly wide awake and landed on the floor, trying to roll under the bed.

Marco poked his head out over the edge and said, "Amanda… I duct-taped all of the curtains shut. There's no sunlight coming in here."

She paused a moment, then looked around. Black-out curtains had been tightly shut. While normal people would have noticed the dark immediately,

Amanda's night vision was so perfect that it might as well have been a clear, sunlit day. "Oh. Sorry."

He smiled at her lightly. "Come on. Let's get you fed, shall we?"

"You have blood around?"

"Well, I make a good snack, if all else fails."

She shook her head, then rolled to her feet. "No. I am good. I was well fed yesterday. I drank heavily so I could get here without a problem."

Marco nodded. "Understandable." He smiled at her. The smile she recognized from last night.

"Listen, Marco," she began, "about last night -"

"I should probably make that more official."

Amanda blinked. "No - wait - what?"

Marco's smile flickered, and so did his eyes. He was almost shy. "Ahem. Amanda Colt… or whatever your actual birth name is… I love you, and -"

"Are you sure?" she cut him off.

Marco blinked, then gave his head a little shake. He looked like he'd been smacked. "Sure about…?"

"Loving me."

His face crumpled - brow furrowed, mouth bunched up like he was thinking hard over a math problem. "I know I love you. I don't get what you mean."

"Have you thought it through?"

He paused. His face was so scrunched up in thought, it may have been the facial manifestation of the blue screen of death. "Now you're just confusing me."

She stepped forward and took his hands. "Marco, have you really *thought* about how long I'm going to live? I'm technically going to live *forever*. Do you understand that? People can get over hurt with time-"

"You're people -"

"- but time heals fewer wounds when you're living forever."

Marco looked at her… strangely. His smile grew just a little and -

She flinched. "Are you laughing at me?"

"Not yet," he said, his tone giving the impression it was a distinct possibility. "Amanda, have I proposed marriage to you?"

"Um, no, but -"

"Are we even *dating* yet?"

"Last night -"

"Could be a fluke for all we know. I'd want to formalize *that* before we talk marriage."

"But we -"

"Did not cross any lines. We came danged close, I'll grant you, but we both stopped short. Because I don't want your body." He blinked, looked at her eyes, her lips, looked her up and down quickly, once, and amended, "Well, I *do* want your body, but only insofar as your body is connected to the rest of you. I'm not asking you to marry me this minute. I'm really not. But you think I haven't thought about this? Haven't imagined where this might go, long-term? I mean, assuming that we survive the next 72 hours?

"Presume that neither of us gets murdered in the coming decades. Trust me, when I'm pushing ninety, I'm figuring that living as a 22-year-old vampire for the rest of my existence is going to look pretty damned good at that point. But that's not a decision I need to make today, tomorrow, or fifty years from now. I hope. That, of course, presumes that we can even stand each other in a few months as a couple. Let's not get too ahead of ourselves, okay?"

"Okay." She smiled at him for no reason she could fathom. She actually felt… tingly. She hadn't been well rested, not as much as she should have been, but she hadn't noticed. "Well, then, what now?"

"To Merle's place."

"How should I get through the streets?"

"Well, Merle has an underground entrance as an escape route, so we can use that." He glanced at the clock himself. "Besides, you have some time before the morning mists burn off. After all, this is San

Francisco. There's a reason I carry a crucifix in the daylight."

Kristen Kelly walked to her office and smiled. The piles of folders that had been dropped on her initially when she was new in the office were finally a thing of the past. Granted, having the FBI walk away with most of the files was a large part of it.

Kelly took off her suit jacket, smoothed out her blouse, and paused. She frowned at the latest folder on top of her inbox. She was certain that it hadn't been there before.

She sighed, then took it off the top. It was another bit for the "odd" file. Apparently, all of the "new guy" syndrome hadn't fully worn off yet.

She opened it up and checked the address… "A vampire club? Burned to charcoal? Not again…"

Detective Kelly flipped the pages. They had a walk-in deliver the tip. No name had been left behind, but the man in question was dressed in a full opera cape, top hat, and a silver wolfs-head cane with ruby eyes.

For a guy who's set up shop in Boston, Dalf gets out here a lot.

Kristen sat back in her chair and went over the past few months in her head. First, there was the scarred hitman in New York who shrugged off bullets but was slowed down by a wooden spear. Then there were the graveyard molestations she was put on back in September. Then this.

Kristen frowned, looked at their active/unsolved murder board, and saw a lot of things she didn't like. Including the method of death.

All of them had their throats ripped out.

Tiffany's head shot up from the till at the ringing of the bell over the door. "Oh, hello," she greeted, slightly disappointed that it wasn't a money-bearing customer.

"Tiffany," said a soft-spoken voice, tinged with annoyance. "What did you do to the stockroom!"

"Organized it," Tiffany called back.

A moment later, Merlin Kraft stalked out from the storeroom. "Fix it. Now."

The retail queen nodded and moved back. Kraft was certainly back, his usual windbreaker in place, along with his dark pants. He then turned to find eyes on him. "Ah, hello."

Marco and Amanda moved inside as one towards the books and Merle looked after them. Charming fellow. Surprised he wasn't strangled at birth.

Merle sat down with the six of them. "Okay, in my flight over from New York, I've been talking with my brother Tal, Jennifer Bosley, and Father Rodgers. They've all been coordinating resources and databases, and sources of information. This is going to be strange."

"Too late," Tara answered.

Marco nodded. "Tell me again, what does your brother Tal do?"

Merle glanced up from his notes. "He's a stage magician. And he runs a little store down in New Orleans."

"Let me guess, another magic shop."

"Funnily enough, yes."

"What's his stage name?"

"Talisman."

Yana blinked. "I actually know that one. But why would he know so much about vampires?"

He smiled slightly. "It's a hobby - he runs the New Orleans Vampire Hunter's Guild."

Marco smiled. Then his eyes flickered to the door. "Merle, do you happen to know a rather attractive woman with blue eyes and honey-blonde hair?"

Kraft blinked, and he didn't even look over his shoulder. "Hello, Kristen. Everyone, this is my wife, Detective Kelly of the SFPD."

"And haven't we already met?" Rory answered.

Merle gave Rory a sidelong look. "You have?"

"Hello," she replied. Kristen stepped into the store, walking down the three steps from the elevated platform at the entrance and scanning the room, noting the vampire and the New Yorker first. "I see that you managed to trust Marco Catalano and Amanda Colt, Merle." Her gaze traveled back to her ex-husband. "I'm glad to see that giving you that information from their FBI files was of some use. So happy that you could call after returning from wherever the hell you were since September."

Kristen's eyes went flat, and her voice dropped to an icy temperature. "May I talk with you for a moment?"

Merle nodded slowly. "Sure. How about the rest of you keep going on this, okay?" he said, tapping his notes.

Kristen pointed at Marco and Amanda. "I want the three of you. Let's step outside, shall we?"

Marco and Amanda shared a glance. Amanda didn't have her sunblock on, and the sun had already burned away the heavy fog of that particular morning. The vampire's eyes flicked to the silver cross hanging around the police Detective's neck and wondered if Kraft's ex knew something she shouldn't.

"How about we talk in the back room?" Merle asked, leaning in that direction. Kristen nodded, letting them go ahead of her.

Detective Kelly closed the door behind her, and she let out a breath of frustration. "Over the past few years, people have been dying in San Francisco, more than average. Most of the killing has been by throat trauma to one degree or another." She glanced at her ex-husband. "Merle, after you called me about the man Marco Catalano, and the possible CIA-based Amanda Colt, deaths with the signature of neck-killings began to fluctuate downward.

"Last August, a woman by the name of Sarah Bell died. Of the people questioned, most if not all of them are out in your store, Merle. Except for George Berkeley... who left to join the Army, unit unknown, at the same time that you told me that you would be out of the state for a while."

Kristen took a breath but continued before any of them could recover. "I know you didn't cause Miss Bell's death, Merle, because you were flying to New York to be with me at the time it happened. However, her death is classified under what we could call 'weird,' torn apart and partially eaten, with bite marks of deceased criminals. When some microscopic organisms were found and sent to the FBI, we were told to back off the case, it was being handled as part of another investigation. That reeks of you - and the day after she died, I know you received a phone call that sent your mood through the basement."

Her eyes pinned Marco to the floor before he could even move, and her hand rested on her hip, right next to her pistol. "Then, Mister Catalano comes to San Francisco, and suddenly, the murder rate plummets, and that kind of killing motif almost disappears once again. On 9/11, this year, after Marco suffers a personal loss of his father's hospital, lots of damage is inflicted on the cemeteries of San Francisco. Nothing comes of it - plenty of fire damage scorching stonework. Big deal, no pressure… but last night, a Goth club rumored to be for people who dress up as vampires got burned to the ground."

Her gaze flicked back and forth between Amanda and Marco. "A tip about a man and a woman matching your descriptions was handed in by a man dressed in a tuxedo, top hat and cape, which sounds like Dalf." Kelly looked directly at Merle. "Sarah Bell hung out here. Catalano hangs out here. Strange unsolved murders, vampire hangouts, and you in the middle. You want to tell me a tale, or the truth?"

Even Marco blinked at the speed, delivery, and easy intelligence on display. He patted Kraft on the back. "Wow. Merle, why are you divorced? She thinks exactly like you."

Kristen smiled slightly. "Because I got tired of playing guessing games about his job."

Amanda smiled and nodded. "And how did you get on this case?"

"I was assigned the cookout at the club. It had been under observation back during the murder spree since we thought there might be some freaks who thought they were vampires. Sarah Bell was part of that murder spree. The dots were easily connected after that."

Marco looked at Merle, brow raised. "She calls that easy?"

Kraft merely gave him a little smile that almost mirrored Kristen's. "That's my… that's Kristen."

Marco looked at his watch. "Before we got here, Amanda wanted to make the rest of my body turn black and blue for a little while to toughen me up for the revenge of the vampire. If anyone needs me, I'll be right here. Merle, you're the expert, you explain things to the nice officer here. I'd like to stay out of it."

Kristen looked at Merle. "Is he serious?"

Kraft shrugged. "Believe it or not, yes. How about I give you the short version - real vampires."

Kelly blinked, sighed, then held her head, rubbing her throbbing temple. "Merle… listen, I'm going to leave, walk around the block for an hour, then come back. Then we'll try this again, okay?"

Marco and Amanda watched the two of them leave. "It's like they're still married," Marco muttered. "Ah well."

Marco slipped his t-shirt over his head and slipped into a combat stance. Amanda had a more relaxed, noncombative stance: one leg straight, the forward leg bent at the knee as though she was leaning against the wall, and her arms fully relaxed. She was almost like a ballerina standing *en pointe*.

"Ready?" he asked.

She snapped into a stance to mirror his own. "Yeah."

"Go… Don't feel you should hold anything back -"

Within mid-blink, Amanda's right cross snapped into the air, but Marco had leaned back a split-second before the blow was launched. He grabbed the wrist, her belt, and threw her across the mat. She landed and rolled to her feet.

She charged and went at him with a flying kick. He had his arm out, waiting for her foot as it left the ground. She kicked right into it, and he latched onto her ankle, spun, and tossed her to the floor, immediately stepping back. She was on her hands and knees and glared at him.

Marco smiled. *Ah, signs of life. She must be feeling better.*

Amanda went from her knees to a burst of speed. Marco dropped and tumbled. She leapt over him before he could cut her legs out from under her. They rolled to their feet at the same time, Marco next to the punching bag and her on the other side of the room. She smiled and ran at him again, this time using a reverse back kick on the punching bag. Marco's smile had turned to a grin as he dropped to the ground as the kick was launched and let the bag fly over him. He swept the redhead's leg as she touched the ground. She dropped to the floor, and he pounced upon her, grabbing her wrists and pinning her legs with his.

"Gotcha!" he cried.

With that, Amanda flipped him over and landed on him, pinning him to the ground. "Try again?"

Marco frowned for a moment, then licked her face.

"Ewww!" she said as she reached up to wipe her cheek.

Marco used that free moment to deck her across the face, grab her shirt, then toss her over his head with his legs.

But Amanda had latched onto him as he grabbed her. She went over his head, but he was also flipped around, straight up against a wall.

Amanda waited for him to land, and he bounced off the wall, coming straight down on top of her. One knee rested gently on her stomach, and he held both her wrists to the mat. His other leg was across one of hers, keeping it to the floor.

"Give up?" he asked, dismissing her heavy breathing as mere exertion. She had taken a habit of keeping her body functions up and running so she could call upon anything as needed - produce tears, sweat to cool off, and even if she wanted to have children someday. So any residual heavy breathing was just a side effect.

Of course, it is. Yeesh, Marco, can you lie to yourself with the best of them...

It's not lying if it keeps me from jumping her on more ways than one.

Amanda smiled gently. "You've gotten better. Honestly."

Marco smiled. "I'm just keeping up with the fencing."

She nodded, her nose brushing his. "Your combative chess."

He nodded. "Like when I sparred with you the first time, I predicted your next move and struck accordingly. With your opening move the other day, I dodged the opening punch, then numbed the muscle so I could avoid a backhand, then step back to avoid a kick - your only move left. Just logically guess where your opponent will move next."

Amanda smiled, peering deeply into his rich blue eyes. She'd heard the sermon before, but she never tired of hearing it. She looked up at him, holding her down, his weight atop her. Her body was starting to warm involuntarily - body parts that hadn't been exerted during the sparring match.

"Marco," she whispered.

He blinked, trying to draw himself out of her eyes, his smile still there. "Amanda?"

"I feel warm now."

He brightened further. "You have what you needed?"

Amanda's head started to lift off the mat, still peering straight into his eyes. "*Da... almost...*"

She leaned forward and started to kiss his neck, giving him light, bloodless bites, and gently sucking on his skin. He mimicked her moves easily, his hand fell away from her wrists and wrapped around her waist, as her arms encircled his neck.

"Are you guys done yet? We want to get back to this thing trying to kill you!" Tiffany called into the back room.

Amanda and Marco instinctively rolled apart from each other. They stopped on hands and knees, each facing the other, staring with surprise. Each had the same thoughts flow through their heads -

Requited love, check…

Mutual interest and attraction, check…

Deal with it this minute, or regroup to kill the bad guy…

"Coming," Amanda called. *Kill the bad guy* had won for now.

Marco's eye twitched. "I am *so* going to kill this bitch."

"The assassin or Tiffany?" Amanda asked.

Marco chuckled darkly. "Don't tempt me."

They walked back to find the image on Merle's iPad: the same tangle of red hair, the green eyes staring out from a demonic vampire face. Tall, lanky body, long fingers ending in sharp nails…

"Yup. That's her." Marco admitted.

Merle glared at him. "Who'd you think we'd find? Bela Lugosi?"

Yana blinked at the words. "Um, anyone here understand this?"

Tara looked at the Irish vampire. "Sean? Have you picked up on any Gaelic since you died?"

Rory blinked. "Aye, but…" He looked at the computer screen. "'Tis a really bad scan…"

Marco sighed. "How about we look at the translation." He scrolled the screen up, then paused. "Ah, Vatican archives. Nice. From Rodgers, I presume."

Merle nodded.

"Her name is Nuala na Connemarragh," Rory said. The "ua" came out with a long "oo" sound.

"Is that some sort of disease?" Tiffany replied. "Sounds nasty."

"Isn't Connemara where they get all that nice marble?" Yana asked.

"'Tis," Rory replied. "But fer her, it might be talking about where she's born - though she could have been born in Belfast for all the name means now, but doesn't it say she was from Ulster in 1183 and made a vampire in 1201?"

"Does it?" Tiffany asked.

Rory glanced at the blonde, wondering if anyone would care if he ate her… and then he pondered why he would go near that much silicone. He looked back at the screen and blinked. "Feck… Before she was turned, it says she hunted the Leanhaum-shee."

Marco raised a hand. "Okay. You win. You have something I don't know. What the bleep is that?"

"One of the *sidhe*," Rory answered, pronouncing it like *she*. "One of the dark ones. The fae. This is a variety of fae that drinks blood.

Marco groaned. "She hunted vampires."

Amanda growled, "*Sukynsin.*"

Marco nodded. "'Son of a bitch' sums it up." He leaned against the wall. "With their ability to spin and believe faery stories, the Irish would have no problem with a woman who hunted bloodsuckers."

Rory nodded. "And back then, they'd enjoy it, too. They spent a lot of days cattle raiding as a pastime… From each other and anyone else around, usually. They even made an epic over one. Hunting down bloodsuckers would have been just grand."

There was a long moment of silence as everyone tried to figure out how to kill a woman who hunted vampires while she was alive, now that she was undead and survived being staked.

"Maybe we need some overkill," Marco commented, thinking out loud.

Everyone gave him curious glances, prompting him to go on. He shrugged. "Well, you know about Rasputin?"

Amanda smiled. "He turned a few people into vampires before they took him down."

Marco blinked. "Okay…"

She continued, "He had to be shot, stabbed, poisoned, beaten and drowned before he finally died, but the wounds are what killed him… that and the frozen water may have simply kept him dormant."

He nodded. "Right. So how about you burn Nuala. Then stake her, toss her into the sunlight, and cut her head off? There's a *reason* my stakes are doused in turpentine."

Amanda nodded. "She probably needs to use massive amounts of energy just to stay together with the stake inside."

Rory lit a new cigarette and pondered the sketch a bit more. "Ya know, I think I know this bitch." He inhaled deeply. "She's an assassin by profession, Nuala. If it's the one rumors talk of, she comes out of the shadows every few years, kills someone important, then disappears again. No-one *knows* exactly what'll kill her."

Merle frowned. "That's the gist of what I've heard. Maybe it's just a matter of putting in the stake and making sure it stays there long enough for it to have an effect."

Rory smiled. "It gets worse. There're rumors that Nuala is directed. Her targets are chosen for her, ya see. She's a vampire, but almost never feeds from her assassinations, or even kills at close range. Her preferred weapon is a rapparre: a light Gaelic spear."

Amanda looked at Marco. "What she used on us last night."

He raised a finger. "*Tried* to use on us last night."

Merle nodded. "She's also used a crossbow, even a gun… her last kill was with a sniper rifle. The rumor mill only knows about it because of a mark she left on the bullet extracted from the victim."

Amanda cocked her head. "How do you know about this, and I don't?"

Merle smiled. "Bosley, for the most part. She's kept her ear to the ground a lot lately."

Rory grinned. "And I associate with the lower echelons more often than you do."

Merle sighed deeply and ignored them. "So she's after Amanda."

"And Marco," Tara interjected. She paused a moment, blinked, and said, "Right?"

Yana glanced at her girlfriend. "What makes you think he's on the vampire hit parade?"

Rory shot her a look. "Do you need to ask? Most vamps would've eaten 'im long ago."

Amanda nodded at Tara's assessment, ignoring Rory. "What about Asmodeus?"

Merle nodded. "You mean blowback, 'You mess with me, you mess with my family'?"

Yana looked over at Marco, who stood off to the side, his eyes staring off into nowhere. He had obviously drifted into his own mind. "Marco? Something wrong?"

His eyes flashed for a moment, and he turned to her, eyes gleaming manically. "Nothing… yet." He stood and whirled in one, smooth motion. "How old did you say our girl was?"

"She's from twelve-oh-one," Tara murmured. Yana smiled and played a little with her girlfriend's hair.

Marco stepped in front of Amanda and smiled. "Back when we were facing Day, he said that our friendly Russian vampire in Brooklyn was trained by someone with 800 years of experience. Sound like anyone we know?"

He whirled toward Rory. "If you were an assassin whose only goal was to kill someone, how would you do it?"

The vampire looked at him funny. "Why the hell are you askin' *me*?"

"Because you were a killer in your former life before you even became a vampire, and you're familiar with modern tactics," Marco snapped at him. "And one of your best qualities is that you aren't a sadist, so *answer my damn question, okay*?"

Amanda inched back a little from Marco, getting a small glimmer of what he'd hidden from her. His eyes sparkled with a distant… something. It was dark, it was scary, and it was her love.

"I'd simply kill you both," Rory stated. "If I was going to do it, I'd do her first, then you, but preferably at the same time -"

"That's why she waited for us to be right next to each other," Amanda noted.

Marco nodded, not looking away from the Irish vampire. "Continue."

"And I'd try to hit you when you're not expectin' it."

Marco nodded again slowly, thoughtfully. Then his eyes widened suddenly, and he jumped on Amanda an instant before the crack of a rifle shot rang through Artful Krafts, breaking through the storefront window, ripping through the shutters, and impacting in Marco's back.

Chapter 14

The Most Dangerous Game

As Amanda moved to roll Marco onto his back, "Stay… down" came hoarsely from his lips.

Another bullet entered his back, followed by the whip-crack of a rifle bullet breaking the sound barrier. The impact pounded into his body, slamming into him like wrestler swinging sheet metal. His arms tightened around Amanda, despite the pain spreading over his body.

Amanda looked toward the back of the store. Everyone else had already dropped to the floor. She reached up and dragged herself and Marco along the wooden boards, moving for cover in the reading niche off to the side - the table alone wouldn't provide cover for the amount of firepower being tossed at them.

For the first time in a long time, Yana muttered a frightened obscenity under her breath. She glanced over at Tara, watched her girlfriend roll towards one of the counters, then turned her attention back to Marco.

"What's she using, a thermal imaging telescopic sight on top of a rifle?" Merle asked from behind the counter. *Damn, I've been in country too long. I'm starting to think like SpecOps.*

Rory smiled, looking down from his chair. He slid back and stood, puffing a little at his cigarette. "Bullets, eh? Well, I guess that leaves me safe -"

The next three rounds hit him square in the chest, knocking him to the floor.

"So much for the thermal imaging idea," Merle remarked. "He's room-temp."

"Whatever happened to traditional old-fashioned fangs?" Rory complained as he staggered to his feet. "Maybe even a battle ax? Bloody banshee, I'm gonna -"

A rapparre flew through the front door and nailed him to the stairs. He looked down at the wooden spear protruding from his body, his eyes radiating pain as he stood there, nailed through the center of his chest.

"She's got an expanded radar," Yana said in awe. "Vampires sense things really well, without looking."

"No kidding…" Amanda rolled Marco off of her and onto his stomach. "And her range is longer than mine. I didn't even feel her coming."

Yana crept to Marco's other side, and they both stripped away his clothes, only to find, under his jacket and shirt, a piece of solid white plastic with several bullets lodged into it.

"What the hell is this?" Yana asked.

Marco groaned and rolled over onto his side. "It's called the Kevlar vest I got out of the *Quartermaster* military surplus catalog… I figured around here, it couldn't exactly hurt."

Yana: "How did you know she'd -"

"I didn't," he moaned as he made his way to a sitting position. "I figured if I jumped Amanda, the worst that could happen would be that I'd look even dumber than usual."

"Good boy, you get a treat later," Amanda told him, patting him on the head. "Assuming we all live."

He groaned. "No fair, you and Rory are already dead."

"Whatever."

Rory slid off the spear, looking really annoyed and in pain. The spear was made of wood but hadn't hit his heart, so he was still undead… for the moment. Any more damage to the shutters, the sun would come through and…

Oy. Merle noted the same thing. He pulled out a little keychain with a laser pointer on it and tossed it at Rory. "Catch!"

Rory grabbed it in mid-flight with one hand, holding the other to the wound in his chest. "What am I supposed to do with it?"

Another spear came through the window and went through the bookcases providing cover for Amanda, Marco, and Yana. It stuck in the bookcase coming out, nearly tipping it over.

Merle called out, "Place it alongside the spear and turn it on."

Rory did so, and the red beam shot through the hole the spear had come through.

Amanda immediately ripped the rapparre from the bookcase and leapt into the center of the shop, throwing the spear along the path of the beam.

The Pyramid Building sat in the "good" part of town, near the piers, and the Embarcadero - a strip of stores that was once almost an outdoor mall. The people along the piers were wealthy, and many owned their own shops. Beyond that was the Bay, and Alcatraz. The Pyramid Building looked just like its name - a pyramid. It was considered by many to be the jewel of the city, the peak of San Francisco 20th century construction.

The long, slender body of the building went nearly straight up, with a gentle slope to all sides. Before the top of the building came to a point, it flared out to a broader, squatter, inverted pyramid, and atop that was another, this one coming fully to a point. It was the lone skyscraper in the middle of the Embarcadero, and the only buildings taller than it were Coit Tower, which lay on one end of the city, and the Lombard Street residential area on the other - the latter inhabited only by the 'best families' in the city.

In a middle floor of the Pyramid building, the vampire assassin known as Nuala looked down at the red dot on her chest and said, "Clever girl."

Then her own spear nailed her in the chest, knocking her off the floor and ramming her to the ceiling.

Yana glanced over at Rory, still clutching a hand to his chest. "You okay?"

He smiled reassuringly at her. "Nothing that won't heal. Eventually." His eyes suddenly widened much like Marco's had before. He tackled her as the door imploded.

Yana felt all of her bones rattle, and her breath was knocked from her body as she met the floor with a heavy vampire on top of her.

"Ow!" she wheezed painfully. "Get the hell off me!"

He had the grace to look embarrassed as he scrambled away. "Sorry."

"Oh, you're sorry all right," a female voice said. "A sorry excuse for a vampire."

They both whirled. The living version of the digital sketch stood in the doorway. Her eyes glowing at them like a pair of deadly gems separated by half-a-nose that was literally hawk-like. Amanda stood before the vampire assassin. Amanda briefly wondered how Nuala could have jumped across the street through sunlight without even a sizzle.

"I've been tearing fockers apart fer a century," Rory retorted, not noticing he was ignored.

Nuala smiled at Amanda. "I too never had the good sense to stay dead either."

Amanda shrugged. "Well, I never did know when to take a hint."

Nuala raised one hand, ready to strike when she flicked it down in time to block a knife blade with the back of her hand. She glanced at Marco. "You and the other mark."

Marco gave her a weak smile as he stood, using the bookcase for support. "Marc-*o*, not Mark." He straightened painfully. "You don't like to die, do you?"

She merely smiled. She stepped toward Amanda and Rory slid into her way.

"Hey bitch, I'm not exactly chopped sweetbreads here."

Nuala glared at Rory with disdain. Without even removing Marco's wooden knife from her left hand, she delivered a sharp uppercut to his stomach. Rory doubled-over in pain, then she slammed her elbow into his back. "My sire talked like you. It took me eight days to kill *him*."

"Only eight?" Marco asked curiously. Rory shot him a pained look from the floor. Nuala stepped onto the vampire's back, then launched herself at Amanda. Amanda had leapt back in anticipation, just like Marco had done to her. Nuala had a longer reach, faster moves, a stronger body, and this was trouble.

At once, Amanda and Rory leapt at her from different sides. Without looking at them, she blocked their blows with lighting limbs and simultaneously hooked her foot around the leg of the table and flung it at Merle, making him duck.

As they fought, Tara searched underneath the countertop. "Come on, where do you keep the crucifixes?" she murmured.

Nuala blocked another of Amanda's blows with her left hand and back-kicked at her, knocking her off her feet. At the same time, she whacked Rory upside the head with her right hand, making him soar toward the beams of sunlight from the street. His back burst into flames. He rolled out of the way, putting out the fire.

In the middle of her next kick, Marco threw another knife at her before stumbling down. His aim was off, and the blade landed in the buttock muscle, making the leg she balanced on collapse. She fell, face first, to the floor. Nuala pulled the knife out and rolled, flinging it away casually.

Nuala pushed off the floor and whirled back to Rory, only to find Tara standing between them with a cross bigger than her torso. "Back, Hellspawn!"

Nuala looked at her like she was insane. "That is so absurd. Can't you get any better lines?"

"I agree," Marco added from the floor. "That was awful."

"Yup," Merle Kraft smiled. "It was really bad."

Nuala turned and looked at him, noting that he was only two feet behind her. She stared down at the shorter man and snickered. "And what do you *want*, *lesser* Kraft?"

Merle shrugged, smiled, and swung. Nuala blocked, as usual, only to find that Merle was swinging a glass gallon jug of holy water right into her face. Her block had shattered the glass, splashing the contents all over her.

Nuala was surrounded in one giant burst of steam and wailed like a damned soul. With blurring speed, she dashed out into the street and leapt through a manhole cover to the sewer below.

Merle sighed. "Well, that was fun."

Marco rolled onto one knee, pushing off the table to his feet. "Think we can expect other tricks, too?"

Rory slowly creaked from the floor. "I've seen vampires with extraordinary powers and abilities: the ability to mesmerize, telekinesis, shape-shifting -"

"Able to leap tall buildings in a single bound," Marco muttered.

"Making earthquakes, calling animals to themselves…" Tara began as she leaned up against the countertop.

Yana looked at her and smiled. "No, honey, that's from those Anita Blake novels you've been reading."

"Yeah." Tara smiled and blinked.

Marco sighed. He'd been beaten more than enough already. "Here's my question. Why couldn't she shape-shift? She did all right last night, turning into mist, and disarmed me without even turning solid."

"Sun's out," Rory explained.

Amanda nodded. "It would be like if she was within range of a crucifix. It would cripple her ability to shift."

Marco nodded slowly. "Gotcha. I don't think we ever discussed that. Though did you notice that she can shift with her clothes? I found that interesting. I've only seen Mikhail do that."

"Why don't I feel so good?" Tara groaned

Everyone turned towards her. The last wooden knife Nuala had so casually flicked away protruded from Tara's stomach.

Chapter 15

Strike of the Minions

Marco swept forward and caught Tara before she fell, pressing his hand around the knife at the point of entry to make sure it didn't move. With luck, the blade was corking the wound. Uncorking would result in a very frothy bloody Champagne.

"Stay with me, Tara," he told her, gently lowering her.

Merle disappeared a moment, then reappeared at Marco's side, holding two needles, a phial of epinephrine and one of saline.

"I have 911," said a voice from the door. Marco barely spared the owner of the voice a glance. But when he did, he saw Merle Kraft's ex-wife Kristen Kelly, cell phone already in her hand, and already talking with the EMTs.

Has it been an hour since she left already? Marco drew a tension knife from a back pocket and used it to cut away the shirt around the entry wound. "Tiffany," Marco barked without even looking up. "Make yourself useful, grab the knife, just like this, and *don't* move it. Amanda, start licking the wound *around* the stake."

Yana grabbed Marco's shoulder, trying to drag him away from Tara. "You're not feeding her to your vampire bitch."

Marco barely spared her a glance as he shoved her back. "Detective, keep her off me. Merle, hand me the epi, and draw the saline."

Detective Kelly grabbed Yana and picked her up with ease, despite the height difference. Merle blinked at the medical speak, and Marco growled, snatched the epinephrine/adrenaline and needle, drawing a hefty amount. "Stay still, darling. Don't move."

She didn't reply, as he expected. He felt her pulse. Nothing.

Both he and Amanda said "Defib," and Marco stabbed down with the needle, plunging it into her heart. He carefully pushed the plunger all the way down, then withdrew it, pushing it off to one side.

"Merle, push the saline, Rory, start CPR." Marco pushed away from Tara so the vampire could take his place. He leapt over the front counter, drawing a wooden knife, then yanked the wire out of a table lamp. With two quick movements, he stripped off the protective covering. Once the wires were properly exposed, he leapt back over the counter and barked, "Clear!"

Everyone backed away seconds before Marco stabbed Tara with the live wires. Her body jumped.

"Detective," Marco called, taking Tara's pulse again. "You'll have to stay here to keep the cops off our people. Merle will fill you in on the details, we'll need local cover." He waited for a second more at the pulse. "Damnit! *Clear*!"

Kristen looked up from her cell phone. "Yes, that's clear," she snapped.

"I wasn't talking to you," he said, stabbing the wires at Tara once more.

Then the front of the building exploded with a stream of bullets.

Marco pulled the wires off of Tara's chest and held them away from everyone as he used his body to cover Tara's. "Damn it to hell, now what?"

"Did I mention that she has minions with machineguns?" Merle said.

"No!" Marco yelled. "It might have been helpful to know that *before*. Rory, Amanda, help me get her into the back room. Tiffany, keep that stake steady."

"I'm great with my hands," the blonde answered, "just ask George."

Marco was too busy to reply. "Everyone else, follow us."

Detective Kelly hurled Yana into the back room. She turned back, staying behind the door frame, drawing her weapon. When everyone was in behind her, she fired out through the windows, one round at a time.

Then the shades and shutters came right off of the front window.

Kristen winced. There were dozens of them, covered in the latest body armor. They were all armed with full machineguns, some of them with 200-round box magazines, and some with chain-fed belts. Those guns were almost all usually put down for emplacements. But they all fired away as though the guns were as light as the average hunting rifle.

She ducked. "I am so not carrying enough rounds. Merle! I hope to God you have another plan. We've got an army of darkness out here, and none of you look like Bruce Campbell to me."

Two men on either side of the semicircle of death made certain to keep the local traffic at bay. Several drivers had approached from around the bend in the Embarcadero Road and were immediately riddled with bullets. The men in the middle of the column of death were only two men deep. There wasn't any need to be subtle about this, and there was no need to conserve ammo.

The first minion to die didn't have a chance. His attacker ran up behind him and broke his neck. With all the noise from the weapons' fire, not even a vampire would have heard him die.

The attacker drew his knife and slashed the throats of the men on either side of him. He dropped down and grabbed two of their guns.

At that point, the minions - linked through their master Nuala - felt their numbers dwindling, a vibration deep in their bones. The three minions in front and one on either side of the attacked all turned to engage. The attacker opened fire with his peripheral vision, starting with the two on either side, sweeping towards the three in front of him. He swept back and forth through the minions, his body moving like he was working a scythe. But that's what happened when there was a wolf among the fold.

Or in this case, a wolfhound.

The minions stopped and turned to engage the large, monstrous killer amongst them. George Berkeley, fresh from the sandbox, was not having any of it.

Then the first BOOM echoed throughout the area, in short time with the second one. Both of them came from the Pyramid Building. It was from a different floor than Nuala though. Two different floors.

On one floor was Merle's sniper from the sandbox, Carl Ramirez, with his .50-caliber anti-material Galil sniper rifle. Each bullet punched through the armor and bounced around inside a bit before coming to rest.

On a different floor was Ibrahim Javaherian, the Vatican Ninja sniper. He was less fancy and just went with headshots all the way.

From behind Artful Krafts, out of sight of everyone except for Alcatraz, Vatican Ninjas rounded from the right, Merle's vampire SpecOps team came around from the left. The minions were caught in the middle.

It was a very short firefight.

"What the hell was that?" Kristen asked as the gunfire died down.

"You asked what I was doing for the last few months," Merle answered, "meet some of my coworkers. I knew there were armed minions afoot, so I called in a favor or three."

Kristen hesitated, then shook her head, dismissing her next thought. "Great. Maybe you can tell me why that woman is licking blood out of that girl's wound?"

"We were attacked, and -"

"I figured that. What's with the licking?"

"She's a vampire," Marco bellowed. "Her saliva has healing properties that I hope will slow the damage and fix the bleeding and - clear!" He shocked Tara once again. "Now will someone get me the damned ambulance!"

* * *

The EMTs has declared Tara dead at the scene - twice - but her time of final departure had been forestalled by Marco, also twice.

In over a hundred years of existence, Amanda had never borne witness to such an event outside of a battlefield. Granted, Amanda Colt, vampire, had to track this amazing feat from under the ambulance, in the sewer system, but her senses were such that she might as well have been next to the wounded Tara. Yana's girlfriend had been kept alive by will alone, and it was almost all Marco's will. When Tara was wheeled into the hospital, Marco rode her chest, beating her heart back to life again.

An hour later, Yana sat next to Tara's dead body.

Amanda and Marco now watched Yana mourn her girlfriend from the hall.

Marco's hand rested on the vampire's shoulder. "I just hope I didn't kill her… I felt several ribs creak while I worked her heart."

Amanda wrapped an arm around her friend's waist. "Normally, it is possible, but I doubt it, Marco. Unless you are worried about my bite?"

He nodded. "I still remember hurling manhole covers for days after the first bite, and you nipped me just yesterday. I'm more worried that I shattered Tara's internal organs."

"This time it was just a small one. The first time, I drank."

He allowed himself a smile. "As long as it's not while I'm moving. I'd hate for you to drink and drive."

Amanda smiled weakly. "You are charming, dear, but not that intoxicating."

"I'll go on a drinking binge sometime," he said smoothly, "then we'll see what you have to say when my blood is a hundred proof."

"I'm Russian. You'd need to trade your plasma for vodka."

"Point." Marco looked at Yana over her dead lover. "Should I have given up on Tara? Slit your wrists open and -"

Amanda squeezed Marco so hard, his ribs creaked. "Stop it. Mine is not a life I wish on anyone *un*willingly."

"Why not? I thought you were happy with your afterlife."

She nodded. "I have managed to keep myself busy." She gazed at him.

"Busy, sure," he said, "but so? Busy isn't happy. As long as I've known you, you've been… well, lively, if you'll forgive the pun."

She sighed. "Marco, you have only ever seen my good days. My bad ones were… very bad. Do you think that vampires are just people with fangs?"

He just looked at her. "You've managed to convince me that they are."

Amanda shook her head slightly, the smile still on her lips. "That is sweet, but not true. We start off blank, yes, but it is hard when you understand our situation. When we are turned, we need blood, are driven to kill, and have no understanding of it. I was a predator, Marco, and in many ways, I still am. Do not forget that."

Marco almost smiled at that irony, but his eyes drifted back to the operating room.

Amanda stared at his face, focused, intent, deadly. His eyes were as cold as Siberia, and somewhere behind those blue irises was a sign reading *Doctor Jekyll is on vacation, but Mister Hyde will see you shortly.* "Where are you?"

Marco glanced back at her, and his eyes softened. "We need to get Yana out of here. Do you think Rory can hold a cross without getting his hand burned off?"

She frowned. "Yes, why?"

"Because you and I are being hunted. Someone needs to be with Yana, and I don't want her on the firing line again - that leaves Rory for night watchman. Maybe even day watchman. If Nuala has done any research, she'll come here to find us, and we need Yana out of this place."

"It is a Roman Catholic hospital. Crosses everywhere, a chapel upstairs -"

Marco shook his head. "Minions, remember? Also, she uses sniper rifles. We would be screwed, and so would Yana if she even went to the bathroom."

Amanda paused a moment. "I'm surprised. You care about her, don't you?"

Marco nodded curtly, at first, as his only answer. Amanda closed her eyes, almost in pain at the idea. She was right, he could never love her, the very idea that she could have believed he could was absurd.

A moment later, he added in a whisper. "She's one of mine. I'm responsible for her. I was responsible for Tara, too. I would do for her what I would for you from our first month together. Before… well, before."

She blinked. One time they had gone into a vampire club, he had taken the first vampire who attacked her and explained how sometimes a "copper cross" inserted a certain way did *not* make it an intra-uterine device. Especially on a guy.

"Before what?" she asked cautiously.

Before I discovered I'm as much of a predator as you are, if not more, he thought. *Before I found I enjoy the hunt, the kill; you don't, not anymore. Before I found out that I've become an animal I can barely control. What I want to do…*

Marco looked at Yana a moment longer, then pivoted to sweep Amanda off her feet. He spun out of the line of sight of the OR window, pressed Amanda against a wall, and kissed her on the lips with all the passion he had been holding back from her, and from himself. His arms wrapped around her, his hands on her back, enjoying each sensation as they washed over him - her warmth, the texture of her skin, how she smelled, how she tasted, and the small sounds of enjoyment he heard from her.

Had Marco narrated that moment, he would have denied that he was scared out of his mind by how much he loved her. How utterly terrified he was by what he might do to her by complete accident. He might have said that he had blacked out and didn't know what he was doing or found himself compelled by irresistible impulse. He would have denied how absolutely in love with her he was, made up some excuse to convince himself…

However, Marco wasn't narrating.

Neither of them knew how long they were there, and Amanda swore she had several small orgasms, but when they parted, they looked deeply into each other's eyes, searching for words to fill in the silence…

Then they realized that Yana was out of the operating room.

And Yana was looking at them, open-mouthed, and a little dazed.

Marco was about to speak when the redheaded San Francisco native smacked him upside the head.

"Took you long enough to figure it out," Yana snapped at him. She stared at him a moment, then her chin began to wrinkle, and she sniffled, and Marco was in deathly fear that she would start to cry on him.

"Yana, I -"

"Ow," she whined. "I hurt my hand. Why's your head so *hard?*"

Kristen Kelly looked around the aftermath of the fight in Artful Krafts. The store had certainly seen better days, nights, afternoons, and most weekends… one time that came to mind was the one Halloween where it overlapped with the weekend and brought a three-day pillaging of his store that only ended at gunpoint.

The best description was "totally destroyed." The front of the store was nonexistent. The glass had been shot out of the window. Every bookcase and shelf had been cut in half. The counter was now a stack of splinters and wood pulp.

Kristen stood outside the perimeter of yellow tape that had marked off the crime scene, gazing over it with a thoughtful gaze. "I hope you have insurance for this."

"I'm not even sure what this is? Act of war? Act of Devil? Sure as Hell ain't an act of God. Murderous rampage? I can't say a terrorist attack, the store isn't blown up. It just looks like it."

"Right. As for the rest? Vampire," she said, making it sound more like a statement than a question. "In daylight?"

"She's a strong vampire," Merle explained. "And minimal light exposure means she could get through without bursting into flames."

"Right," she said, not overly affected, just acknowledging the simple fact. "And your Amanda Colt is what?"

"A good vampire," Merle told her, "but not as far up on the power scale as this one."

"Uh huh," she nodded.

Overall, Merle thought, *she's taking this rather calmly.*

"You've been dealing with this stuff for years?" she asked.

"Just since that time in New York with you, me and Demers."

Kristen spared him a glance. "The scarred creature that you decapitated with the stop sign?"

He nodded. "Apparently, they're up to something. What… is beyond me."

Detective Kelly didn't say much. The gears of thoughts were evidently turning behind her eyes. "I know you've been busy and out of town since this 9/11, does that mean that they were involved?"

Kraft smiled. *God, I love this woman. Why can't I still be married to her?* Then he remembered - he couldn't tell her everything about his job, and the number of creatures he had to contend with were things he wouldn't discuss with her even if the government paid him to tell her everything. "Yes. Some vampires work with the Taliban. Some are even recycled suicide bombers."

"Huh." She shrugged. "Well, that's one use for vampire foot soldiers. They can pick up a gun even after they blow up."

"And I know there are some pulling strings behind the scenes. Unfortunately, I'm not even entirely certain which strings are being yanked by who." *Amazingly enough,* he thought. *I think all of that was the truth.*

"Now my question becomes how do we cover this up?" Kristen asked.

Merle gave a small smile. "I'm already in the middle of that. The FBI will want this, for reasons they won't state to the SFPD, which will piss off the SFPD, but it'll be one less unsolved murder that they have to look at on their books."

"*My* books," she corrected him.

"Point taken."

Kristen sighed, shaking her head. "And what am I supposed to do with the rest of it, Merle?"

"Well, I know it's a lot to get used to -"

She laughed wryly. "Oh, don't even start with the vampires, start with the pragmatic problems. You and your guys have been leaving a lot of damage to clean up. San Francisco isn't as big as New York. We're getting smaller all the time. Remember all that bull I've had to deal with lately? The odd little assignments I've had, like all those crypts destroyed in a reign of what looks like bum-burning gone mental? Not your style, but given what I saw of Marco just now, I could believe that was his. There was also an entire pier wrecked. He burned down a nightclub and attracted a vampiric assassin from the back end of Hell. Will the FBI be taking all of *that*, too?"

Kraft winced. He hadn't expected that Kristen of all people would be taking the brunt of the damage that Marco Catalano had left behind. The man was a one-man wrecking crew. "Yeah, sorry about that. Look, I'm not sure what we're going to do about this right now. Hell, I can't even imagine what pretense we're going to use for having Tara's murder just go away." He sighed. "Sorry… but, you know, you're taking this very well."

Kristen raised an eyebrow. "Merle, I was married to you for years, and my two brothers-in-law… one's the head of the New Orleans guild of vampire hunters, and the other is a Boston Brahman Lord of the Sith who never comes out in daylight and scares me and every animal in a 10 block radius. Not to mention that my ex-husband walks through locked doors without tools, and…" She smiled at the thought. "On our honeymoon, managed to disappear my clothing while it was still on me. Explain to me where *vampires* should strike me as weird?"

Chapter 16

Angels of December

George Berkeley felt strange, sprawled out on a couch in a hotel suite, just chilling in his body armor and weapons. Then again, with his girlfriend Tiffany draped over him *while* he was covered in weapons, it felt even stranger.

One of the Vatican Ninjas, a redhead named Timothy Doughtery, was sprawled out on the floor. "Dang, it feels good to be on a soft carpet this time, don't you think?" he asked in a thick brogue that made Rory's sound soft and gentle.

"There's a carpet," George answered. "That's new for me lately."

"Point taken, lad."

On the opposite couch, Marco and Amanda sat in a similar position to George and Tiffany. "So, George, I'm getting the impression you're embracing your inner dog."

George gave a little shrug. Ever since he had been bitten by a lycanthrope, he'd never really had an opportunity to use his invulnerability or strength in a day-to-day situation. But then there was a good reason he turned into an Irish wolfhound - he didn't get more laid back short of being dead, and if someone touched any of his people, George would utterly destroy them.

Technically, he hadn't needed his Ka-Bar knife to attack the minions, but it was easier to explain than ripping throats out with his bare hands. And he didn't want to spend the next few hours digging human flesh out from under his fingernails.

"It's been useful," George answered.

Marco smiled. "I don't ever remember *Dracula Versus the Wolfman* as a Universal monster film, but it sounds like it'll work. Especially if you're armed. You guys generally carry silver bullets, or what?"

George shrugged. "One of everything, really. I'm just glad we didn't need the flamethrower today. Those things can make a mess."

Amanda smiled, looking up from Marco's chest. "I know. World War I. Such a train wreck."

Over Marco's shoulder, Carl Ramirez stopped dealing cards between himself and Bram. He looked at his Vatican Ninja counterpart with a raised eyebrow. Ibrahim just smiled, shook his head, and nodded to the pile of cards. Carl rolled his eyes, sighed, and kept dealing.

"I guess your guys aren't used to working with vampires yet?" Marco asked.

"In the sandbox," George said, "only good vamp is a dead one."

Dougherty raised a hand straight up, volunteering an answer. "Aye, lad, 'tis true. Most of them? Stake on sight."

Amanda sighed. "I must concur. I was the only vampire in Afghanistan in the 80s that I trusted. Not even my CIA handlers would trust the others, and with good reason. Most Afghanis? If they want to live their life, they don't want one like mine."

Marco nodded slowly and thoughtfully. He looked over his shoulder. "Hey, Bram, where's Hendershot? Isn't he coming along? Or did you leave him in his crypt?"

"Crypt?" Carl asked. "He's another vampire?"

Bram gave a little smile. "Captain Hendershot is not a vampire, he is my commanding officer. He and Marco don't get along. They occasionally differ on how best to proceed. It leads to conflict."

Marco scoffed. "Hey, I would have had him that one time if Father Rodgers hadn't zapped me with the Taser."

Carl's eyebrows shot straight up. "Really, dude?"

Dougherty laughed. "Marco can be a tad touchy, can't ye, lad?"

Carl looked over at the couch again, with Marco cuddled up to Amanda. "Doesn't *look* that scary."

Bram chuckled and shook his head. "Don't go there. Just don't."

"Please don't," Marco said, waving it away, "I have no interest in proving anything today. I had enough blood on my hands just this morning." He paused, looking at his hand. "I think I still do. Huh. Funny that. Guess I gotta scrub a little better."

Carl leaned forward to Bram and whispered, "She can always lick them clean for him. Heh."

Marco groaned. "Mister Ramirez, I just met you, don't make me murder you. Just, seriously, don't."

"*Da*," Amanda agreed. "Has been long day already."

Dougherty nodded. "I concur, kids."

"I'm just glad that this creature can't track us," Ibrahim said, looking at the cards in his hand. He started sorting them by suit. "After all, she can operate well enough in daylight, and the only reason we've won so far is a surprise and, literally, the Grace of God Almighty. We should all be counting our blessings."

"I am," Marco said, as he slowly stroked Amanda's hair. *I'm counting the hairs on her head. Each one's a blessing as far as I'm concerned.* "Trust me, I'm glad I have a hefty prayer life."

George's languid face reacted, allowing himself a quick smile, which just as quickly faded under his mustache. "I'm glad you do, too. Otherwise, that bit with the demon wouldn't have ended well for any of us."

"Demon?" Carl asked with a laugh. He tossed in a paperclip as his bet. "Is that the big scary demon who turned into a dragon, George? Something out of *The Hobbit?*"

"Actually, it was more like *Sleeping Beauty,*" Marco corrected.

"Aye," Dougherty added. "We had to kill the host… who was hard to tell from the actual demon at that point, to tell the truth."

"Freeze with liquid nitrogen," Amanda added, "then exorcise."

"Then hit with guardian angel," Ibrahim said.

"With what?" Amanda asked.

Marco cringed. *Oh drat.*

"Oh yeah, you had to go misty for that part of the battle," the Ninja explained, "and weren't there when Marco's angel come out. Pretty much punched a hole in Asmodeus."

Amanda lowered her head into Marco's lap, then turned over so she could look at him. "No-one told me that."

"It wasn't like it was going to add anything to the story," Marco reasoned.

"Some boyfriends hide former girlfriends, you hide a visit from a guardian angel?"

Marco held his hands up, palms up. "Eh?"

"Amanda," George said, eager to change the subject, "tell us how bad this could get."

"With the assassin?" She gave one last look to Marco, then, glanced at George. "Worst case scenario? Soul fire."

"Which is?"

"Two varieties: black and white," Amanda explained. "Vicious and virtuous. Black soul fire is corrosive, explosive, and can punch through a cinderblock wall. White soul fire can destroy corruption and heal people. Soul fire is literally powered by the soul. But it is just a myth. A vampire rumor. If Nuala could use it, she would have killed all of us by now. And there would be nothing left of our bodies. Or clothes. Or even guns."

Marco said nothing for a long moment, processing everything. What would the next move be? For the vampire, not them.

"First question: why did she go easy on us?" Marco asked. "Of all the weapons on the planet she could have opened with, had she used an RPG, we would all be dead now. She certainly wasn't shy about sacrificing minions left, right and center, so why not send in two suicide bombers and have them scream *'Allahu Akbar,'* just in case there were any survivors?"

"Too much attention," George explained. "I know that much. Either one is terrorism all over. Guys with machine guns aren't that unusual in California— see the LA gunfight in and aren't necessarily something the FBI should look into. The way Merle puts it? So few people know he's an agent, it wouldn't blink on the FBI's radar otherwise."

"See," Bram continued, "while we don't want the general public to know about vampires for safety concerns, vampires have stayed a secret for the same reason. They don't want every idiot running around with a crucifix and stakes. If an FBI investigation turns up something while digging into an obvious terrorist attack, the vampires would have problems of their own."

"Aye," Dougherty said, laughing from the carpet. "When Satan appears in a puff of smoke, the general populace makes a run for the nearest church. Vamps generally don't like that. At least not the ones Abe and I are called in to kill."

Marco nodded, taking this all in. "Except they weren't that shy when they blew up my father's hospital a few months ago."

Doughty nodded. "But the late 'Mister Day' had distinct ties to the Taliban. He was a terrorist and could be written off as such. It's New York - people want to destroy New York all the time. But San Francisco? It's not worth it."

"Right now," George added, "from what we've gathered, all of the gunmen are mercenaries, not terrorists. They won't strap bombs to themselves for a paycheck. They could be hired by the mob, a competitor, someone who wants Merle's building space. The possibilities are endless. An RPG elevates that threat."

Marco processed all this and wasn't entirely certain he bought it, especially if they were this frantic to kill him. "Hmm. Okay, thanks. That makes a certain kind of sense. At the least, it puts a cap on the type of force that can be leveled by her. Second question: she could sense us through the walls of the store without seeing any of us. What keeps her from sensing us here? In this hotel room?"

Everyone in the room suddenly became very, very thoughtful.

A second later, the bullets hit the window.

New York

Jennifer Bosley looked perfectly immaculate, even at this hour of the morning, with the sun shining. Her blonde hair was perfectly coiffed, stopping just above her shoulders. As her car pulled up to the Veterans of Foreign Wars Hall in Queens Village, New York. She closed her binder, slid her Monte Blanc Mozart pen away, and waited to come to a stop. She would, as usual, leap from the car and into the front door, being exposed to sunlight for only a moment.

Sigh. The things I go through just to ensure some peace and quiet around here.

Bureaucracy never slept, especially for a vampire. As President of the New York City Vampires Association, Bosley was as much a moderator and referee as a player. Sometimes multiple problems solved each other - but only if one knew about them.

When Vampire X hides a secret for twenty years which creates an immediate problem, it was hard to say one size fit all.

But Jennifer Bosley was President for many reasons. Few could keep a secret from her, but fewer tried. When spies didn't work, she could chameleon herself so that most would open up to her. She had a great memory - she recalled who hated who, who owed which favor to what acquaintance from what decade. It was almost a flowchart in her head. She knew how to leverage people with that information.

Though all that changed with Amanda Colt. During her development, Jennifer found a route to power through pragmatism and politics. Other vampires, like Lynch, found it through hard work and the sweat of his brow. Other businessmen, like the schmuck Kalsey, found it through vice and cultured sins. Everything about Amanda Colt said that she found a way via plain, simple good works, civic duty, prayer, and, well, virtue. Jennifer had never had to lie to her to get Amanda to do what Jennifer wanted. As long as Jennifer wanted the most correct and moral choice to happen, Amanda was the one to talk to. With others, Jennifer had to tell either the right truth (or half) to get things done. Luckily, Jennifer had long found that the ethical thing was the most pragmatic so Amanda might have been the best friend that Jennifer never had.

Granted "ethical treatment of vampires" was different than what normal people would consider. Capital offenses were executed in a quick and final way. Cardinal rules included "Don't get caught," "Don't mess with other vampires," and "If you must kill each other, do it quietly, where no-one else will be bothered."

But Amanda was just… a good person. *Huh.*

And Jennifer had no problem helping Amanda. When there was a problem between Amanda, her pet human, and Kalsey, well, Kalsey had needed to learn manners and discretion. When Jennifer decided to help Doctor Catalano… well, hospitals made no enemies (and created new and safer sources of blood banks). Whatever doomsday scenario that "Mister Day," Mikhail, and this assassin had on the agenda… well, Jennifer liked the world the way it was.

Then there was Amanda's pet, Marco. She really wanted to meet him one day soon. She expected it to be interesting. Someone like Marco with someone like Amanda.

I wonder if they'll ever manage. Then again, there was Jennifer's own relationship with a pet human. In this case, Enrico. He was more middle management of his organization, but he understood her troubles. Better yet, her confidentiality was guaranteed by his indifference. She even considered advancing their relationship to… something… but she couldn't yet imagine an endgame. Neither were really people persons - heck, she was barely "people."

Ironically, the last person she felt that way about would probably put Enrico in jail.

Speaking of which, time to call him.

She dialed the private number. It rang once before he answered.

"Hey Jen, how are you?" came the voice of the New York City Police Commissioner.

Jennifer smiled. "I'm just lovely, Commissioner Wilson," she said in her put-on, eloquent English accent. She liked the man and always had. Granted, the two of them had met during a murder investigation in the 70s, after he had returned from Vietnam. There were more than a few murder cases that had been deliberately put on the back burner because the killer had been reliably dealt with off the books by Jennifer. He had taken it as a compliment when she compared him to a young, taller Teddy Roosevelt.

"Oh come now, Jen," Wilson answered, "if you start with that, I'm going to have to call you Madam President."

Jennifer laughed. "All right, if you insist. I just wanted to update you on a few things. Nothing to worry about, but -"

"Does any of it have to do with your boyfriend's house in Bensonhurst? And the reports of machinegun fire?"

Jennifer blinked. She hadn't considered that the PC would have heard about the attack of the minions on Enrico's house. "Oh. You heard about that."

"I should say so, Jen. And not twelve hours later, there were six highly-trained mercenaries found dead in the East River, most of them drained of blood. Oh, and get this. If *that* wasn't enough, they've all been declared dead at least once before."

Jennifer blinked. "Oh? Really? Well, that's frightfully interesting, Ray. I should have thought to run fingerprints."

"Well, I'm so happy I could help, but would you please tell me what's going on? In my experience, vampires don't stay around after you kill them."

"True, Ray. But then, these are minions."

"Great. Just great."

There was the screech of tires outside, and Jennifer blinked. That didn't sound like any traffic pattern on that intersection, especially not at that time of day.

Jennifer strode from her desk to the window.

Two hummers had stopped outside the VFW hall. "Oh no… Ray, I'm at the VFW Hall in Queens, on Braddock and the Cross Island. I think the minions from yesterday have decided I'm a threat."

"Can you take them in daylight?" Ray asked.

"Not impossible, I -" Jennifer was cut off by the sight of men piling out of the Hummers. "Ray, tell your men at the 105th that they have RPGs!"

Ten seconds later, the rocket-propelled grenades destroyed the wall Jennifer had been standing at, flooding the room with sunlight and fire.

Chapter 17
Bullets Over Grant Street

San Francisco

The bullet was a nice, heavy load. When it impacts on a human head, the hydrostatic shock is literally a shock wave. Just imagine a bullet that is around three inches long, flying at a speed faster than sound, transferring all of its energy into a human head. The result is an entry wound the size of a dime, and the exit wound an explosion out the opposite side of the skull. It would quite literally blow a large chunk of the victim's brains out, suddenly, violently, and all over the place.

It is a messy, ugly way to go. Wherever it struck on the skull, place money on a closed-casket funeral.

On the other hand, when that same bullet strikes the surface of a pane of bullet-resistant glass the length and depth of a hotel suite's windows, the damage is spread out, like someone swinging a baseball bat into mesh netting.

"And that," the sniper Ibrahim said, "is why I pick the seating arrangements."

The hotel room phone rang. Carl Ramirez reached over and picked it up. "Yo." He listened and nodded. "Marco. It's for you."

Marco smiled down at Amanda, her head still in his lap. "Should we chat with her?"

Amanda frowned. "Could not hurt."

Carl passed the phone. Marco answered.

"Well played, lad," came the lyrical accent of the vampire assassin.

"Can't take all the credit. The Vatican Ninja I'm closest to happens to be a sniper. And you prefer to be low-key about all of this, so we weren't exactly expecting a rocket launcher."

"That won't last forever, you know. I've had to take out my fair share of men who thought they were invulnerable. You're one of the few who's made it so far that they even knew they were being hunted, never mind by me. Are you going to make this a fight? Or are you just going to keep running like prey until I run you down and murder you?"

"Haven't decided yet," Marco answered honestly. "I considered inviting you inside the hotel room and then beating you to death with my bare hands, but I'm not sure if that would be enough fun, Nuala."

The assassin laughed. "Not that you lack confidence, do ye, laddie?"

"I beat Mikhail, the Bear just by having him look deep into my eyes. I took out your precious Mister Day with basic chemistry and a lot of anticoagulants. What makes you think that I can't drop you by blowing hard on you?"

Nuala laughed even harder this time. "I might just take you up on that. After I kill your pretty little playmate, you'll be needing someone to help with that."

Marco's omnipresent smile became cool. His eyes hooded. An objective observer might call the expression snakelike. "Oh goody. I didn't have sufficient enough an excuse to murder you. You had to go there, too, didn't you?"

"Oh, she's on my list, just like you are. I'm going to kill you both. The how is the only question. But I prefer to end things in a timely fashion. Sundown's in a matter of hours. When it goes down, we'll have this conversation again. And you're not going to be nearly so cocky."

"Gotta ask you, Nuala, how does a hideous creature of the night like you end up as a lackey for the Council?"

There was a long pause. Marco had hit the target. She finally said, "Who said anything about the Council?"

"Your long pregnant pause did, right now. The next question is simple: why me?"

Marco could hear the smile in Nuala's voice. "You kill a creator of armies, and slay a demon, and you're asking me? I thought it would be obvious even to an idiot."

"Yes, it would be. Except an idiot would forget that a demon was specifically sent after him in the first place. And while I took down Mikhail, it was a tag team effort that finally neutralized him - until you offed him, of course, to keep him from talking. That means that *the Council* knew I was a threat after I went a few rounds with him."

The line went dead silent for a moment. It went on for so long, Marco half-expected to hear the dial tone next.

Marco continued. "They're afraid that there's something for me to figure out, isn't there? And that I'm going to figure it out. Thanks. This helps. I'll talk to you in a few hours when you're going to try to kill me."

Marco slammed the phone down. "From now on, presume that she can hear everything we say in this room." He looked right at George. "We need to fall back to the secondary location."

George nodded.

"No-one type anything, different keys send out different signals and frequencies, and if she can pick them up, she'll know everything we do."

Amanda tapped Marco on the shoulder, and she looked up from his lap into his eyes. Marco knew what she was doing, and this was the best way to secure communications.

She may be able to follow your scent, Amanda thought into his brain.

Marco nodded. *Understood. I'll lose these clothes, borrow some from the SpecOps and the Ninjas, some deodorant as well, just to make certain that I smell like someone else. Mine are covered in all sorts of crap. As for your scent, if they get a scented spray, you should be good with a quick spritz.*

Do I get to watch you change clothes? She asked with a decided sardonic edge.

Only if I get to watch you, too, he answered with a chuckle.

Okay. Amanda smiled right back at him. *Remember, I was a spy. I was trained to be comfortable nude, lest I be captured and stripped naked.*

Marco blinked. His smile faded. His pulse spiked. He pursed his lips, tensed them, and thought, *Amanda, you're going to want to get your head off of my lap. Otherwise, we're going to be in an embarrassing situation in another minute. Or less.*

Amanda was grateful that they weren't in a situation where she could tease him right back. But listening to the inside of Marco's mind, she could tell that he wasn't bluffing. Now that he wasn't editing his thoughts, the things he was trying not to say, or think, or feel, or act on (especially act on).

Amanda slid from his lap, and his arms stayed around her waist, keeping her against his side. He placed his chin on her shoulder and whispered huskily in her ear. "When this is over, you and I will continue the chat from last night."

Amanda shuddered at that thought, and she didn't know if it was good or bad.

Marco rose and went to change. Amanda watched him move, and just appreciated his graceful, lethal movements.

On the one hand, knowing about how Marco felt was liberating, and even joyous. But she couldn't tell if his homicide-inclined reflexes to protect her were sweet or scary. She could protect her own self, thanks, but he knew that… and he still jumped in front of a bullet for her, even though 1) he just presumed there would be one and 2) it probably wouldn't have harmed her.

But it was nice to have someone who was decisive, thoughtful, and that he would literally kill for her was… refreshing? It was certainly different.

Then again, Marco knew her - even more than she had thought. Most men were easily intimidated - either by her looks, her fangs, her desire to have a relationship, or her ability to lift a car.

One day, Marco may learn to be intimidated by… something.

When Marco returned, the clothes were so baggy on him, they were obviously George's. He casually tossed her a spray can, and she gave herself a once-over. She tossed it back to George, who caught it easily.

She and Marco waited by the door, watching the commandos pack up.

Marco slid the back of his hand down her arm, and gently took her hand, giving it a comfortable little squeeze.

Yes, she thought. *We will finish that conversation later.*

She blinked. Yes, she wanted the conversation, but she had no idea where she wanted it to go. She had never actually been in a relationship before. Okay, there were a few dates here and there, but the majority of them were spy-related, and none had gotten to the "I'm a vampire" stage.

A joke Marco liked to tell was simple: Once the dog catches the bus, what does the dog do with it? Marco always answered "Take hostages."

But this time, Marco was the bus… or was he the dog? She couldn't tell if he had chased her until she caught him, or vice versa. She was so used to being the hunter, she never once remembered being chased when she desired to be caught.

Okay, she did that *once*, but only because he wanted to assassinate Pope Pius XII.

Now? She and Marco had caught each other - more or less by complete accident.

Hopefully, one of us has some idea of what to do next.

Ibrahim's cell phone chirped. He picked up the cell phone and winced. He raised the phone up, facing Amanda and Marco. Marco stiffened beside her, and Amanda could feel the temperature in the room drop as he gripped her hand tightly.

Hospital is under attack. Doctor Catalano & Enrico are inside. Minions have RPGs.

New York

Doctor Robert Catalano had never figured that he would be walking around a hospital with the man who had held him at gunpoint over a year ago. No one would have guessed that the tall, elegant man with the high cheekbones was a mobster. He wasn't even dressed as gaudily as some black-and-white movie gangsters.

"Did anyone ever tell you, you bear a passing resemblance to Michael Rennie?" one of the nurses asked.

Enrico simply smiled and shrugged, and kept moving to keep up with the tall, thin doctor.

"I'll have to make sure none of them know where your money comes from," Robert said casually, with a surprising lack of judgment in his voice.

Enrico walked into the new wing of the hospital and grabbed a hard hat. "Gambling, smuggling, and black market cigarettes, mostly."

Robert arched a brow as he put his own hard had on. "Really? Not prostitution? Drugs?"

Enrico shrugged as he looked around. He liked the look of the place. It was still antiseptic white, but that was to be expected. It would help if the walls had rooms, but those would come sooner or later. They were probably the next to go up.

"You know how the *Godfather* films tried to perpetuate a myth that said that the Mafia didn't deal drugs? That's a lie. However, my branch of the family had great reasons to get out of drugs. The market is flooded, the cartels who are the competition are psycho, the kind we would have to go to war with, and war is bad for business. Two, we do a lot of business with Chicago, and the Outfit really, really hates drugs. They kill people who deal drugs, even their own people, so that's a problem."

Robert arched a brow. "And the rest?"

"High-end prostitution is getting crowded out by the Internet. I'm not really interested in streetwalking - too hard to control - and sanitation is a cliché. I'm not Tony Soprano. Frankly, as long as New York has utterly insane taxes, we can make a killing just by circumventing them. It's why we back Democrats. They *love* hiking up taxes on everything. The trade-off comes when they're totally inept, and we won't even go into that."

Robert frowned, thinking over the price of cigarettes. "I didn't think that would be profitable enough to sustain your business."

Enrico shrugged. "You'd be surprised. I think Jen was the one who said it best— just because you're doing something illegal doesn't mean you also have to be immoral, too. But sometimes, it's just good business." Enrico smiled slyly. "We occasionally supplement our income by stealing from the competition. We may not like going to war with cartels, but that doesn't mean we can't avail ourselves of their profits every once in a while. Heh."

Enrico's pocket beeped, and he stopped, picking the phone out of his pocket. He clicked it on, then blinked. "We should go now."

"What's wrong?"

Enrico passed Robert the phone as he jogged down the hallway. Robert read the text. It was from "Jen," and it read simply: *Under Attack. They're after us. U, Me, doc. RUN!!!*

Robert's eyes narrowed. He frowned grimly and looked up. Enrico was already rushing back, a micro-Uzi in hand.

"Two can play that game," Robert said. He gave Enrico his cell phone back, and he drew his own. Robert tapped three buttons on the phone.

Then the walls exploded.

San Francisco

"White noise generators. Now," Marco stated.

Bram nodded, then headed over for his duffel. He spent a minute digging, then pressed a button. "It's on. It should be safe to talk."

Amanda winced at the pain in her head. Being this close to the thing wasn't pleasant. "It's safe."

Marco nodded, and pulled out his cell phone, reassembling it, with the battery in place. It immediately lit up with a text message. "Good. Everything's already been set in motion." He looked up to Bram. "Can we get to the van and load Amanda into it? On the one hand, it's great to transport her through the sunlight, on the other, I'm not sure it's safe to drive off in a vehicle Nuala might be able to identify. Or have one of her minions plant a bomb on. Or a tracker."

The sniper merely smiled. "We've got that covered. This isn't my first time, you know."

Marco narrowed his eyes. "How, exactly?"

"Four-panel vans rented from different companies by different people using different identities, parked in different levels of underground parking. Good enough?"

Marco raised an eyebrow. "I'm really not used to people thinking things through as much as I do."

Ibrahim nodded. "Thanks. I'll take the compliment and run with it. Preferably all the way out of town, if we can manage."

Amanda put a hand on Marco's shoulder. "Can we stop talking now? I am getting headache."

It had the desired effect. Marco knew that when Amanda dropped articles, as in her native Russian, it was a sign that something was wrong. He looked at her strangely, then signaled to Ibrahim to cut it. The Ninja killed the white noise generator. Marco turned back to Amanda, and she was able to finally pick up what was wrong. He was no longer smiling, his eyes slightly wider as he studied her.

He's afraid. And looking at me like I've got cancer.

Marco stepped forward, sliding his arms around her waist, hugging her close. Had this been anyone else, she would have thought he was *trying* to press her chest to his. But he was starting to breathe a little heavier. He was…

"I'm not going to lose you, Amanda," he whispered gently into her ear.

She hugged him right back, held him close, and came to a very simple solution. It was easier to confuse him than reassure him.

"You're not that lucky," she whispered back. Amanda reached down and squeezed his butt.

Marco pulled back, blinking, confused. He mouthed "What?"

Amanda just gave him a small, amused little smile of her own.

Chapter 18

Battle of Brooklyn

Brooklyn, NY

Doctor Robert Catalano's first thought was that he had fallen asleep and awoke in a Michael Bay movie. The far wall of the hallway exploded, with several more ripping apart.

Enrico grabbed Robert and pulled him away from the exploding hallway. "Come on, we have to leave."

"I'm hip."

The two men ran for their lives, back toward the finished parts of the hospital.

Which is the point where the first two men stepped into the construction zone, machine guns raised.

Enrico suddenly changed direction, hurling the doctor into a room where the walls were at least finished. "Aw crap!"

The mobster fired a short burst from his Uzi down the hall and wounded both of them. They staggered, and then kept coming as though nothing had happened.

This could be bad. Enrico fired again, catching one center mass, the other in the throat. That one fell to his knees, coughing, gagging, and dying.

The second one fired again, nailing Enrico in the chest.

Enrico dropped backward, sprawled over the floor.

The minion that shot him walked past his body and wheeled into the room with Doctor Catalano.

Robert, standing just inside the door, was waiting and grabbed the machine gun with his left hand, then jammed a nail gun into the minion's temple, firing. Since head wounds were tricky things, even with normal human beings, Robert punched the nail gun into the minion's skull repeatedly, firing a nail each time. There were nails in the minion's temple, ear, eye, and three in the neck before he went down.

I'm glad Marco decided to show off some of his Krav Maga.

Robert pulled back, taking the machinegun with him, a moment before the walls exploded, this time with bullets cutting through the wall like a saw. Robert dropped and cursed.

Time to figure out how to use a machine gun.

The minions kept coming down the hallway. This time there were three of them. They all started firing at the same time. They were not going to stop this time until the good doctor was dead.

The minions ignored the body of Enrico as they passed him. A corpse with a gun that small wasn't worth the time.

As the third minion started to pass Enrico's body, the arm with the Uzi came straight up, jamming the muzzle into the minion's crotch. Enrico fired a burst right into him. The bullets passed by the pelvic bone, bounced off the rib cage, cut into the spinal cord, and essentially turned organs into puree.

Enrico grabbed the body with his other hand and dragged it down on top of him. He left the minion's corpse down to shield himself as he aimed for the next minion in the formation. That minion went down without making a sound.

The lead minion, the last one left, wheeled back around.

Robert leapt out and jammed his nail gun into the minion's gun hand, throwing it off course. The next strike of the nail gun was into the minion's eye.

Robert looked around, saw there was no-one left, and rushed for Enrico.

"Thanks," Enrico groaned. "I wasn't sure I could take that one."

Robert grabbed the minion on top of Enrico, hauled him off, then helped Enrico to his feet.

"I need better body armor," the mobster moaned.

"Can you stand on your own?"

Enrico leaned heavily on him. "I'd rather not. We need to take some weapons and ammo."

Robert nodded. He knew exactly what the mobster was thinking. Five minions had shown up almost on top of each other. But there were still men outside who had fired RPGs at the building only seconds before. There would be more of them.

As they passed the last man Robert had killed, Enrico said, "Aw crap. I know why they think they can get away with the ordinance."

"Why?"

"They're MS-13. These are the guys I said we'd rather not deal with. And this is right up there with their level of weaponry."

"Thankfully, I called for help," Robert told him.

San Francisco

As the panel van pulled out from the hotel's underground parking lot, Marco sat against the wall, one arm wrapped around Amanda, almost protectively.

"I'm not going anywhere," she said.

"I know. I'm just worried. I'm not in Brooklyn, doing what I need to. Instead, I'm running around San Francisco trying not to get my head blown off, waiting for the crap to hit the fan. I don't like feeling I haven't done everything I could with everything I have on the line. I don't want to lose Dad, and I'm just hoping that they don't know to go after Mom."

"Marco, you've already *done* everything. You did it *months* ago."

Brooklyn, NY

Officer Donald "Duck" Tolbert of the NYPD sat back in his patrol car, wondering what the next bit of strangeness in his day was going to be. He made certain the window was cracked open, just to make sure he had something like ventilation. He didn't bother keeping the heater on, even in December, especially since he was in full uniform. He was a tall, light-skinned officer of Jamaican heritage, two generations removed.

When his cell phone chimed at him, he answered it immediately, because he also had a supplementary position to his job as a cop. He was also hunting vampires.

When he saw that the text came from Robert Catalano, Don read it at once.

Don grabbed his radio, identified his patrol car, gave the address of the hospital, demanded ESU backup, then started his car.

Don did nothing else. He didn't call one additional car, any other special backup or ground forces.

Because the text message sent out by Robert Catalano had gone to *everyone* in their vampire hunting league.

* * *

The first person to arrive on the scene was not a cop. It was, in fact, a short, sturdy fellow, bald with a green Chinese water dragon tattooed on the back of his scalp.

Zeng Nyugen, leader of a street gang called "The Dragons" (shut up, he liked the name, and the jackets looked *awesome*), had been relaxing on the roof of the apartment building across the street from the hospital and keeping an eye on the place. After the hospital had been blown up in September, Marco would probably be slightly mollified to learn that the gangs were keeping an eye on the place.

The attack first caught Zeng's attention with the sudden braking of several cars, one right after another. Two vans had parked in front of the wing still under construction. Another two had parked across the street from the hospital.

Zeng studied them. The panel door of the van faced away from him so he couldn't see who was getting out. The ones in the street had parked right beneath him. He couldn't watch them unless he leaned over the edge of the roof.

After a minute, the vans nearest him popped open. One van emptied eight men with machineguns - light machineguns, with box magazines.

The others had RPGs.

Two RPGs were sent off before Zeng knew what was happening. When the third one fired, Zeng was already in motion. Because Zeng wasn't the book type. He needed something for his hands to do while he was watching the hospital. So he had spent the day preparing Molotov cocktails.

The first target was the van with the RPGs and the RPG team. Two bottles hit the van - one inside, and one beneath. The men firing the RPGs, alerted to his presence, dodged out of the way. The men with the light machineguns opened fire just as Zeng got out of the way.

So, while the machine gunners were busy blasting at Zeng, a Lincoln town car in the hospital's front parking lot ejected two men. They had simple M4 fully-automatic assault rifles - because Enrico wasn't going to go traipsing about New York City *without* bodyguards watching his back.

The minions with machineguns returned fire at the Mafia thugs, while two of the RPG team kept their eyes on the roof, the rest keeping an eye on the street for further from anyone else.

Then the cops showed up. And things got even worse.

The usual procedure in a police firefight starts with establishing a perimeter. Whether it was the historical 40+ minute shootout in LA or a liquor store, it served to prevent the escape of the perpetrators and contain the potential havoc.

Unfortunately, the first people on the scene were two regular patrol cars, each closing in from opposite sides of the street.

The machinegun minions turned and shredded their cars with precision and no mercy.

When ESU arrived with their armored Lenco BearCats (Ballistic Engineered Armored Response Counter Attack Truck), the box was better established. That's what happened when you had armor an inch and a half thick.

When Don Tolbert showed up, his phone rang. It was Zeng. "Can I get back to you?"

"What the hell is going on here?"

"Here?" Don looked around. "You're here? At the hospital?"

"I'm right behind the guys with the Uzis."

Don looked up. The bullets had made pockmarks all over. There was no Zeng. *Must be ducking out of sight.* "Can you get down?"

"Even better," Zeng answered. "I can get you guys up here. I have a rope ladder I can drop down the back. But you need to get someone inside. I think there are more of them after the Doc and the mob guy."

The classic three options as far as enemy action went were simple: run, fight, hide.

With Enrico's chest a solid black and blue, running was an invalid option. Caught in the open hallway, they'd be vulnerable. If men came up the emergency stairs, they'd be boxed in.

So they grabbed all of the weapons that they could find on the bodies and fled to the most undamaged room at the farthest end of the wing.

This time, though, flash-bangs were tossed into the hallway, filling it with enough light and sound that it would blind anyone too close and looking at it.

But no-one was looking at it. Enrico and Robert stayed in the room - it may have been an exam room or an ICU when it grew up - just waiting for the minions to come to them.

When they got close enough, Robert was going to throw the grenades from the previous batch of minions.

Every half-minute, there would be another sound of a flash-bang. From the sound of it, they were clearing every section of the wing systematically.

After three minutes, the flash-bang was the closest yet, rattling his teeth. Robert raised the first grenade. The moment he heard the first footstep, he would start hurling grenades.

Robert waited, bracing himself for the end. He had no illusions about how this would happen. He wouldn't go down without a fight, but he knew he would be going down.

Dear Lord, no offense, but do me a favor and keep Marco safe, and my wife, and Amanda, too. Whatever it is that's doing this, please assist Marco and all of his people by sending them straight to Hell. Thank You.

Robert listened, working hard to control his breathing. He couldn't hear anything on the half-finished floor. There were no footsteps or sounds of breathing. There wasn't even a breeze.

Though for a second, Robert would have sworn he heard the sound of something splashing - like water droplets hitting a wall.

"Doctor Catalano," came a European-accented voice, "you can come out now."

Robert blinked.

"I think you know my friend Ibrahim. I am his commanding officer, Hendershot. We got your text message."

Robert peeked out. There were dead minions in the hallway, not five feet from the door.

And blood all over the place.

Commander Hendershot leaned against a wall at the opposite end of the room, cleaning his knife on the shirt of one of the dead. "Sorry. Arterial spray is so messy."

"How did you do all this? We didn't hear anything."

The Swiss Guard Commander blinked, confused. "What part of 'Vatican Ninja' did you not understand?"

"What's happening outside?"

Hendershot sighed. "That is… a little more complicated."

It took a few minutes for the police officers to scale Zeng's rope ladder. They made it to the edge of the roof (or what was left of it after the previous barrage of RPGs) and coordinated with the ESU trucks. At the same time, snipers circled around and took up positions across the street, in buildings next to the hospital.

At which point, the two ESU Cadillac Gage Rangers pulled in on either side of the street. The guns mounted on the top of the trucks were M60 7.62mm machineguns.

The first thing that happened was the rooftop cops dropped Zeng's Molotov cocktails on the minions below, herding them out of their positions. The cops opened fire immediately after the firebombs dropped - and opened fire from the roof, the streets, and the trucks.

In any other context, this would have been considered overkill. In this case, the minions were barely put down by the hailstorm of gunfire.

"What about Jennifer Bosley?" Enrico asked.

Hendershot blinked. "What about her?"

"She was under attack at the same time. She warned us, which is the only reason we're still alive."

The Ninja Commander frowned. "I don't know. I heard nothing."

Enrico's phone rang again. He reached into his jacket and answered. "Yes?"

"Could someone please come by the VFW in Queens Village and dig me out of here?" Jennifer asked.

"You're okay!"

"Of course I'm okay. I didn't get to be President of the NYC-VA by being unprepared for something as mundane as an ambush by minions, of all things. Now, will someone come and dig me out of this basement? And call the Police Commissioner. I don't want Ray to be worried."

San Francisco

"Where the hell were you?" Marco asked Merle Kraft.

The government spy for the strange sat on the steps of the home Tiffany shared with George. Marco would consider how a beautiful home came with being a tightfisted dime-counter, but that would be later.

Merle pointed at the step below him. "First, I should mention that I picked up Amanda's stuff from her stay at Rory's little crypt. Second, Kristen is *seriously* concerned about your rampaging all over the place, so if you could please be a little quieter about being a human wrecking ball, that would be *great*. Third, I've been working on a trap for our little-redheaded problem."

Marco arched a brow. "*Really?*" he drawled. "Is this going to be better than the *last* trap you planned? You know, the one where *we* were the bait?"

Merle cleared his throat. "Yeah, well, you might still be the bait."

Marco's eyes narrowed. "Now listen here, you -"

"New message," Bram interjected, not wanting this to turn into a *Marco-gets-cranky-and-hurts-people moment.* He raised his phone. "The minions are dealt with. Most everyone on our side is safe and sound. You know, in case anyone cares about that."

Marco took a deep breath and suddenly deflated.

"Marco," Amanda said, "if I could, I need to eat."

His smile flickered back to life. "Sure. Of course."

Amanda gave him a little squeeze, and broke away, sweeping up her bag, and heading for the kitchen. It was a nice little kitchen, complete with an island in the center. It struck her as strange since Tiffany did *not* come off as the domestic type… or the cooking type… or the human type, come to think of it. She placed the bag on the kitchen counter.

Amanda took a deep breath and was surprised to realize that she'd been running on prayer and adrenaline all day. She hadn't even had time to visit the nearest church. Sure, a healthy sip from the chalice fed her for days, maybe even a week if she spent enough time in prayerful meditation, but usually, not when she'd been breaking up vampire bars, fighting off a vampire assassin, and spending a large part of the day moving under the sun.

She pulled out one of the Chinese soup containers where she kept her blood from the bag, then popped it open. She figured it would be best to go for the whole quart this time.

Amanda stopped breathing and started to drink. It was going to taste, well, like expired blood. And she wasn't going to be looking around the house for something alcoholic to spike it with. *Maybe next time, I can try it with a little mint Listerine.*

Amanda was almost done when she felt a little blood trickling out of the corner of her mouth. She quickly lowered the quart and caught it with the back of her free hand.

That could have been embarrassing.

Amanda licked the blood off her skin. *I'll need a napkin to get all of this.* She swiped at the blood with her finger, into her mouth.

"Problem?"

Amanda blinked and gave Marco a quick glance over her shoulder. *Not again.* "*Nyet.*"

He gave a quick chuckle as he slid up behind her, taking her by the shoulders. He turned her around, turning it into a hug.

"You missed some," he said, swiping it gently with his thumb, drawing it across her lips.

Amanda instinctively sucked his thumb into her mouth, cleaning it off. His hand slid up her cheek, his fingers combing into her hair. Her head tilted back as his face closed with hers.

Amanda started to breathe again and realized that her mouth still smelled of blood. "I need to wash out my mouth," she whispered.

"No," he whispered back. "You don't."

Their kiss this time was gentle. Marco's tongue barely touched hers. His lips moved lower and caught Amanda's lip, sucking it into his mouth. He ran his tongue along her lower lip, then, let it go. Then he dipped down for her lips one more time.

Amanda tried to think as they kissed. Marco was making a point, and something she hadn't even known she was concerned about - he didn't care about her eating habits, even though it meant that he was, technically, food.

You never have to hide who you are from me, Marco couldn't have possibly said, but Amanda could have *sworn* she heard him say it, even though his lips were on hers. She couldn't have heard him think it, because his eyes were elsewhere.

But I drink blood, she thought.

Marco chuckled, as his lips moved from hers, then, kissed down her jawline to her neck. His teeth very gently grazed the nerve running down the side. *I'll happily devour you first if it makes you feel better.*

"You can hear me?"

Yup, he thought back at her.

Amanda blinked, grabbed him by the shoulder, his planned romantic moment sent off-track by the sudden telepathy. She pushed him away, holding him by the shoulders. "This does not concern you?"

Marco blinked, wondering why he wasn't indulging in making his point. "You're a vampire. Your powers and abilities fluctuate and vary. We've been in each other's heads before, I just roll with it." His smile grew more teasing. "Have I made my point, though? Because I'd be happy to continue making it for as long as I need to. And for a few hours after that."

Amanda rolled her eyes. "I need to finish eating."

Marco shrugged. "If you must." He leaned against the kitchen island, and he waited.

"Are you going to leave?"

"No." He crossed his arms casually. "I'll wait."

She sighed. Marco really was going to push the point home. She grabbed the quart and slugged back what was left of the blood. "Better?"

"I'm not kissing you, so no. But I assume you want to go back and talk to Merle about his grand plan and hope that *this one* doesn't kill us?"

"The last one didn't either, but yes."

"Oh, all right." Marco offered Amanda his arm, and she took it. Together, they headed out of the kitchen.

"Considering everything that happened today, do you think we've forgotten anything?" Marco asked.

Yana was thrown into the crypt by two of Nuala's minions. Yana looked up, finding herself at the feet of the vampire assassin.

Nuala grinned at Yana, which looked fairly terrifying, considering that all of her teeth looked razor sharp.

"Stay there," Nuala told her. "You should get used to that position."

"What do you want?"

Nuala leered. "You're the addict. The weak link. I could smell the drugs on your skin." Nuala took her left nail and slit the skin on the webbing of her right thumb. She reached down, grabbed Yana by her hair, and yanked her head back, jamming her bloody hand into Yana's mouth.

"Start licking. You should be good at that," Nuala growled. "And if you're very good," the vampire added, "you can service me. I haven't had a good lay in a while, and I hear that you play that side of the street."

Chapter 19

My Minion Can Beat Up Your Minion

Marco listened with half an ear to Merle's grand plan, studying just how lovely Amanda was. He had never taken the time before, lest Amanda figure out he was enamored with her - but that was a concern long since past.

"Look at the bright side," Tiffany said, her voice piercing Marco's mental shroud. "We could take her."

Kraft raised a brow, glancing at her. "With Rory's help … and Tara's help … and Amanda's help … and Marco's throwing knife into her leg didn't hurt either. Not to mention her minions, for which we had some minions of our own."

Marco sighed and nodded, allowing himself into the discussion. "Let's face it, even I'll admit she's a little more than my match, and I'll deny that under any future questioning."

Amanda nodded. "It could be worse."

Merlin Kraft shook his head and groaned. "Oh, no, don't tell me that! How much worse could it get?"

"She could have soul fire."

Merle and Tiffany simply blinked. Marco sighed. "Yeah, that would be bad. Thankfully, it's virtually impossible, from what you told me."

Merle ground his teeth. "What *is* it?"

Marco chuckled. "It's not possible, that's what it is. It's a myth, a characteristic only shared by the demonic or the angelic."

Tiffany blinked. "What?"

Marco shook his head. "Merle, didn't you explain this to her?"

Kraft nodded. "Tiffany… you know where vampires get their powers from?"

"Blood?"

He rolled his eyes. "Simply, their souls are connected to their bodies. In-between humans and angels… imagine if your soul was something that you could actively tap into as a power source. The more evil you are, or the more good you are, the more access you have." He looked at Amanda. "Now, where does soul fire come in?"

"White soul fire," Amanda said, "is for those who are so good, almost saintly, that their souls are almost perfectly aligned with their bodies. They cannot be more than 'almost' since perfection is God's alone. White soul fire requires not only talent but incredible strength of will. It can heal, and it can destroy evil, at will. Sometimes both at once."

Merle nodded slowly. "If you believe the myths."

"Right," Marco added. "Black soul fire is obviously evil. It burns with cold, and it kills any who get in the way. A vampire who wields it would have to be almost literally demonic in character, and really, really good at what he does. If Nuala had it, we'd be dead already. Simple as that."

At which point, the front door opened.

Everyone with a gun pulled it, including Marco with his squirt gun.

Yana walked in and smiled. "Hey everybody!" She took three steps towards the dining room.

Marco barked, "Freeze, bitch! Bram, shoot her if she doesn't!"

Yana stopped moving and blinked. "Marco, I know you were upset with me earlier, but -"

Amanda hissed. "You walk like a martial artist now. You didn't this morning."

Ibrahim didn't even hesitate and shot her twice, once in each leg. Yana fell with a gasp of surprise, not a scream of pain, onto her front.

Marco burst forward and brought both of his feet down on Yana's hands. "Frisk her!"

Amanda was on Yana in a flash, and in thirty seconds came away with two stakes and three Desert Eagles with extra magazines. The Ninja Doughtery came in and zip-tied her right hand at the base of her spine, then grabbed the other hand, bending it back, over her shoulder, pressing it against her spine, and tied it to the other wrist. He then followed it up with metal handcuffs. It was uncomfortable, but any attempt to break the cuffs would essentially break her arms.

"I'm going to kill this useless little twit if you don't come to me tonight," Yana said, this time with a bit of an Irish brogue in her voice. She rolled over, and her eyes were glowing green.

Marco lowered himself down to a crouch. His smile had grown cold, and one might even say evil. "Good. Do it."

Amanda touched Marco on the shoulder. "Marco…"

The thing possessing Yana blinked. "What? You wouldn't dare."

"You're in her head," Marco said, almost cheerfully. "You can play back her memories, can't you? This is the 12th, right? Go back to the night of the 10th. Start with the words 'You listen to me, you petty little witch,' and fast forward through the evening. Heck, playback the development of our entire relationship. You tell me, Nuala, am I bluffing?"

After a moment's hesitation, Yana's eyes narrowed. "You can watch her die."

Marco narrowed his own eyes. He reached up for one of the guns Amanda had, and without a doubt or hesitancy, she slapped the grip into his hand. Marco jammed the gun under Yana's chin.

Tiffany shouted, "Not on the carpet! Do it on the tile! I can replace those, and they're easier to clean!"

Marco's smiled tightened. "You may have gotten her to drink, but Yana is one of *my* minions. She belongs to *me*. Kill her, I will blend in, disappear, and you will never find me until I want to be found, and that's the day that you're going to find yourself in a corridor of claymore mines for your minions and Holy Water for you. If anyone's going to kill her -"

A dart hit Marco in the arm. He blinked, looked up at the shooter, and said, "I hate you, Merle," just before keeling over.

Merle stepped forward and smiled into Yana's face. "I now have Marco. You want to kill him? Come get him."

Yana narrowed her glowing green eyes. "You think you can trick me into a trap."

Merle nodded. "Yes, I can. Because if you don't come after him tonight, I'm taking him out of the city. I'm a spy, I can take him anywhere in the world. I'll keep him in a nice little room under, I don't know, maybe the Vatican, and feed him intel. I'll plug him into everything I do, everything I find, and he'll be as problematic as he is now. You want him dead. Not out of the way. Not off the battlefield. *Dead.* Either you can come, and kill him tonight, or fail." Merle smiled. "I would love to know what the consequence for failure is in your world. There's a nice little mansion off of Sea Cliff. We'll be there. Come and get us, sucker."

Merle looked at Ibrahim. "Bram, could you help Carl with Yana here? He'll explain about the sealed coffin in the basement. A sensory deprivation chamber for when we need to interrogate some vampires but want to hold onto them for a bit."

Ibrahim shrugged, grabbed Yana's legs, Carl grabbed her shoulders, and they hauled her away.

When Carl and Bram returned, Merle nodded. "Okay, Marco, you can get up now."

"Good," Marco said, "this floor is uncomfortable." He pushed to his feet. "I thought it would actually be *harder* to get that message to Nuala."

Merle laughed. "I know, right?"

Amanda raised a hand. "Excuse me. Have you not thought about what happens to a minion when the leader dies? Where do you think the minions get their strength from?"

Marco and Merle exchange a glance. Marco said, "I figured that it was from the blood - you know, more of the vampire virus than from the saliva, and it creates a bond between vampire and minion."

"But the minions can also power the vampire. If we don't kill Nuala immediately, she could try to suck the life out of all of her minions trying to stay alive. Yana might actually die."

Marco stared at Amanda clinically for a moment. "Methadone."

Both Amanda and Merle cocked their heads.

"What about it?" Merle asked.

"Methadone works by competing for the same sites in the brain as heroin. What we need is something to complete with Nuala's blood."

Amanda blinked, wondering if she really wanted to have a minion.

Marco could read the look on her face. "I meant Rory. I have no idea how the effect could ripple from Nuala, into Yana, into the competing vampire - if there *is* any effect."

Amanda frowned, her brow crinkling in the way he loved so much. "There *should* not be one."

"Better safe than sorry. If there's an unknown variable, I'd rather risk Rory than you…"

Amanda cocked her head. "You mean risking me in a battle with a vampire assassin *isn't* a risk?"

Marco laughed. "We at least know what the battle with Nuala is going to be. Just you, me, and maybe Rory if we feel like it -"

Merle, who felt like he had been demoted to a third wheel, shook his head. "We'll do one better. We'll give her all three of *us*." He frowned. "I met Nuala in Afghanistan."

The entire room looked at him. Amanda raised a brow. "Say that again?"

Kraft walked to the other side of the room, looking at the silverware. "I was on a mission to knock off a few terrorists who were using high-level vampires to do some of their dirtier work." He picked up a knife and absentmindedly made it appear and disappear as he paced. "This includes ISIS and spread to Afghanistan."

Marco: "Should I ask?"

Merle shook his head. "I wouldn't. Short version is that vampires have no problem getting favors out of local governments - city, province, anywhere. The one that we're talking about can read minds, from what I can tell, so they know exactly what evil lurks in the hearts of men. Who can be leveraged, and how they can be leveraged." He glanced at Tiffany. "That's what George has been helping me with, mostly the vampire problems."

Marco frowned. "Should I presume that Mikhail helped set up these nests?"

Amanda shook her head before Merle could answer. "*Nyet*, it would have to be Day. He worked with governments, remember?"

The magician shrugged. "I don't know, but one or the both of them probably had something to do with it. I nearly didn't make it out alive, but I had help…" He looked away. "There's also the matter of the daisy cutter."

Even Marco jerked at this. "You've got to be kidding me."

Tiffany sighed. "What's the matter with a simple lawn trimmer?"

Kraft spared her a look. "A daisy cutter is basically a firebomb that can destroy San Francisco."

"Oh."

Ibrahim blinked and leaned against a wall. "Tell me that she doesn't have one of these."

Kraft smiled. "Oh, she doesn't have one… I *dropped* one *on* her."

The Ninja rolled his eyes. "Of *course* you did."

Kraft nodded. "Exactly. That's why I started working on this particular trap as soon as I got back. I've learned my lesson from the Mount Olivet incident."

"Here's hoping," Marco said. "I don't think that this would work as well as last time. We can't have any mistakes."

Marco dressed in a neat black turtleneck and pants - he could never abide jeans - securing all of his weapons.

"Marco?"

He turned to look at Amanda. She smiled at him. "Are you all right?"

He shrugged. "I'm not sure. You?"

"Good… so far." She stepped toward him. "Are you sure you want to do this?"

He smirked and gently touched her arm. "It's like with Day. I need her guard down just enough to sneak in and get her. For that to happen, you can't be within a city block of us at least. Hell, *Merle* can't be within a city block of us. I need her to underestimate me for maybe ten seconds. Possibly less."

Amanda slowly reached for him, putting a gentle hand on his arm, sliding it up to his shoulder, and around the back of his neck, to draw him in again.

"I've been told," he whispered, allowing himself to be brought closer, "that a vampire can be made stronger depending on how far she goes into the dark or the light."

She smiled. "Textbook vampirism."

His hand went up and combed through her hair. "You'd think being a vamp would kinda suck, wouldn't you?"

"Let's find out."

This time, Amanda pulled him into a kiss, and she let him have it. He didn't object. Heck, he felt like he was getting stronger as they pulled each other into an embrace - and he didn't think it was that he was drawing in vampire bacteria via saliva, but it helped.

There was a deep sigh from the doorway. "Oh, for God's sake, not now!"

Marco and Amanda broke, and they both gave Merle a slightly embarrassed look.

With a roll of the eyes, Merle jerked a thumb over his shoulder. "Amanda, come on. If lover boy over here is right, we don't want to be here anytime soon. In this case, I think I'll want to go with him on that. Don't you?"

She nodded. Merle smiled at Marco, then, shook his hand. "God be with you."

He smiled and pumped Merle's hand once. "*E tu spiritu tuo.*"

"Heh. That too." Merle looked around the place where the trap would be sprung. It was an ancient bathroom straight out of the 1920s, with a cast iron bathtub. The darkness was so complete, Marco's head looked as though it floated without a body.

"It looks like you picked the right color scheme."

Amanda chuckled. "I picked it out for him. Even a vampire would have trouble picking him out."

Merle nodded, then looked at the door. A slot was cut into the wooden door at eye level so he could see out into the hallway. "Looks like everything's put together."

Marco nodded. "Time to have cooked vampire."

Chapter 20
Great Balls of Fire

The mansion at Sea Cliff was old and run-down, but if one avoided the various and sundry patches of dilapidated walls and floors, it was in good shape.

Nuala's senses pinpointed, relatively, where Marco was. But where was everyone else? She had trouble believing that Marco would come here alone.

She smiled at the arrogance of the trap. She could smell Marco. She couldn't sense him though. Or anyone else, really. That was odd…

But if we have a legion of Vatican Ninjas at prayer, I wouldn't be able to sense any of them… but I should be able to smell them, surely. Unless they've sprayed themselves in something to help them blend in.

Nuala reached out to her minions to make certain that all of them spread out and secured the area. She wasn't going to be ambushed any worse than she had to be. She *knew* it had to be a trap, but where was it?

Nuala walked up to the front of the old mansion and tried to mist her way through the doors.

She couldn't.

Nuala frowned, then reared back and kicked the door in. The door shattered off the hinges. She took two steps in and stopped dead.

The house was made entirely of wood. Either the wood hadn't been finished, or something had been done to it to make it retain water. Because everything - the floors, the walls, the ceilings - had all been coated in holy water.

Nuala frowned. Technically, it shouldn't really hurt her, though it explained why she couldn't mist through the door. The holiness wasn't as bad as, say, a church, where her feet would probably be on fire already. But she probably wouldn't be able to punch through cinderblock - Marco's skull, sure, but not cinderblock. And shape-shifting was out entirely. Her power was great enough to keep her in one piece throughout, but this would put a damper on most of her abilities.

She briefly considered turning around and letting her minions head in and at least trigger the boobytraps, if not level the place - RPGs could be dismissed in New York, but blowing up a random abandoned place in San Francisco? Too much attention, too many loose ends. But that wouldn't guarantee anything, especially since Marco had contingency plans all over the place.

The only guarantee would be to rip his throat out with her teeth.

Nuala took a deep breath. She smelled Marco.

As Nuala looked down the hallway from the second-floor landing, she frowned to herself. It was a corner room of the building, so three of the walls had windows in them. The fourth wall had no window, only the opening to the hallway and a closet.

The vampire stopped in front of the bathroom and turned. Nuala crouched a little to look into the door.

Marco stood in front of her, ready and waiting for her. For death.

And she would give it to him.

Nuala stood and tilted to the side, curling one leg beneath her, ready to push her energy into one kick that would turn the door to shrapnel and kill the target easily.

She kicked, and the door exploded… *toward* her.

Deadly splinters ripped into flesh, tore and shredded.

Nuala was knocked backward by the explosion and slammed into the wall, her left side a mass of splinters. The clothes around her arm, leg, buttock, and parts of her back were pincushions. She had solidified her skin so that she could not be harmed by flame, wood or steel, but she was still impressed by the method of the trap. The holy water in the wood had nullified that defense and penetrated her flesh.

Nuala looked up. Marco wore a black turtleneck against the darkness, giving the illusion that he was disembodied head floating in the mist.

Marco stood serenely in the door frame, eyes peaceful, and smiling broadly. He launched himself at her, kicking into the splinters, driving his fist down into her back. She sprang away from him, the push from her leg sent her all the way down the hall, back the way she'd come. With a pivot the speed of sound, she twirled, sending half the splinters from her clothes into the hall toward Marco with the centrifugal force.

Marco darted back inside the bathroom, letting the splinters go by.

Nuala drew her twin Desert Eagles and called out, "Here, Marco. Don't you want to come out and play, lad?"

Marco stayed inside the bathroom door as he fished in his pockets for the car key fob. "Nope. I'm pretty certain that you're parked where you can shoot me if I stick my head out, right?"

"Of course."

Marco's little smile widened just a bit. He clicked the key fob. It triggered the claymore mine that was perfectly aligned with the hallway.

It had been in the ceiling of the hallway, pointed into the center of the little room. The concussive force launched a hundred ball bearings into the room like a giant shotgun. It didn't destroy Nuala, though it did shred her clothing.

The important part was that it destroyed her guns.

Marco charged into the hall, crossbow up and ready, and running straight for Nuala, still shaky from the explosion. Marco fired off the crossbow bolt. The bolt - its shaft coated with holy water - slashed through the nerve center of her shoulder. Marco dropped the crossbow as Nuala turned on him, hands bare and teeth bared. Her left arm hung dead by her side.

Her roar had dropped to a low growl. She hadn't felt such pain for centuries, and yet this annoyance had hurt her more than a contingent of crusaders. However, she was curious how he even managed to penetrate her skin. "What did you do to me?"

"I soaked the shaft in holy water. I suspect it stings a bit."

The vampire growled, broke off the back of the shaft, and slowly pushed it through the wound. Nuala would have to cut out the bad flesh later, then regrow everything. She considered doing it now, but that would delay her too long, and her arm in its current state could still rip Marco's head off with a backhand swing if she wanted.

"I'd hate to put you at a disadvantage."

"Disadvantage?"

He slid into an easy combat stance, waiting. "I'm already a genius, you're no match for me."

"Listen, child, I'm a Ph.D. six times over. So we'll have no talk of you being smarter until you manage to finish me."

"Have at ye, then."

Nuala exploded at him, and he leapt backward. Her reach was as long as his, and he wanted to stay out of it.

He ducked before she threw a right cross through a wall, and he kicked into her diaphragm and pushed off, back out of reach. Nuala's body froze with the impact, and he swung once more, smashing his palm across her face. He leapt back as she spun, sending a roundhouse punch to tear his head off; she missed by a hair as he leapt underneath it, and behind her. By the time Nuala finished her roundhouse, he had secured a grip on her collar and belt.

Marco lifted her off the floor and over his head. He turned toward the closet and threw her, hoping the door would break and the C4 trap he had planted there would rip forth and through her, in her weakened state. The explosion could rip through the both of them, but at that moment, Marco just wanted the vampire *dead*.

Nuala bounced off the wooden door and back at him.

Why couldn't this place be ready to simply fall down*!*

He crouched as she flew overhead, and sprang up, into her stomach, and grabbed her crotch and chest. He charged at the door, slamming her against it, cursing it as the only thing in that house that had held up so far.

The vampire rolled from his grip and onto the floor, grabbing him in a bear hug, holding him face to face with the ghastly visage of her almost-mangled countenance. Her green eyes glowed like crystals as she sank her teeth into the collar of his turtleneck.

The nerves of Nuala's teeth sent shocks of pain shooting through her head, and she staggered into the middle of the room, a curved piece of wood in her mouth.

Marco smiled, wrapped his legs around Nuala, and held her tight against his body. "Ever read the book *Dune?*"

The belt buckle at Marco's waist, activated by the pressure against it, shot forward with a needle, stabbing straight into Nuala's stomach, automatically injecting a small flask of holy water into her.

Nuala roared and dropped him. Marco straightened and smiled as he touched his ruined turtleneck. Even though it was a risk to fight Nuala without the benefit of holy objects, he thought it was worth the risk - she had a tendency to *run* from holiness, and he wanted this to be a decisive battle.

"Got something stuck in your teeth?" he asked, a smirk evident in his voice. "It's a wooden collar, soaked in holy water. Hope you don't mind."

Nuala reached into her own stomach. With a growl, she literally ripped out her own guts and threw them across the room. Marco watched them disintegrate before it even hit the wall.

Before Nuala could charge Marco, a fist connected with the wood in her mouth, knocking it from her head, taking her canines with it. Her head snapped back as she rocked with the blow.

"Like that, bitch?" Rory growled, punching her in the arm Marco had shot with the crossbow. More pain ripped through her mind, and she punched Rory with her palm, snapping his head back with enough force to cause brain damage in a human. Since brain damage had never stopped him before, he whirled with a flourish of his duster and whipped a foot past her face.

She grabbed him with her best hand and raised him over her head.

"If you had just stayed out of the way, you might have lived. Now you don't get that much."

Nuala threw Rory against the wall so hard that he broke it.

The window behind her smashed in, and both of Amanda's feet crushed Nuala's side as the Russian swung in on a rope from the roof - she came running as soon as the older vampire entered the building. Nuala rolled and came to her feet, her body on fire. She cringed, her entire side on fire with refreshed pain. She looked down at the shoes that Amanda wore, and then at her side. They had strapped cleats to Amanda's shoes… wooden ones, also soaked in holy water. The cumulative damage made her entire body feel as though it was starting to disintegrate.

"Spry little thing," Nuala growled, "aren't you?"

Rory groaned and moved to his feet. "You noticed that, did ya?"

Nuala felt movement behind her, and whirled, punching before she looked. Her fist cracked the Kevlar plates in Marco's bulletproof vest as Marco rammed a stake into her brain. She fell to the ground in agony, screaming, her head burning with pain. She ripped out the stake and threw it at Marco, who had ducked in anticipation. The stake ricocheted off the wall (breaking the wall), and the blunt end landed in the back of Marco's skull. He forward, blinking, unsteady, and immediately fell back against the wall, concussed.

Nuala was back on her feet, woozy. It took her a moment, but she understood that Marco had soaked his stakes in holy water, as he had soaked that wooden collar. He had almost fried her brain - had she been stabbed in the frontal lobe instead of the temporal lobe above her ear, she would have been a personality-less zombie, like a member of the Kennedy family. As it was, she wouldn't hear well out of one ear for a long while.

Nuala shot forward and punched Marco again, solidly, in the diaphragm, slamming him against a wall. This time, Marco went down and stayed down. That done, she dismissed him and whirled on the other two vampires. Without looking, Nuala's bad arm ripped across Rory's throat, tearing it out, and delivered a backhand to his face so hard his neck broke. He fell to the ground, out cold again.

The taller, evil vampire smiled as she turned on Amanda. "You can run, little one, but you can't -"

Amanda had already moved in, a roundhouse punch delivered solidly to Nuala's side, and another to her face. Nuala whipped a right cross at Amanda, but Amanda parried it with her left hand, deflecting it to one side. The assassin slashed across and would have decapitated Amanda had she not already bent her knees to duck her head. Amanda burst forward, her left arm up in a block to ward off the next strike. Her right hand shot forward at the same time, driving a fist through Nuala's face, snapping the elder vampire's head back.

Amanda grabbed the back of Nuala's head and drove herself forward, bringing their skulls together in a resounding crack that sounded like one of Nuala's rifles. With her left hand, Amanda grabbed Nuala's right wrist, digging into the wound track in Nuala's left shoulder with her right hand, and hurled her to the other side of the room, crashing head-first into the heavy wooden windowsill.

Amanda leapt on her back and continued to pound into the assassin's wounded side. Nuala reared up and threw Amanda off of her so violently that Amanda was the one to visit the other end of the room, smashing into a wooden wall. The assassin turned on her and smiled. Marco was wounded, Rory was unconscious, and they were the only two left standing.

"And now, you face me, young bitch, and all the forces of hell!"

Amanda didn't move for a moment. Nuala had driven her back so hard, she had created a crater in the wall. She felt her ribs broken, she felt her shoulder dislocated, and she… couldn't feel her legs. The damage had been by wood… it would heal, in time, but not fast enough. Amanda looked her straight in the eye and said, "I saw that Disney picture."

Nuala laughed. "It is just the two of us."

Amanda looked around and stared only at Marco. She could still hear the heartbeat, but she could also smell the blood.

Amanda's heart rate sped up, and she didn't feel any pain anymore. She could taste Marco's lips on hers, his surprisingly gentle hands over her body, hugging her, touching her, caressing her to sleep… and she thought of never feeling it again.

Amanda's eyes glowed as she looked at Nuala, and the other vampire took a step back. The assassin realized what was happening, even if Amanda didn't.

She didn't even notice something was different when she slowly rose to her feet. "You may defeat me, Nuala. You may even kill me. You might even be able to get one other person here. But if I die, you are going to have my teeth in your throat!"

Nuala grinned.

A fist landed a solid punch on her jaw, and Nuala staggered back, hurting from the blow. A second hit landed on her shoulder. It felt like she had been set on fire as a vial of holy water crushed inside her wound. A double-punch and an uppercut sent her sprawling. She suddenly felt weaker, almost like a human. Merle Kraft stood before her, a little smile on his face, two sets of rosaries wrapped around his knuckles. He reached down and picked up two glass jars filled with fluid, rags sticking out of the top.

"I'd like to talk with you, you reject from Mordor," he said simply. "More importantly, I'd like to know where I can find the man who sent you."

She smiled and kicked up to her feet. "You know where to find him already, little Kraft. What you don't know is who. And those Molotov cocktails won't hurt me, no matter how many holy artifacts you have with you."

"Fine." He dropkicked one of the bottles into her chest, and a cloud of steam rose up as she realized that the bottles were filled with holy water.

She screamed and dodged the next bottle. Her skin was blistering, her body was in unimaginable pain. She was about to leap out the window when -

Marco's cavalry sword ran through Nuala's side and pinned her to the wall. Nuala looked down, grabbed

Merle by the collar and tossed him over Amanda's head, on the other side of the room. Nuala slid off the sword and was about to strike again when a searing pain ripped through her chest.

Nuala looked down and saw a cross sticking out of her heart.

Amanda smiled and stood back. "Death does not feel so great, *da*?" she asked, and fired a palm into the top of the cross, driving the longer, sharpened end deeper into Nuala's chest.

Nuala's knees wavered as she grasped for the cross, her hands, and torso on fire. She slowly burned with agony and staggered away. Nuala looked at Amanda, then Marco behind her, stirring slightly, and then at the closet - the closet that Marco had been so desperate to smash her through. The one with the C4 behind it.

The vampire's eyes glowed. If Nuala took out the closet door, the flames would ignite and possibly consume Marco. That would prompt Amanda to save him, and both would die in the process.

The vampire charged the closet and broke through the door.

The room filled with fire. The windows blew out with the sudden pressure. A wall of flame cut off Marco from everyone else in the room.

Amanda instinctively backed away from the flames. While she was strong enough to survive flames for a few seconds - which, for a vampire, is usually enough to put it out - diving into an inferno like that would be enough to make her go up like flash paper. One minute, she would be a real person, the next, she'd make an ash out of herself.

But Marco was on the other side of the inferno.

"Merle?" Amanda asked.

Merle shook his head. "I'm not going to try that. I'm good, but I'm not a miracle worker. Not to mention that Marco's probably already toasted or suffocated."

Amanda's head whipped towards him, and she shot him a look that made him step back. She had to repress the urge to hurt him.

Fix problem, not blame, she thought. She looked back at the wall of flame, then the wall of stone. *Dear God, let this work.*

Without any thought, Amanda burst forward, slamming into the stone wall.

To everyone's surprise, she crashed right through it.

Amanda didn't hesitate, but turned to mist, redirected herself to the outside of the building, and rematerialized past the hole in the wall generated by the explosion. Going through there would have only landed her in fire. Amanda grabbed hold of untouched wall, driving her fingernails into it. She anchored herself with one hand, then punched through with the other. She turned her fist into a claw, then ripped the hole open so she could get through.

Amanda grabbed Marco and jumped back out through the hole she'd created, landing outside, on her feet.

"Didn't know you could do that," Merle said over her shoulder.

Amanda wasn't even surprised that he was there already. He moved so fast, she didn't even want to ask how he did it. "I turned to mist. Big deal."

Merle arched a brow. "Except you did it quickly. And you took your clothes with you."

Amanda blinked, looked down. She at least had her shirt on. Her pants were still in place. When she usually changed form, she had to leave her clothing behind. It was usually a trick that someone of a higher power level could achieve, like Mikhail or Nuala. "First time that happened."

Merle nodded. "Whatever. Good news: She's dead, Jim."

Chapter 21

Bloody Details

December 13th

Marco awoke in a hospital, blearily looking up into the smiling face of an intern. In the background, the stern voice of a doctor lectured on the dangers of hanging around old buildings: "You have gas pipes all over the place, running thither, running hither. You have no idea of how dangerous those old places are," et cetera.

Amanda glided alongside Marco's gurney. "Hello. So nice of you to join us. We thought you were cooked for a moment there."

"What?" He blinked, confused. "Is the bitch dead?"

"Vampire, *da*. Yana, no such luck. You are little crispy, and you will have bad headache, but you'll stay overnight for now. There are cracked ribs, and concussion and they want to check you for internal bleeding."

Marco smiled and reached up for her, taking her hand. "Hey," he whispered. "Imagine if you hadn't bitten me a few days ago. I'd probably be a broken mess."

She chuckled. "You *are* broken mess."

Marco closed his eyes for a moment, and then it became even longer than a moment.

"Marco?" Amanda asked softly.

Marco started awake. "Hi. Is she dead? No, wait, you told me that, didn't you?"

Amanda nodded. Her brow furrowed, and her mouth became tight, concerned, and trying not to say anything.

Marco gave a laugh - or maybe a scoff. "Don't worry. Not going to die today. Tell me how she died."

"Your sharpened crucifix to her heart. She then ran into closet with the claymore."

Marco's eyes closed, and he sighed. "Nobody."

Amanda smiled. "Usually not with a vampire."

He paused long enough to make her wonder if he fell asleep again. "But we usually see them die. What about all the minions? Did they put up a fight?"

Amanda shook her head. "They were still moving in when Nuala died. They fell down dead."

Marco arched a brow. "Really? Good thing that we made certain Yana wasn't part of that. Except there's only one problem."

Amanda blinked, staring at him intently. Drawing power had to be the act of a conscious vampire. Had she been instantly killed, would that have worked?

Had she been in our Faraday cage trap in the house, with the walls painted with holy water, could she have pulled on that power regardless?

"You think she survived long enough to make it outside, and drain life out of her minions, and stayed alive?"

Marco smiled tiredly. "Would you be surprised at this point?"

"Barely twelve hours after I told you that you had to be more subtle, you blow up a house? Wasn't there a quieter way to say that you were going to ignore me?"

Merle shrugged. "We tried to find a nuclear bomb, but they were all taken."

SFPD Detective Kristen Kelly sighed, looking down the length of his magic shop. The crime scene tape was still up, marking the place where Tara had fallen before being taken to the hospital. "The FBI hasn't taken down the tape yet?"

"No, mainly because they want to keep the illusion that it's a real, ongoing investigation," he explained. "They couldn't do that if they simply packed up everything and went home. Besides, someone is terrifying the FBI Director, and the terror just moves its way down the chain of command. There will be a few FBI agents floating around who will be very confused, but aside from that, there will be no fingerprints on this anywhere." Merle dismissed it with a wave of a hand. "As far as the mansion, the explosion will be dismissed by agents from Homeland Security as a matter of old gas pipes gone bad."

Kelly raised a brow. "Why would DHS be involved?"

Merle waved it away again. "Oh, the suspicion that it was a terrorist plot gone wrong, you know, that sort of thing. So many problems lately in San Francisco, it's a possibility, right? Heh."

She smiled slightly. "Makes you wonder how vampires survived without help from the authorities."

"Bribery, I suspect," he murmured as he stepped over a bit of the crime scene. "Not to mention other factors that Miss Colt mentioned before."

Detective Kelly chuckled. "I like that. You're still calling a vampire 'Miss.' You're polite even with bloodsucking fiends."

Merle hopped to the other side of the scene tape and offered her a helping hand over it. "Well, she hasn't sucked me yet, so I have no evidence on the matter."

She gave him a sidelong look as she took his hand. "I can't believe you said that."

He blinked, clueless. "What?"

She rolled her eyes, then hopped over the tape. "Never mind. Speaking of people she *is* sucking, what about Marco? How's he?"

"Catalano will live." He grinned. "Damnit."

"And his friend the bloodsucker?"

Merle shook his head, wandering towards the back and away from the crime scene tape. "I don't know. I can't read her, really. Marco isn't talking, which, for him, is a first. But that's mostly because he's on painkillers and sleeping it off."

"Hmm… What is their problem, I wonder. What do you think he did?"

He turned back to her and raised a brow. "You think he did something? It's Marco. If Amanda isn't used to him by now, he would have been dead long before we met him."

She wrinkled her brow in thought. "True. And neither one of them seems the type to run away from something they want."

Merle smiled. "Yeah. You'd think that two people as bright as they are would recognize love when it smacks them over the head and bites them. In their case, literally."

"Right," his ex-wife replied vaguely. "Although they could very well know it already."

He opened the door to the back room, and Kelly followed. He started to unpack the weapons collected from the latest outing. *I really needed to get some of my supplies from my overseas job diverted to the magic shop.* He grabbed two handfuls of sharp objects and put them aside on the bench.

Knives and stakes… where could I put them? "What exactly are you implying?"

"Think about it," she said, closing the door behind her. "What's the *best* that could happen?" She moved next to him, watching the various and sundry weapons begin to pile up on the gym bench. "Say they fall in love, they get together, maybe they even get married? Then what?" She reached into the bag and pulled out a stake that looked rather nasty. She placed it with the others. "Will Amanda want to live forever *without* him by her side? If they're really in love, and it's going well, would he want to stay a vampire with her? Since no-one wants to be an eternal seventy-year-old, even as a vampire, that decision would have to be made soon, even sooner if he gets nearly killed over the course of one of their little raids. Will either one really want to live with the consequences of that decision if he says no?"

Merle gently placed a bundle of crossbow bolts over in the corner and reached for a long blade. "You haven't known them for long, but you've got their numbers down perfectly."

Kristen smiled, amused. "I don't need to know them, Merle, all I need is to see is they're in love. I mean, come on, when was the last time you were in love? Don't you remember how scary it can be sometimes?"

He paused a sharpened cross in one hand, one of the machetes in the other. He glanced at her for one long moment, wondering, just for a moment, if she had seriously inquired. He slowly placed both weapons down, and turned towards the wall, digging into a gym bag for something else to unpack. Anything else.

"I don't need to remember. I've never been out of love."

Kristen blinked. "Isn't that a line from *Romeo and Juliet*?"

Merle shook his head, rummaging through the occasional rags to wrap the weapons in. *Why can't I find anything more to store, stack or put away?* "No. The line is that Romeo is 'out of her favor, where I am in love.' Such a schmuck. Just because someone dislikes you doesn't mean you stop loving them."

Hands roughly pushed through the contents. Couldn't he find *something*? He needed a distraction… English Lit would not manage it.

"Besides, that *schlemiel*…Romeo…was dumb enough to ditch his love out the nearest window for the next pretty thing to come along. In the case of *our* lovebirds, I guess I'm going to have to hit the both of them over the head," he muttered. "They're both in love. To be honest, they most likely know that they're in love. However, the likelihood of them following through is as likely my contention for lead rebounder for the Chicago Bulls. Besides, they should both be more aware of the overall situation; after all, it's not as though finding someone to love is as easy as—"

He felt Kristen step up behind him. "Merle."

Pause. "Kris?"

"Speak Yiddish to me."

He raised a brow and… to be honest, he was half afraid to face her. She didn't leave him an option and assaulted him by wrapping her arms around him, kissing him as she drew Merle in.

Of course, that sort of assault he could prepare for. He only had three black belts. His reflexes were pretty good - he immediately responded in kind, then started kissing along Kristen's jawline.

"*Oy vey.*"

They didn't fall on each other so much as simply fall, though he made certain he landed on the bottom. He didn't slow down or stop to think. He didn't allow himself to be surprised at all of this, or that Kristen removed his windbreaker and other elements of clothing…

Merle kissed her neck gently, then right behind her left ear, moving to suck on Kristen's earlobe. She drew him closer, her mouth latching on to whatever it could. When she tired of that, she grabbed his head in both hands and kissed him deeply. She wrapped her tongue around his and drew it into her mouth, massaging it with hers and sucking on it gently. Kraft's hands wandered up and down her spine, lightly stroking as they made love with their mouths.

Kristen moaned lightly, and Merle increased the passion in his own kiss. His hands traveled up her sides, thumbs lightly brushing the curve of her breasts as they passed. They wandered up her arms, drawing them up above her head. He moved up to kiss the inside of her wrist, and slowly moved down her arm with kisses, wanting to taste every bit of her. He moved to her, latched onto it and sucked on the spot right behind her ear, then kissed, lightly bit and licked his way down her neck, following the nerve down her shoulder. He kissed at the hollow of her throat, sucking at the skin.

Somehow, and she didn't even notice until then, all of her buttons had come off her blouse.

They moved over each other with practiced skill. They had been married for years and divorced for less than half that time, so they had forgotten very little about one another. The movements were deliberate but no less passionate - they wanted this more than they needed it, a distinction they had made not long after they were married.

About an hour later, they lay on the floor, on the training mat, finally worn out and breathless.

Merle stayed with Kristen, wrapped around her to keep her warm. "Were we trying for the marathon?" he whispered.

"You're a black belt," Kristen answered, "I played sports, and I practice self-defense daily. We're athletic, and besides, we were having fun. What do you think?"

He smiled. "I definitely think we're having fun."

"Almost makes me wish I locked the door on my way in."

"It's locked, don't worry about it."

She stared at him a moment. "Should I ask how you did that?"

"I'm magic, remember?" He moved his fingers over her, and she twitched in surprise.

"Oh. Yeah," Kristen said.

They lay there a little longer in silence before Merle said, "Normally, I would ask if you and Arthur would want to move back in, but your place is nicer than my apartment, so that would be insulting, and I'm not going to invite myself into your place, so -"

"We can't, Merle." She moved her hand to his face. "I didn't divorce you because I stopped loving you, and you know that."

He sighed. "I know."

"It's why I never got an annulment. You want to be 'technical'? We're still married."

Merle remembered the divorce vividly. She had served him the papers herself and explained it to him all too simply - the secrecy of his job had spilled over into his home life. He didn't only stop talking about his work, he'd stopped talking. He had known he'd always been in danger of falling into his own head, especially since his mother raised him like a toy to be played with instead of a child to be raised, but as his job took him out and across the country with greater and greater frequency, the problem worsened. Kristen had issued the divorce as a warning shot across his head.

There were still days he didn't notice they were gone.

And that was something that terrified him about himself. He fell into a world of monsters and came back to a world of freaks… and those were just his customers. He hadn't wanted Kristen in that world any more than she had wanted him to hide it from her.

Merle blinked. If he was simply terrified of being unable to talk to the woman he loved, who he married, what must someone like Marco and Amanda be going through? They were both predators, and they both knew they were predators - and that was their problem!

Who would want the person they loved to move in with a killer? Despite whether or not the killer was one of the lovers themselves? Answer: a sociopath.

Neither of them fit that bill.

Merle pulled himself out of his thoughts and joined Kristen before she could note he had drifted off into his own head again. "Yeah, I know. I'm not exactly greatly improved on the personal stuff, am I?"

She graced him with a smile. "Well, it's at least a start."

Merle laughed. "No." He moved his hand down her body. "That is, though."

She laughed. "Well, I always said you were magic."

After Marco fell asleep again, Amanda watched him. Aside from looking as though he'd been savagely beaten, he seemed rather peaceful. He looked cute, almost cuddly, almost angelic…

She closed her eyes tightly. She had already lost control twice around Marco. She couldn't lose control a third time. She'd allowed herself once, and that was self-indulgence as far as she was concerned. She had to get out for a few minutes. He'd be fine without her, if only for a little while.

Marco's eyes opened before the door did. He slowly reached above him and grabbed the headboard, pulling himself up. To his right, there was a janitorial cart with a bucket precariously balanced on edge, and a mop leaning on it.

Marco closed his eyes for a moment and let the scent waft into his nostrils. The annoyance smiled. "Hello, Nuala, I'm so glad you could come and visit me."

The tall vampire stood at the foot of his bed.

Marco looked at Nuala for the first time, studying her. Her primary biting teeth had yet to grow back, but the rest of them were sharp enough for the task. Despite her face belonging to the most gruesome creature in existence, her body… well, might have once been quite attractive without the necrotic look. It made him wonder what she had been like before the vampy look.

But right now, even despite her normal appearance, she looked like hell. She was naked, though she was as erotic as an unfinished statue. Her entire body looked like the surface of an overdone London broil, burned and blackened. There was a giant hole in her shoulder he could see through, her side looked like it was about to break off of her, half of her hair had been burned off, and there was a hole in the side of her skull just above and behind the ear.

"You know," Marco stated weakly, "I'm disappointed that no-one checked for remains."

Nuala shrugged. "They found a sharpened cross and assumed I was dust."

"Your minions managed to keep you alive," Marco whispered, suddenly tired. "But it didn't heal everything."

"Doesn't need to, does it? I just need to suck the life out of you, and won't that be a grand start?"

"Heh. Amanda's going to figure it out, you know. You don't incinerate a vampire and have *nothing*."

She cocked her head. She may have cocked her eyebrow, but Marco couldn't actually see one. "And she'll think this through in time for her to save you?"

He thought a moment. "Probably not. But, truthfully, I'm surprised. I mean, doesn't anyone read Jeffery Deaver? It could be one of his books."

Nuala nodded. "True… like *The Devil's Teardrop*."

Marco's eyes lit up. "You've read that! Thank you!"

She blinked. "Fer what?"

"For being the only literate vampire I've ever met… well, aside from Amanda, that is."

Marco jerked his foot to one side, and the bucket leapt off the janitorial cart, drawn by the string around his ankle. The contents of holy water slashed up and down Nuala's leg. The vampire screamed and leapt backwards, into the wall. He reached behind the headboard.

"You bast-"

Nuala was cut off by the foot-long throwing knife entering her chest. The vampire reached for it, ready to break off the handle and slide off when the next one landed in her throat.

Nuala looked ready to pound Marco into dust.

The door to the room burst open, and Nuala just saw Amanda right before she pounded both stakes into Nuala. The first punch into the large knife in her chest pinned Nuala to the wall. The second punch pounded the stake through Nuala's spine.

Nuala's entire body went numb.

The assassin stared at the two of them blankly. All of her strength left her, being invested in solely keeping her in existence. She was dying …

She was dead. Her body was just slow to catch up to that fact.

All of the knives had been soaked in holy water beforehand.

Marco slowly made his way out of the bed, walking on the dry side of the floor. He sat down on the edge of his bed. "You want to tell me who sent you?"

Nuala gritted her teeth against the pain and merely glared with her green cat eyes.

He smiled. "Then I'll tell *you*: The Council sent you after me."

Nuala's eyes narrowed, and she choked a little, as though she were trying to breathe, but just fighting the inevitable.

"What is their problem, huh? We pissed them off by killing Mikhail? Really?" He cocked his head. "First him, then Mister Day, now you. We must have honked them off something awful. What are they? Master vampires? Legions of Hell? The French?"

Nuala smiled. "You'll… never… guess."

His smile changed to a smirk. "No? You see, I know you're involved in a few problems over at the United Nations. Has someone been brokering a deal with some politicians?" He sagged. He hurt, but he wanted this over. "A few months ago, someone ate an FBI agent pointing a laser microphone at UN windows. I don't know whose office, but I know a vampire heard the laser mike, then killed the agent. Maybe the Council has been dealing with the UN Human Rights Commission? Make a deal to eat all of those unwanted people in Sudan, Syria, Libya?"

Nuala just blinked and said nothing. Marco sighed, unsure of how much time he had before the vampire finally died on him in mid-interrogation. "You took a bad risk coming into a Catholic hospital as you did. I even moved my room closer to the chapel so you would be at your weakest. I can only conclude that you must be really out to kill me. Why? Did I kill someone's relative or something?"

"You are… what you want to be," she choked out. "You do what you want to."

Marco sighed. She *had* to be delirious. "If I am whatever I want to be, then I want to be a millionaire. But for right now, I'll settle for this…" He reached down, under the bed, and drew the crucifix he had Amanda take off the wall. He reached out and pressed it to her face, making a sharp sizzling sound, and the pain was so excruciating that Nuala couldn't even cry out.

Amanda watched Marco's eyes burn into Nuala's face as he held it there. The eyes widened, and his ever-present smile grew a little.

He's enjoying this, *she thought.*

He ripped it away after a second. "That should wake you up." He held it close to her. "Feel free not to answer. Please don't. I want to hurt you. I want to make you suffer. You wanted to kill Amanda, you foul creature from Hell, and I want to personally send you back there, as slowly as I can. You want to go quickly, then answer my questions. You were sent by the Council, yes or no? I want you to say it."

Nuala blinked, still reeling from the pain. She considered playing deaf and dumb again but looked at the crucifix Marco held. "I was."

He smiled. Ah, progress. "And they want me dead because I'm dangerous?"

She smiled. "You… could say that."

Marco moved the crucifix closer to her skin, and she whimpered. "How?"

"You're too flexible. You're open-minded enough to do what you set out to but certain enough to set your mind to something and do it."

Marco stopped a moment. He couldn't tell if she was delirious or making perfect sense. "So, is there anything you want to say before you die?"

"I don't… want to die…"

He nodded thoughtfully. "Reasonable. After all, after the people you've killed, you won't exactly be going to a highly pleasant resort." He looked over the crippled vampire. "We don't know how long this will last, it hasn't exactly been done before, so you might want to say a few prayers, assuming you remember any."

Her eyes filled with sadness. "I… I…"

Marco sighed, trying to remember what language they would have prayed in, in the 1200s. Latin perhaps, and the closest derivative he knew was Italian.

"Padre Nostro…" he prompted, starting with the Our Father. She took up the prayer in time with Marco, and they prayed together, him leading her along.

As it progressed, Nuala's face changed, turning humanesque once more. Her hawkish nose slid in further, and the skin that looked like it had been burned off slowly started to reform, covering the exposed facial muscles. Her eyebrows grew back in…

Overall, Marco decided that Nuala's human face was as beautiful as her vampire face was ugly. Her green eyes sparkled with moistness, making them gleam with light. She had wonderful cheekbones. As it was, he merely smiled at her. He bent over slowly, dipped his fingers into the holy water on the floor.

"Humor me… and just one more prayer."

She began again as he drew his damp thumb over her head, one line vertical, the other horizontal, in the shape of a cross. Though the flesh sizzled, Nuala's eyes only glowed brighter as the prayer went smoothly, rapidly.

"Amen," she finished.

Marco quickly whipped out a rosary from underneath the bed sheets and looped it around her neck, pulling it tightly around her throat. The holy object burned through her skin as though it was a lightsaber, and he snapped it straight through her neck.

"Oh," she said innocently. "I see."

Nuala became a pile of dust on the floor.

Marco shrugged. "Maybe she won't go to Hell after all."

Marco slumped forward, and Amanda caught him.

Chapter 22

A Theory of Everything

Amanda took Marco and gently pulled him up to rest on the pillow. She examined him carefully for extra damage. She gently ran her fingertips along Marco's skin - her senses strong enough to have felt a ruptured capillary or anything worse, like a ruptured organ.

As for Marco, he had been conscious of Amanda's touch, ever since she dragged him along the bed - he just wasn't able to open his eyes, and most of his conscious functions were recovering from the past 24 hours with Nuala. Despite having been beaten bloody, he felt an electric charge buzz through him wherever Amanda touched. He longed to reach out and touch her back, but uncooperative limbs held him down.

Amanda trailed fingers down his abdomen, stopping short halfway past his navel. She knew nothing could be broken down there, she had already checked the bones.

She smiled to herself. But it always paid to be thorough, *da*?

"Am I interrupting something?" Merle asked.

Amanda looked up. Merle wasn't even at the doorway, but on the other side of the bed from both her *and* the entrance.

How does he do *that?* "I'm checking for wounds," she answered. "You're going to tell us what you're dealing with. You must."

Merle raised a brow. "National security at stake and I'm going to tell classified information to a vampire and a man crazy enough to be certifiable? Give me a reason."

Amanda narrowed her eyes, took out a business card from her well-fitted jeans, then wrote a number on the back. "This card? Belongs to a man you should call to verify. The number is my security clearance."

The vampire handed the card to Merle, and he blinked. "Oy."

At that moment, a hoarse voice whispered, "Bring… Rodgers…"

Marco tried to open his eyes and failed.

Marco opened his eyes hours later, staring up at the delicate face of Yana. "Hey dahlin," he rasped.

The redheaded lesbian looked up, into his eyes. She had nice green irises. Yana leaned forward and touched his hand. "Hey. You saved my life. Thank you."

He smiled. "A pleasure," he croaked. Dear Lord, did he really sound that bad?

Yana patted his shoulder. "Can I do anything for you?"

"Stay alive."

She smiled. "What are you, Marco?"

He blinked. Yana might have been slipping into her San Fran-Wicca mode again… but after the ominous little discussion with Nuala, he wasn't so quick to laugh as usual. "Whatever do you mean?"

"You know what I mean. You're not super-wacko guy, yet you are. You scare me to death half the time, and now you're… you. What are you?"

He flashed the smile. What was he exactly? Great question. Nuala had said he was whatever he wanted to be. But that wasn't true - he couldn't be three inches taller, for one thing. But there was something about what the assassin said that echoed with him still… something Yana may have picked up on that he hadn't… maybe Nuala got it wrong… It wasn't whatever he *wanted* to be.

"Whatever I *need* to be."

* * *

Merle stood in the hall, outside of Marco Catalano's room, speaking low into his cellular phone. Finding an old spy's business card with Amanda didn't worry him as much as it confused him.

Also, he went through what was left of Nuala's clothing. Among her pocket litter included several business cards from multiple Ambassadors that work at the UN. Seriously, Ambassadors at the United Nations and a vampiric assassin who tried to kill a random US citizen? It made no sense.

And if Merle took the initial assumption that Nuala was sent after Marco as retribution for the destruction of Mister Day, it was even more confusing.

But then Marco had found a way to put himself into the thick of the situation. So now, Merle was going to have to talk with Marco, primarily about what he talked about with Nuala. Merle needed to know what the vampire said before Marco axed her. And Marco was making demands to see his priest.

So all in all, this was going to be fun.

"You have an odd definition of fun."

Merle sighed and closed his eyes. He slowly closed the cell phone, not even looking up at his half-brother. "Dalf. Not now. I've got the Pentagon yelling that I return to Afghanistan to lay waste to ISIS vampire hordes. I'm up to my neck in vampires over here, mysteries on the East Coast. Amanda Colt handed me a number that has the CIA breathing down my neck, wondering why I've dug up something so old the dust cloud has taken on a mushroom shape. So now isn't the time for your cryptic 'I am demon hear me roar' act." Merle turned to face Dalf and had to pause in appreciation - half the hospital hallway had gone dark. "Cute trick."

"I tell you not to trifle with me, little brother," Dalf's voice wafted out from the darkness. *He would make a great ventriloquist.* "I come for your own good."

Merle said nothing. First of all, what could he say? Second, Dalf *had* been helpful from time to time. Why he could never figure, but it was most likely for his own profit. "And what vague bits of wisdom have you to offer today?"

"*Ignore* posse comitatus."

Merle arched a brow. What could the ban against Army or Air Force actions on US soil have to do with anything?

He shook his head. Dalf was being vague again, and mysterious, and he could be dealt with later. *Right now, Marco has all the cards. Though Dalf may have a few more that don't belong to him, and a spare deck just in case. But first things first. Kristen would have to know about all of this, and would probably want her own, separate interview. As long as Marco knows not to tell anything about national security, Kristen won't ask about it.*

But one never knew what would come out of Marco's mouth.

In her career, Detective Kristen Kelly had performed numerous interrogations with various levels of New York City scum, up to and including white-collar thugs. *These* two were something completely different.

Then again, they were also in love.

Kristen could tell that just from the way they were around each other. The annoying subtle glances, the light touching as though they reassured themselves that the other was still there. Even the way Amanda sat on the upper edge of Marco's bed gave off signals of intimacy.

Kristen leaned against the wall, standing next to where Nuala had been executed. "So, Miss Colt, just to be clear, you're a vampire?"

Amanda smiled. "*Da*, I am. Why, does that surprise you?"

Kelly shook her head. "I'm a New Yorker, I deal with people who are far scarier than you are."

"I don't know," Marco said, "I don't think you'd like me when I'm angry. That's generally when people start to die, and things explode."

Kristen smiled and raised a brow. "Who do you think you are, Bruce Banner?

"I prefer Jack Bauer." He smiled dreamily for a moment, then, thought aloud, "Hmm, Jack Bauer, vampire…a V-CTU…Vampiric Counter Terrorist Unit. I can see it now. A crossover series with *24* and *Buffy: The Vampire Slayer*: all the daylight scenes take place indoors. Kiefer Sutherland can get his makeup from one of his previous films—*The Lost Boys*, was it? And the interrogations, heh…" His voice lowered slightly, becoming a bad imitation of Sutherland, "'Tell me where the bomb is, *now*, or I eat you!'" He coughed to clear his throat. "Or maybe 'Jack, this is Chloe, you have ten minutes to stop the bomb and get back to your coffin, it's almost daylight.' Then one of the terrorists trying to stop him waves a Koran in his face, screaming 'Allahu akbar, *Allahu Akbar*!' 'Wrong Deity,' chomp!"

Amanda leaned forward and ruffled his hair. "He can be cute at times. Especially on painkillers."

Kelly smiled. "Let me know when the cute starts. Now, Merle has explained a lot of this to me regarding vampires and assassination. My question comes down to motive - why do these people keep hunting you down?"

Marco blinked and exchanged glances with Amanda. "Well," he started, "the first problem was local."

"The second problem followed patterns of rage to Marco," the vampire added.

He nodded to himself. "And the third... was a contract hit, we know that much. Then again, the second one was also directed at us." He hesitated.

Amanda even blinked. "Good question. Why would they send them after you? Revenge for previous problems? For Mikhail and Day? It seems too petty."

"I know, that's been our problem. Unless they think we really are a danger to them," Marco thought out loud. "But *why* would that be? Merle's certainly scarier, and he's got a government behind him. Merle's entire crew should have cooler toys. Not even discussing some ninjas we know." He tried to shrug, then winced. "I just do some tricks as seen on *MacGyver* reruns."

Kristen arched a brow. "How many vampires have you two been responsible for killing, personally or otherwise?"

They both blinked. Marco suggested, "Maybe a few hundred… well, how many people did the club hold before it was burned down?"

"Three hundred people."

He blinked. "Um, maybe five hundred, more or less… simply because we warned two street gangs about vampires, and they've been busy."

Amanda nodded. "Add another five hundred for me… I've lived longer."

The detective shook her head. "And you wonder why people are out to kill you. Your continued existence was disruptive before, and now it's meddled in the plans of some obviously powerful people. Killing underlings is one thing, especially since they can literally make more. But to do that, plus screw up their point man in New York by bringing in Merle, plus take out two of their heavy hitters? Whoever or whatever Merle's investigating is not happy with either one of you. First, you were annoying, now you're a threat. Since you've just taken out what I can only assume was an assassination specialist, I'd watch your backs if I were you."

Marco frowned. "Great. It took blowing up half a building to even slow this one down, and you want us to be quieter and more subtle even though the necessary force required goes up exponentially."

Amanda agreed. "It takes time, money and resources to perform surgical strike. If we were lucky, could have cut head off last one with heavy-caliber sniper rifle and uranium high-explosive charge. Maybe. Otherwise, we will need something bigger."

Marco frowned to himself. "But we can't bring in an air strike. And they tried that already."

Kristen sighed. "Do me a favor first… try minimal force to start with, before blowing up half my city?"

"We'll do our best."

Chapter 23
Complications

December 14th

Merle Kraft sat next to the hospital room door, lounging in his blue windbreaker, reading a magazine.

At the foot of the hospital bed, was Father William Rodgers.

Marco saw the priest when he opened his eyes and blinked. "Time to start," he said, still groggy. He tried to sit up in bed, and Amanda reached over and helped pull him up. He smiled at her and said, "Amanda, I need to know everything about your history. You know more than you're telling; you've at least suspected something for quite some time."

She blinked at him, then, her lips tightened in thought. She patted him on the shoulder and then sat in the chair next to his bed. "You never wanted to know my history before."

He rolled his eyes. "Mainly because I think it's rude to ask a woman's age. But now I need to know, especially since this is even better than the Mount

Olivet incident. Maybe I should start with what are you, really? You're a vampire, but how many other vampires do you hang out with? Not many, and I've been around you a while. The only one you've mentioned has been Jennifer Bosley. I suspect - I don't know how, but I suspect - you know about a lot of it firsthand."

Amanda leaned forward, touched his hand, and she smiled gently. "Relax, Marco. This will be a while."

Once Marco was settled in, Amanda did not even look away from him as she simply began, "Has anyone noticed an increase in devil worship?"

Caught off guard, Kraft chuckled. "You mean the nutcases out in Haight Ashbury? Yeah, we've noticed."

The vampire smiled. She tore her glance from Marco to the shorter Kraft brother. "I do not mean Goths, 'nature worshipers,' and people who indulge in 'mystic crystal revelations'; they are generally harmless. Fools swearing oaths to causes they cannot possibly understand, and many of them are too stupid to be accepted by any they swear to. Maybe we would like to discuss abortion clinics where they pay members per head, and then sell the body parts for profit?" She smiled wryly. "God takes everyone, but the Devil is picky."

Marco leaned forward, almost falling off the bed, then fell back to the mattress, giving up. "What are you referring to? Pick a starting point."

"I mean the French Revolution."

Father Rodgers nodded. "That's where I'd start."

Amanda nodded and spoke to Merle - the only one in the room who might not know what she was talking about. "In the Christian liturgy," she continued, "there is always bread and wine - body and blood of God Himself. In the French Revolution, once the Roman Catholic priests had been removed from the revolution, and the Terror had started, after a victim of the guillotine had been decapitated, peasants, 'proud citizens' of *great, People's, Republic*," she articulated with so thick a coat of sarcasm, Merle expected the words to drip onto the tile and burn a hole in the floor, "they would take their hard-earned bread and then dip it in blood of executed and eat it. If that is not perversion of religion, what is?"

Merle shrugged, "No offense to my brother's French connection, but it's the French. They have an anticlerical streak going back five hundred years, but I don't hear you accusing Henry of Navarre of being satanic."

Amanda's eyes narrowed to slits. "How about the resurrection of Moloch?"

Marco raised his eyebrows. "Moloch? Huh…"

Merle chuckled. "Yeah, that's the primary demon from that *Sleepy Hollow* show, right?"

"Moloch's been *technically* out of the mainstream for three thousand years," Rodgers boomed. "A deity of the ancient world, he was the god of money in Carthage - you may remember Hannibal and his elephants fighting Imperial Rome? Hannibal fought for them, and they so loved their money, they sacrificed to Moloch any impediment, any *inconvenience* to money - starting with throwing their children into a pit of fire."

Merle winced at where this was going. "So, Amanda, you're talking about abortion?"

The vampire snorted. "You think I would go from 1789 to 1967? *Nyet*, Merle. That is too easy. If you wish to talk about that, we can tie it to the foundation of your Planned Parenthood. But I mean America, Cold Spring Harbor, 1920s, where they sterilized, euthanized, and murdered the mentally deficient…the *inconvenient*. What Margaret Sanger, *founder* of Planned Parenthood, supported. It is also the Weimar Republic, where eugenics programs did the same thing ten years before anyone heard of an Austrian art-school reject named Adolf Hitler.

"It was those years, from 1917 to 1927, that evil rose to power in the 20th century. The Soviet Union, after Lenin died, grew to worship Lenin, taking from Russian Orthodoxy all their religious symbols and icons and ceremonies, and transferred them, almost whole, to worship the dead Lenin. 'Lenin Lived, Lenin has lived, Lenin Lives!' was their battle cry."

Marco slunk back into the headboard and murmured, "Mimicking 'Christ has died, Christ is risen, Christ will come again,' from Church. What next, train whistles for church bells?"

Amanda looked at him and nodded. "Correct. The sounds of factory and industry. And I will not even get into Hitler's attempt to resurrect the Norse gods." She leaned back in her chair. "I suppose it is time to tell you all that I am a World War I–era vampire."

Merle blinked. "I hope they don't classify all of you by eras."

Amanda smiled. "You mean Generation X or Y isn't a classification? Baby boomers? Hippies, Yippies and Yuppies?"

"As opposed to Yippie, Yappie, and Yahooie?" He smiled. "And while a Hippie is more of a disease than a generation, your point is well taken."

The vampire laughed lightly and shook her head gently. "I was made vampire in 1918 when Bolsheviks came to power." She squeezed Marco's hand. "I had been turned by one of Lenin's vampires."

Merle held up his hand. "Lenin *had* vampires?"

Rodgers nodded. "The entire Soviet Union did. Especially after the Gulags were set up - if vampires existed, the Gulags are free food. And the Russians have winter almost year-round, making for perfect conditions: permanent overcast."

Amanda nodded. "I never made it to Gulags. I was bitten during Russian Civil War, and -"

Marco smiled. "Being Russian, you bit him back?"

She grinned, baring all of her teeth, and gave a slight nod. "Exactly. A day or two later, I woke up and found the entire world upside down. There was a foreign army on Russian soil, sitting there, doing nothing, and getting shot at all the time. The United Expeditionary Force, an American-British joint project sent into Russia, supposedly to stop the Bolsheviks, but with orders so deliberately vague no-one did anything except hang around and get shot at."

Merle leaned back in his chair, narrowing his eyes. "As I remember, there were two UEF groups, one of them being helped out of there by some of the locals."

Amanda Colt interlaced her fingers in front of her. "I did what I could."

Rodgers sat a little straighter. "You?" He glanced at Merle. "I'm starting to think that my histories are incomplete."

Amanda nodded. "You have yet to understand the full extent of it. It had been some time since I had been turned, and I…went through a bad time."

Her eyes flickered down to the floor a moment, before she blinked, looking back at the two men across the room. If she even glanced Marco's way, he would undoubtedly have her elaborate, and she couldn't have that." By the time they needed to evacuate, I helped them get out, and the British unit was happy to get me out as well." She chuckled. "Thankfully, the London fog is almost as eternal as Russian dusk, so I was right at home."

Merle thought a moment. "Did they know what you were?"

She nodded. "After a while, yes. I had to explain to them what I was, why I needed the sleeping arrangements that I did, and I didn't want to scare anyone with the whole biting prospect. And Churchill was ecstatic about it."

Marco raised a finger. "Wait, wasn't Churchill out of power by then?"

"*Da*, but we still managed to work out an arrangement, since I did not trust the new government." She shrugged. "The new government thought that the Communists were a non-issue, and the Americans—President Wilson—was inept. I reported to Churchill, for the most part. He sent me back in to kill vampires as we heard of them. When 1935 rolled around, I was almost full-time employed—Stalin had made deals with vampires, and I spent four years in-country until Hitler had declared war on Europe, and Winnie sent me into Germany—"

"Winnie?" Merle asked. "Churchill?"

"*Da.*" She shifted in her chair. "You see, vampires had been playing both sides of the Eastern Front in two different wars. They ate people in the concentration camps and in the Gulags. I made sure that vampires weren't used on the battlefield."

Marco blinked and sat up straight, even though that hurt his back, as well as the rest of his body. "Wait a second, they fed Jews to vampires? Wouldn't a bite make them stronger? And if any bite back, like you did, the Nazis would have a *real* problem on their hands. In the mass graves, they were shot or gassed."

Amanda nodded. "That's what the furnaces were for. Any prisoner who died from biting would be incinerated. In the Gulags, they made for excellent fuel for the fire. As for biting back…that's what happened to Treblinka. There was a prisoner uprising." She grinned. "It was a camp torn down by the Nazis themselves. They had good reason for it."

Marco leaned forward, curious, and fell back when something hurt in his back. "I'm surprised you got through enemy lines so easily…other vampires never caught you."

She smiled. "In part, the vampires who were against me could not touch me because of whom I worked with. Because I was also, briefly, under the employ of the Vatican. Pius XI and XII were both very understanding, and I used their life-saving networks to smuggle myself in and out. From 1939 to 1945, I was the shared property of three people at any one time, the Popes Pius, Churchill, and John Foster Dulles."

Merle smiled. "Dulles ran the OSS and set up the CIA after the war."

She nodded. "Which is how I came to America after Churchill was voted out of power after the war ended. From 1945, I worked for the CIA in a 'special capacity.' I never technically worked for the US government, but for intelligence. Not many people knew what I was, just that I had special talents.

"During the 1950s, when Khrushchev came to power, I was a double-agent—Khrushchev wanted the evil vampires out of his domain…it was part of his de-Stalinization process."

"But you were working primarily for the CIA," Merle stated.

Amanda nodded. "*Da.*"

"Police Commissioner Wilson says hello from Vietnam."

Amanda blinked, then smiled. "I am so glad he remembers."

Marco cleared his throat. "You were saying?"

"Yes. Well, when Brezhnev moved in, I was 'fired' from the Soviet end of the job and had to work undercover like every other spy. President Carter all but had me staked, and I did nothing until the 1980s when Reagan sent me into Poland. I worked with Solidarity, later some time in Afghanistan, and I was eventually sent back into Russia…when Gorbachev came to the throne, we had the same arrangement I had with Khrushchev to kill vampires."

Marco took a deep breath and said, "Your clearance." He took another deep breath. "In September. You got 'round the no-fly ban and got the Ninjas here. Your old spy clearance."

Amanda nodded. "I was surprised it still worked. In 1993, I was fired by the US government. Years later, I was replaced." She looked at Merle. "You."

The Kraft brother sighed. "Yeah." He looked at the others. "The New York Police Commissioner said something similar to me not too long ago."

"If that's the case, then why didn't we know about the vampires before?" Marco asked. "Merle needed to be told when he came to New York, but if all of these people had hired you before…"

Amanda growled, tiger-like. "I had never worked with all that many people, and even fewer knew what I was. After I was fired, the President had the documents shredded. He thought they were too *scary*. Most of the ones who knew me or of me were old and died off…and no, I didn't eat them."

Marco nodded, letting things fall into place. "Asmodeus had you fired."

Amanda, Merle, and Rodgers all looked to him.

"Excuse me?" the priest boomed.

Marco leaned back on the bed, relaxing slightly, careful that he didn't hurt himself further. "Mister Day, our 'unkillable' friend from September, mentioned to me that he was on good terms with politicians in the 90s. He specifically mentioned taking out large portions of our military and intelligence. Amanda, you saw him blown apart by a chain gun. I guess he saw you, too; after Afghanistan, he probably found out who you worked for and had the President cut you from the budget."

Merle winced at the thought, then frowned thoughtfully. "Asmodeus knew any replacement would be human," Merle murmured. "Not as dangerous as Amanda."

"*Da.*" Amanda sighed. "But, aside from my own personal history, there has been a slippery slope of demonic activity even into this century."

Merle cocked an eyebrow. "Really? Anything in particular? Should I worry about Obama now?" he joked.

Amanda pulled out a smartphone, tapped in a few things, and showed it to Merle. The screen had the headline about Planned Parenthood cutting up and selling fetal body parts, somewhere the child in question still had a heartbeat as it was being cut to pieces. "You wish to debate the demonic nature of this?"

"Not particularly," he muttered. "Okay, I guess all this makes sense, but what has this to do with Nuala?"

Marco smiled. "You first."

Amanda raised an eyebrow as she followed Marco's thoughts. "We first met you as you sniffed around the UN. You were in Afghanistan, but came back here on business… United Nations business?"

Marco paused, thinking things through; he could play his trump card now, and bluff Merle into thinking he had more… that was assuming his analysis didn't add up to Merle's total knowledge. "Nuala told me the Council sent her for us. So there's her, the Council, and Day, who was tied to political world evil. And you can't spell Unholy without UN."

Merle blinked. "The what?"

Amanda smiled. "Have you never heard of the Council?"

Rodgers looked to Merle. "The Council is generally considered the leader of vile vampire control. It is evil, almost all-powerful, and really bad news unless you live in the Vatican, which is the one place on Earth none of them want to go… Though I hear there's a spot in Jerusalem they don't want to go near, either."

Merle blinked, then sighed. "Damnit," he muttered, thinking of the card in the assassin's pocket. "I was hoping I was wrong. Unfortunately, that's all even I know. I can't make any other connections. I -"

He stopped and blinked. Nuala's employer, the UN business card. The United Nations was a vast organization, with tens of thousands of workers, clerks, secretaries, and enough layers of bureaucracy to flatten several small countries, so it wasn't hard to imagine that some of them had been corrupt, and even co-opted by "the dark side," but the Ambassadors? That required more access than a friendly relationship with a secretary, more like a seat at the table with a world power…

But then they already had it, didn't they? Vampires had brokered a deal with Stalin—Amanda *just* told him so. Stalin had not only set up the United Nations with the Allies, he also had Alger Hiss—who worked the American side of the setup—spying for him. When the Soviets fell, Day had fallen right into the Middle East.

"How long has word of 'the Council' been around?" Merle asked.

Rodgers: "Hundreds of years."

Marco nodded. "Pretty much the point. And for some reason, there's something in all of this that never quite added up, right? And that was Asmodeus making all of those contacts and connections for a take over the world deal with, well, making an Axis of Evil, heavy on the evil. But we've all ignored the simple concept of how Day was able to get into the UN."

Rodgers blinked. "Didn't we already discuss him having major government contacts?"

Amanda nodded, catching on. "But he spent most of his time in the Soviet Union for most of the previous century. How much time could he have spent

Post-Cold War aiding terrorists while developing relations with the UN?"

"Unless," Merle concluded, "he already had a connection to the UN. If *he* worked with Stalin after World War II, then he would have had what Stalin had - an in with the United Nations."

Amanda smiled. "Alger Hiss was on the committee designing the UN, and Hiss was in Stalin's pocket. Stalin and Hiss had them put a council together… a council like the Council on Human Rights -"

"Once manned by the Sudan," Merle interjected. "Irony only a demon could love. Since the Soviet Union, the Middle East and Africa seem to be getting a lot of work on the Councils, all of the Councils they shouldn't be on, like Sudan or Syria on the Arms Council. They would do for replacements in a pinch… or a decade of cultivation. Convenient," Merle murmured. It happened to fit neatly into a pattern - Security, Human Rights, Arms Proliferation… all parts of the United Nations.

Councils…each and every one of them. *Dalf said to ignore* posse comitatus…*now I know why.* We're going to war.

"Exactly," Marco said. "The council… is now a Council. A UN Council."

Merle looked at them both a moment. "You're going home when the semester is over," he stated.

Marco raised his brows. "They want me dead… so I'm bait?" He glanced at Amanda and shrugged. He turned back to Merle and discovered he had vanished. "I have simply *got* to learn how he does that."

Father Rodgers slid out a cigar, and then stopped, looking around the hospital. "I guess I should take a walk outside. Can I leave you two alone in here?"

Marco chuckled weakly. "What could we do? I might fall asleep."

Rodgers looked like he was about to say something, but shook his head, stood, and left.

Marco suddenly noted that he was left all alone with Amanda. He didn't look back at her, though… not completely. His eyes glanced back at her, but he didn't want to turn towards her. That would mean he'd be committed to the conversation, and he didn't know if he wanted to be just yet - simply staring at the door would at least provide him with the excuse that he simply fell deep into thought and got lost.

Mainly because he didn't know how it would go. The temptation would be to resume their make-out session from before Nuala attacked in the first place, though that was out of the question.

Amanda caught his eye movements, however, and her heart stopped - literally stopped, she momentarily forgot to make it beat. She was a hundred-year-old vampire, and he was barely a quarter her age. How could she…?

Marco turned his head towards her and met her eyes. She had been looking at him… watching him. And he wanted to…wow, he really did want to…

No, Amanda thought, she couldn't do that…certainly not *that*…she'd break him in two. She could bite him, of course, but eating in bed never appealed to her, and it would put a damper on the mood… *God, am I crazy?*

Marco felt so excited…

Amanda felt… alive…

They were both truly, madly, deeply terrified.

It was ironic that they were both terrified for the same reason, with the same thought. A thought common to those who were fanged creatures of the night or to those whose minds acted like killing computers thinking five moves ahead…

What if I hurt him?

What if I hurt her?

For the first time in years, Marco couldn't predict what would happen next, and he didn't have a prepackaged, prepared reply. He froze, and for the first time in his career of hunting vampires, he was scared - of himself, of what he'd do, what would happen if he lost all control and loved her with all the passion he felt for her.

Amanda froze, and for the first time in her life as a vampire, she was scared - of herself, of what she'd do, what would happen if she lost all control and loved him with all the passion she felt for him.

"I have to go," Amanda said quickly. She got up and almost bolted for the door.

"No, you don't."

Amanda paused at the door. She looked over her shoulder. "Marco?"

"I need to tell you something."

Amanda's mouth strained. She wanted to frown. Then again, she also wanted to run screaming from the room. She could still do that.

But damnit, Marco is still in a hospital bed. She took a few steps towards him, then gave up, and then sat down next to him. She took his hand. "Yes, Marco?"

Marco made a conscious effort to look Amanda in the eye. "I love you."

She gave him a small smile. During the incident in September, they had made an exchange like that. She had meant it. He'd said, "I love you, buddy."

But this time, Marco closed his eyes and shook his head from side-to-side. "No. I *love* you." He squeezed her hand. "And I mean it." He swallowed, making sure he could finish this one. "I want to marry you."

Amanda blinked. That couldn't be right. Could it? Wasn't their first conversation "Let's just be friends"? "But we were just friends. You said -"

"Preemptive strike," he explained. "So you couldn't say it first." His trademark smile flickered back on. "I'm modest about... how soft and cuddly I am. Heh." His eyes drifted off again, his eyes closing on him. He was fading. "I want you, Amanda Colt, to be... happy. And I don't know how to make you happy. And I wish I did. And I want to marry you and... Amanda..."

Marco fell asleep.

Amanda blinked. She leaned over, lightly kissed him on the lips, and said, "It's Alina. Alina Savinkova. I love you, too, Marco."

Epilogue

Cry Havoc

December 14th, New York

J ennifer Bosley was *pissed*.

The blonde British President of the New York City Vampires Association normally looked well-coiffed, elegant and immaculately dressed.

Now she looked like she had crawled up from the bowels of Hell. Which wasn't that far from the truth.

Back in September, Amanda Colt had survived having an entire hospital wing dropped on her in a massive explosion. She had been dug out in a matter of hours. Multiple factors had been brought to bear. Enrico had supplied the construction equipment and the massive tent that blacked out the sun around the dig site. Bosley had been there to pinpoint Amanda's exact location.

Instead, the VFW didn't want a known mobster digging out *their* facility. No tent, no construction crew. More importantly, there were *no* vampires who volunteered to find President Bosley who were strong enough to sense her in the ground—several vampires who wanted her job thought this would be a *great* time to make their move. She countered all of them by text messages. Jennifer would have merely turned to mist and gotten herself out, but that was stopped by one simple fact—the air ducts had been sealed shut by *tons* of rock that she had no leverage on. She didn't even have the room to punch and claw her way out.

So it was left to normal firemen to come to her aid.

The Police Commissioner explained that his "close friend" had a severe allergy to sunlight, and porphyria, and needed special medication.

Jennifer was found near dusk, which is why, after a construction crane carefully moved several tons of stonework, the firemen were surprised by a fist coming through the ground.

As Jennifer Bosley pulled herself from the ground like Dracula risen from the grave—*1968 film, Christopher Lee, God I wanted to do that man*, she thought—everyone on the scene thought that her eyes were glowing red. But, *obviously*, that was just the light from the setting sun. Her clothes were torn, dirty, and she would have suffocated to death days ago if she hadn't been a vampire.

Luckily for all concerned, both Enrico *and* Police Commissioner Ray Wilson were on hand. Wilson kept the fire department back as Enrico approached Bosley and tossed a blanket around her shoulders - which hid the thermos of blood she downed like a shot of vodka.

Jennifer huddled close to Enrico. She didn't like being clingy, but she'd just spent two days buried alive, she'd worry about how it looked later.

"Where is Amanda Colt?" she asked, her voice shaky with both nerves *and* rage.

"Right now? San Francisco," Enrico answered.

"Get her back here. She is going to tell me *everything* she knows about this Evil Council of Bastards. Because you and I, love? We're going to find them, and we are going to kill every… last… one of them."

To Be Concluded in
Good to the Last Drop

If you've liked the series thus far,
Please, leave a review.
Thanks.

About Declan Finn

Declan Finn lives in a part of New York City unreachable by bus or subway. Who's Who has no record of him, his family, or his education. He has been trained in hand to hand combat and weapons at the most elite schools in Long Island, and figured out nine ways to kill with a pen when he was only fifteen. He escaped a free man from Fordham University's PhD program and has been on the run ever since. There was a brief incident where he was branded a terrorist, but only a court order can unseal those records, and really, why would you want to know?

He can be contacted at DeclanFinnInc@aol.com

Follow him on Facebook and Twitter @DeclanFinnBooks

Read his personal blog: http://apiusmannovel.blogspot.com

Live and Let Bite

Listen to his podcast, The Catholic Geek, on Blog Talk Radio, Sunday evenings at 7:00 pm EST

More From Declan Finn

Love At First Bite
Honor At Stake
Demons Are Forever
Live and Let Bite
Good to the Last Drop

The Pius Trilogy
A Pius Man
A Pius Legacy
A Pius Stand
Pius Tales
Pius History

The Convention Killings
It Was Only On Stun
Set To Kill

If you've enjoyed this title, please check out the rest of the books in this Dragon award nominated series at https://threeravenspublishing.com/love-at-first-bite/.

Or check out some of our other Urban Fantasy titles at https://threeravenspublishing.com/urban-fantasy/
Such as the Lady of Death, Nightshade Series, or Paranormal City

STEPHEN OLIVER
PARANORMAL
CITY

J.F. POSTHUMUS
THE
FAE'S
AMULET
A LADY OF DEATH NOVEL

Or take a look at some of our other award winning series at https://threeravenspublishing.com/series-universes/

Visit us at

Https://www.threeravenspublishing.com and sign up for our newsletter for the latest and greatest news on upcoming titles and events.

THE NORTH
TEXAS
TROUBLEMAKERS

www.ingramcontent.com/pod-product-compliance
Lightning Source LLC
Chambersburg PA
CBHW061620210726
48287CB00001B/209